THE

SHELL

MEMOIRS OF A HIDDEN OBSERVER

BY MUSTAFA KHALIFA

TRANSLATED BY PAUL STARKEY

Interlink Books

An imprint of Interlink Publishing Group, Inc.
Northampton, Massachusetts

D1319119

First published 2017 by

Interlink Books
An imprint of Interlink Publishing Group, Inc.
46 Crosby Street, Northampton, Massachusetts 01060
www.interlinkbooks.com

Library of Congress Cataloging-in-Publication Data available

Cover image: dirty jail cell © Typhoonski | Dreamstime.com

Printed and bound in the United States of America

This book has been translated partially with the assistance of the Sharjah International Book Fair Translation Grand Fund.

To request our complete 48-page catalog, please call us
toll free at 1-800-238-LINK, visit our website at
www.interlinkbooks.com, or write to
Interlink Publishing, 46 Crosby Street, Northampton, MA 01060

I WAS SITTING WITH SUZANNE IN THE CAFÉ in Orly Airport in Paris, waiting for the departure of the plane that would take me home after an absence of six years. Until this last quarter of an hour, Suzanne hadn't given up hope of trying to persuade me to stay in France. She was repeating the same arguments I'd been hearing for months, ever since I told her that I'd definitely made up my mind to return to my native country and work there.

I belong to an Arab Catholic Christian family. Half the family lives in Paris, so the door was open for me to study there. My studies were straightforward and successful, not least because I spoke French well, even before coming to Paris. I studied film directing and was an outstanding student. So here I was, going back to my own country and city after graduating.

Suzanne also belonged to an Arab family, but they had all emigrated and were living in France. We'd become close friends in the last two years of my studies, and we might have married with the blessing of both our families if I hadn't insisted on returning home and she'd insisted on staying in France.

"Suzanne," I said to her, as I put an end to our final discussion of the subject in the airport: "I love my country, I love my city. I love its streets and its hidden corners. This isn't just empty romanticism, it's a genuine feeling. I remember the graffiti on the walls of the old houses in our quarter, I love them, I miss them. That's one thing. And the second is that I want to be an outstanding director. I've got lots of plans and schemes in my head, and I'm very

1

ambitious, but in France I'll always be a foreigner, working among the French like any old refugee, picking up a few scraps that they deign to give me. No, I don't want that. In my own country I've got rights, and no one will have to give me anything. With a bit of effort I'll be able to confirm my own existence. That's leaving aside the fact that the country needs me and others like me.

"That's why my decision to go back is a final one, and any attempt to persuade me otherwise will be useless."

A silence followed, which lasted for several minutes. We heard the announcement. It was time to board the plane. We stood up and gulped down the remains of the beer in our glasses. I gave her an emotional look and glimpsed the beginnings of a tear in her eyes. She threw herself into my arms and I kissed her hurriedly. I couldn't bear situations like this.

"All the best," I said.

"And to you. Be careful and look after yourself!"

I boarded the plane.

Diary of a Hidden Observer

The peeping that I indulged in wasn't of a sexual nature, even though that aspect wasn't entirely absent.

I wrote most of these diaries in the Desert Prison—the word "wrote" earlier in the sentence not being entirely accurate, since there were no pens or writing paper in the Desert Prison. This enormous complex, which contained seven yards and thirty-seven dormitories, as well as several new, unnumbered dormitories, and the older French rooms and cells in Yard 5, held within its walls at any one moment more than ten thousand prisoners. It contained the highest proportion of holders of university degrees in the entire country, but the prisoners, some of whom spent more than twenty years there, never saw pen or paper.

"Mental writing" was a technique developed by the Islamists. One of them could memorize more than ten thousand of the people who'd entered the Desert Prison, with the names of their families, their towns or villages, the date of their arrest, their sentences, and their fate.

When I decided to write this diary, I'd already gradually converted my mind into a tape recorder on which I recorded everything I saw and some of what I heard. And now I am downloading "some" of what this tape contains.

Am I the same person I was thirteen years ago? Yes and no. A small yes and a big no. Yes, because I am downloading and faithfully transcribing some part of these diaries. And no, because I cannot write and say everything. That requires an act of confession, and confession has its conditions. Objective circumstances and another party.

April 20

I stood on the airplane steps for a little while, looking at the airport buildings. I looked at the lights in the distance, the lights of my city. It was a magical moment. I climbed down and collected my luggage, passport in hand. A feeling of contentment enveloped me, the feeling of someone who is returning home to his familiar haunts after a long absence.

The official told me to wait. He read my passport, went back to his papers then told me to wait again. I waited. Two security men took the passport and with exaggerated politeness told me to come with them.

It was just me and my case (which I never saw again) on a ride in the security van along the long airport highway, watching the lights on both sides of the road, watching the lights of my city as they came closer. I turned to the security man sitting next to me and asked him: "Everything's OK, I hope? Why all these procedures?"

He said nothing, but put his finger firmly on his lips, as a sign to me to be quiet. So I said nothing more.

The journey from the airport to that dingy building in the center of the capital was a journey in space as well as in time. Since that moment, thirteen years have gone by. I later found out that somebody, a student who was with us in Paris, had written a report and submitted it to the security organization he was attached to. The report said that I'd made some remarks hostile to the current regime and disparaging to the President—an act that was reckoned among the worst of crimes, as bad as treason if not worse.

This had happened three years before I returned from Paris.

That report had brought me to this building in the center of the capital, near our house—a building that I knew well, as I'd often walked past it and been disturbed by the secrecy and the heavy guard that surrounded it.

The two security men kept me under guard, tightening their grip on my arms as we went through the door to the long corridor. There was a young man at the end of it. "Hi, Musa, what's the latest?" he shouted when he saw us. "Green or red?"

"It's all the same shit."

From the first corridor to another, then an inside staircase, an upstairs corridor, a room to the right. A knock on the door, a voice from inside: "Come in!"

My companion opened the door gently, then stamped hard on the ground. "My respects, sir! This is a wanted man we've brought from the airport. Sir!" My nose caught a whiff of a distinctive smell, the sort that is only found in security men's offices—a mixture of different perfumes, high quality cigarettes, human sweat, the smell of feet. All mixed with the scent of torture. Human torture. The smell of cruelty.

As soon as that smell reaches a man's nose, he feels fear and terror. I felt fear and terror despite my belief that there must be some mistake behind all this.

A giant of a man with white hair and a red face turned toward us. I noticed a blindfolded young man squatting at his feet. "Take him to Abu Ramzat," the giant said.

My two companions dragged me off, with obvious force this time. More corridors and staircases. The building looked so small from the outside, but inside it was vast. I could hear the sounds of men shouting and of cries for help, which became louder and clearer the further on we walked. We went down to the basement, I think. One of my companions opened the door and I saw the source of the shouting. Someone had been laid out on the floor and stuffed into a car tire, with his feet raised in the air. There was a blow of a cable to his feet and immediately a loud cry of pain hit me. I felt my thing between my thighs twitch.

The black cable rose and fell on the feet of the young man stuffed into the black car tire then rose again, scattering specks of blood and fragments of human flesh as it did so. Still numb from the sight, I was frozen rigid by the sound of screaming. Reluctantly, I turned around toward the source of the noise. In a corner of the room there was a man with a flushed, ruddy face, foaming at both corners of his mouth.

"Blindfold him, you ass!"

One of my companions jumped one step forward and one step back. Then suddenly something was being placed over my eyes and fastened with elastic behind my head. I could no longer see anything.

"Stand him against the wall."

5

A blow on my back, a slap on my neck, hands behind my back and I was being forced to walk, my head colliding with the wall. I stopped.

"Put your hands up, damn you!"

I put them up.

"Raise your right leg, and stand on your left leg, you son of a whore!"

I raised my leg and stood there.

Behind me, things were continuing as before. I could hear the sound of the cable, the noise when it struck the feet, the voice of the young man in pain, the sound of the executioner's panting. I could almost hear the sound of the fragments of flesh I'd seen flying around a few minutes ago… sounds, sounds.

For the blind man, sound is master.

The armchair in Orly Airport, Suzanne, refreshments, beer, the comfortable seat in the plane, the air hostess who exuded beauty and kindness, the juice, the tea!

My left leg, which was supporting the whole of my body, was growing tired. If I swapped it for the right one, would the man with the ruddy face notice? And if he noticed, what would he do?

My left leg was growing numb and I could no longer stand it. I would risk it and swap it. Nothing happened, no one noticed. I felt I had won. Later, after several years of prison, I would discover that in the endless struggle between the prisoner and the jailer, all the prisoner's victories would be like this.

Time weighed heavily, and I found myself in a state of disbelief. What was happening? Why was I here? Thousands of questions. I tried to prop myself up against the wall with my hands, touching it with my fingertips. Suddenly, the young man stuffed into the black car tire screamed: "Enough, sir! Enough, for God's sake! I can't take it any longer, I'll tell you everything!"

"That's enough, Ibrahim," said the man with the flushed face, calmly and in the tone of a victor. "Leave him, get him out of the tire and take him to the major."

I heard him speaking on the telephone with the major. "Now my turn has come," I thought.

I was right. I heard the sound of the receiver being put down and the flushed man shouting: "Hey, Ayyoub, Ayyoub!"

"Yes, sir!"

"Come and take care of this customer!"

I could sense Ayyoub behind me.

"Put him in the tire, quickly, for heaven's sake!"

I felt more than five men grab me and throw me to the ground. To this day, fourteen years after that moment, I have never been able to understand or imagine how Ayyoub managed to stuff me into that car tire in such a way that my legs were sticking up in the air, unable to escape no matter how much I tried, nor how he managed to get my shoes and socks off.

"Cable or cane, sir?"

"Cane, cane. It seems the professor is a little sensitive!"

A rod of fire stung the soles of my feet. Before I could finish screaming the cane had stung again. The beating went on, and with it the screaming. Despite that, I could hear the voice of the flushed man say: "Ayyoub, when he's ready, call me!"

I didn't know why they were beating me. I didn't know what they wanted from me. "What do you want from me, brother?" I asked, plucking up my courage.

"Eat shit, you queer!" replied Ayyoub, whose face I never saw. Screaming in agony, I started to count the blows. Later, some more experienced people told me that counting the blows was the first sign of weakness and an indication that the *mujahid* or resistance fighter would give in to the interrogator. (But I'm not a mujahid or

7

a resistance fighter, I told myself!) They told me that in these situations it was best if you could concentrate hard mentally, focus on something dear to you and try to forget your feet. At number forty I lost count and began to lose any physical feeling. My screams grew quieter, and I began to lose my sense of balance and feel sick. Despite the blindfold, clouds started to float in front of my eyes. Was I losing consciousness? *Clouds, nausea, Orly Airport, juice, beer, the plane and the charming hostess...*

A vague feeling that everything had come to a stop. I began to reassess the situation. Yes, even the beating had stopped. A numbness, a numbness, for some minutes, maybe long, maybe short, I didn't know. I woke up.

The red-faced man's voice again: "What's happening, Ayyoub? Has he come to, or not?"

"Yes, sir, only he's wet himself."

"Damn his eyes! It seems the gentleman's really got problems!"

I felt a kick on my hip and heard the interrogator's voice: "Come on! What's wrong with you? Aren't you embarrassed to wet yourself? What's your name?"

I told him my name.

"Look here, you dog, we haven't started with you yet, this isn't all a joke, we haven't got serious yet. It's best to satisfy us and give yourself some peace right from the start. You need to talk, I mean, you need to talk. Here with us, everyone talks! You need to tell everything, from 'tak tak' to 'al-salamu 'alaykum'. Come on, are you ready to talk?"

"I'll tell you whatever you want, sir," I said. "Just tell me what I need to tell you!"

"Okay, let's see, first of all, what are the names of your family?"

I started to list the names of my family, beginning with my father and mother, but he cut me short, shouting in fury: "No, you

8

ass! Are you pretending to be stupid? I want the names of your people. Shit on you and your people, tell me the names of your family in the organization, you ass!"

"What organization, sir? What organization?"

"Ayyoub, it looks like this goat is trying to beat about the bush. He's torturing us and making his situation worse!"

"Sir, by God, by God, I don't know what you're asking me! What organization are you talking about?"

The sound of footsteps. I was conscious he'd come nearer to me. His breath skimmed my face. "The organization of queers like yourself," he said, completely calmly. "The Muslim Brotherhood. Don't you know your organization?" I noticed that his mouth smelled extremely unpleasant.

I didn't know. Should I be happy that the confusion now seemed crystal clear? Or curse my passing fate that had thrown me into this tricky situation? Or curse the coincidences that had determined that I land up directly with Abu Ramzat? If they had searched me and taken my things, as they do with most people, anyone could have worked out who I was and what my crime was. But to arrive at the security services department at a time when hundreds of Muslim Brotherhood detainees were coming in every day, and to be lumped together with them, when the officers and staff were working 24/7 and the department was so utterly chaotic—all this made it impossible for me to clarify or end the confusion. And on top of all this, there was my name, which didn't suggest that I wasn't a Muslim.

"But sir, I'm a Christian, a Christian!" I screamed, nonetheless.

"What? A Christian? Heavens, why didn't you say you're a Christian? Why did they bring you here? You must have done something really serious! A Christian?"

"You didn't ask me, sir. And not just a Christian! An atheist! I don't believe in God!"

9

To this day I have found no explanation for this outburst of mine. What was the point in proclaiming my atheism in front of this interrogator? I don't know.

"An atheist as well?" he asked in a slightly pensive tone.

"Yes, sir, yes, by God! Look at my passport!"

The interrogator said nothing for what seemed to me a very long time. I heard the sound of his footsteps moving away, before he spoke again in a clear voice. "An atheist, he says. But we're an Islamic country. Ayyoub, finish your job!"

Ayyoub's cane resumed its work.

From the first moments of my involvement with these people, I had used the term "brother" when replying to a question, but Ayyoub slapped me and asked: "Am I your brother, you dog? Your brother's in the slum!" I corrected myself and addressed him as "*Ustaz*" but he slapped me again. "*Ustaz*? An ustaz in your family? Between your mother's thighs!" From that time on, they told me just to say "Sir!"

This word was not used here in the same way as it is used between cultured people. When it was used here, the word carried implications of humiliation and servitude.

APRIL 21

I slowly opened my eyes, almost choking from the smells that surrounded me. I was stretched out on the floor in a forest of legs and feet, crowded together, with the smell of dirty feet, the smell of blood, the smell of festering wounds, and the smell of a floor that had not been cleaned for a long time. The heavy breath of people standing jammed together. I found out shortly afterwards by a process of counting and observation that there were eighty-six of us. I looked at the ceiling and calculated that the room was no more than twenty-five square meters!

Conversations were conducted in a whisper, which meant that a continuous buzz dominated everything. I wanted to stand up to breathe some air. There were dreadful pains through my entire body. I summoned all my strength, but when I tried to stand on my feet I screamed in pain. The people around me noticed and several hands stretched out, grabbed me under my arms and helped me up. I stood leaning on the outstretched arms. "Patience, brother!" said a young man standing beside me. "Patience. It's hard, but it will pass!"

"Whoever is with God, God will be with him," said someone else. "Don't despair, my brother!"

The pain eased a little with the movement, and I looked around me. Grown men, younger men, boys of twelve and thirteen, middle-aged men and older men... I turned to the man who'd tried to strengthen my resolve a little earlier and asked him: "Who are these people? Why are we here? Why are these people standing here?" The man looked at me in astonishment, almost doltishly, as if to say, "How to explain something so obvious?" But instead he answered with a question: "Don't you know what's going on in the country?"

When I was in France I had heard news of political demonstrations going on in Syria, and of a party called the Muslim Brotherhood that was responsible for terrorist incidents both here and there. But I hadn't attached much importance to these reports, which remained vague, and I didn't know the details. I had never taken much interest in news reports, or organized political activities, despite the fact that at secondary school and afterwards I was close to some Marxists and was influenced by their ideas—and especially the ideas of my uncle, who occupied an important leadership position in the Communist Party, so it appeared.

"No, I don't know. What's going on?" I replied.

"Why, don't you live in your own country?"

I wanted to put an end to all these questions, so I replied in a way that I thought would answer them all at once. "No, I've been living in France. And now I've been back..." (I looked at my watch) "for just fourteen hours."

"Good heavens, you've got a watch? Hide it, my brother, hide it! You see all these people here? They're the pick of the believers and defenders of Islam in this country. It's a trial, my brother, a trial from God, may He be blessed and exalted!"

"Okay, but what's that got to do with me?" I inquired, interrupting him in a slightly provocative way. "I'm a Christian, not a Muslim, and I'm an atheist, not a believer!"

This was the second time I'd announced that I was an atheist, and again, it was just a curt announcement. The first time, it had cost me an extra helping of Ayyoub's cane, on the orders of Abu Ramzat who butchered Muslims because "we're living in a Muslim country." The second time, it was to cost me several years of total isolation, and treatment like that accorded to insects, if not worse!

I noticed that my interrogator seemed to have jumped back, though because we were squeezed so tightly together, only his top half moved. "I take refuge with God from Satan, the accursed!" he exclaimed without thinking, then in a louder voice: "My friends, there's a Christian, a non-believer, there's a spy among us!"

Several eyes turned in my direction, and at the same time I heard a voice behind me, a voice of authority: "Who's that raising his voice? Silence, silence! Come on, it's time for the changeover!"

I couldn't work out what was going on. At the far end of the room was a group of people sprawled on the floor, in odd but regular lines. As if they were cigarettes lined up in a packet. Between the men lying down and those of us who were standing, there was a third group, a group of people squatting on the ground.

After the man with the loud voice had spoken—I discovered he was the dormitory head—the three groups all moved. In just a few seconds, those lying down stood up and gradually occupied the corner where we were. We squatted down, while the third group moved over to the sleeping place. "Come on, everyone that's lying down, fence, fence!" It seemed that "fencing" meant sleeping on one's side. The first person lay down on his side beside the wall with his back to it, then the second lay down in front of him, front to front, each one's head at the other's feet. The third one "fenced" and put his back against the second man's back, then the fourth went front to front with the third, always head against feet. People carried on lying down until the row reached the other wall of the room but there were still six or seven people with no places left. "Come on, crammer," shouted the dormitory head. "Do your job!"

The second huge man—he looked like a wrestler—got up quietly, went over to the first man lying by the wall, and gently put his feet between the wall and the man lying down. Then he leaned his back against the wall and started to push the man with the soles of his feet, harder and harder. The people lying down contracted a bit until there was room for another man. "Get down here," he called to one of those left over. The man got down on his side between the first man and the feet of the crammer; then the crammer started to push the new man, once again creating a space large enough for someone else. Again, a call of "Come on, get down here," pushing again, and a new man, until eventually all those originally without a place had been accommodated. The crammer went back to his place just as quietly as before, rubbing his hands. I looked at the men lying there. Some had gone to sleep instantly.

I spent three days in this room. I heard that some people, both earlier and later, spent many months there, and that sometimes it was even more crowded with people than when I was there. During those days I got to know the room well.

A short while after we'd squatted down I felt the need to urinate. I turned to my neighbor and asked him: "Where do we pee?" He turned his face away from me without replying. I asked my other neighbor, who again didn't reply. I remembered I was a Christian, an unbeliever, and a spy, and that these charges would follow me everywhere.

My place was near the dormitory head, so I asked him and he showed me the lavatory. At least there was one. I had to wait for more than an hour. One lavatory, one water tap, eighty-six people. I went back to my place. Something moved above. I looked. The wastepipe, which apparently served the whole building, cut through the room from one end to the other. Between the pipe and the roof was about half a meter. Two youths of about fifteen were sleeping on the pipe. One of them had his chest and arms around the pipe, legs hanging down, while his head relaxed to the sound of the water gurgling in the pipe.

"I've never slept so well in my life!" one of them said the next day.

April 22

I woke up. After eight hours of squatting, our turn had come to lie down. Some of the more experienced squatters warned the others that you should go to the lavatory before lying down. If you lay down after the "crammer" had finished his work, then whatever the reason for your getting up, your place would disappear.

I lay down, one man's back pressing on my back, and another man's belly against my own. I remembered my girlfriend who liked the French position! There were two feet behind my head, and two in front of it. How can a man sleep with this smell in his nose? Despite that, I slept soundly. Then I woke, woke up completely. Everything in my body was being pressed. But the pressure on the base of my abdomen was intense, almost painful. It seemed that the bladder of my neighbor in front had become so full that he had an erection, which naturally stuck into my belly. In circumstances like that it would be shameful to think of other possibilities! I tried to dislodge it to no avail, and with every movement it became more and more stuck. I could hear him snoring. I thought of putting out my hand, despite the difficulty of doing so, but I was afraid he might wake up at that very moment. What would he say if he woke with his penis in my hand? With some difficulty I extracted myself from where I was lying, and went to the lavatory.

Three nights… three times a day the door was opened and closed, and on every occasion when the door was opened, food would arrive in containers, or kettles, which they called *qasa'at*. In the morning everyone got a loaf of bread with a piece of halva, distributed by the dormitory head, and there were five qasa'at containing a black liquid. It was supposed to be tea. We got the same in the evening. The kettle would be passed round from one person to another, who would lift it up, sip from it, then pass it on to the person beside him. At midday the kettles were full of *burghul* wheat, and there was a kettle full of tomato soup with some vegetables.

I will never forget the way people tried to snatch the pieces of meat from each other, the only time they brought us meat. Even during the two morning and evening meals, I thought that if it hadn't been for the dormitory head, the dormitory would have turned into a jungle.

During these hours—which seemed to me like an eternity—I was like someone floating in time and space, holding on to a wish (which seemed to me like a firm belief) that all this should just be a stupid mistake that would end soon. My professional and artistic sensibility was crouching in a far-off corner, watching but not intervening—a sensibility that remained beyond the domain of pain and anxiety, awake and neutral, observing and recording however great my own psychological and physical pain.

I remember one of my eminent professors saying that no matter how small the incident, a good director could make a good film out of it; the incident was the skeleton and it was for the director to clothe it in flesh and blood. This sensibility captured the scene of the battle for the pieces of meat. I was conscious of the screaming disconnect between, on one hand, a number of things about the incident that invited nausea (or at least total withdrawal), and on the other, the material actions undertaken by the people snatching the meat. What was it that made those people lose any sense of decency and taste—and as a consequence, their sense of honor, and pride, and humanity? Was it the struggle for survival? Perhaps.

For three days and nights, I ate half a loaf with a piece of halva.

April 23

I woke up. The second period of lying down, sleeping on the floor, was a little better. I woke before the end of the eight-hour period, but didn't feel like getting up. I dreamed I'd had enough sleep but was just continuing to relax and take it easy. I wished I could stretch out a bit. I wanted a coffee and a cigarette.

My place was near that of the dormitory head, and I could hear his conversations with the "crammer." The jailer opened the spyhole, a small window at the top of the door. The dormitory head jumped up and had a long conversation with the jailer who had opened the spyhole, then came back and whispered to the "crammer": "There's some big consignments coming in from the provinces. And this bunch of ours—they'll be leaving the Desert Prison today or tomorrow."

"Heavens, why should all these people be in jail?" asked the "crammer" in astonishment. "My God, there'll soon be no one left outside prison!"

"Shut up, be careful no one can hear you! It's none of our business, my friend!"

The dormitory head and the "crammer" were in prison for smuggling.

In the evening, when our group was moving from standing to squatting, I deliberately squatted down beside the dormitory head. I waited until just before the third meal, then asked him: "Excuse me, ustaz, can I have a word with you?" I tried to make my face look cheerful, as I addressed him with a term usually reserved for respected elders and scholars.

"Ustaz? Why on earth do you call me ustaz? Yes, what do you want?"

"Sir, then, there's been a mistake, for sure!"

"Where's the mistake, ustaz?"

"I'm not a Muslim, brother, so I can't belong to the Muslim Brotherhood. I'm a Christian. Why did they put me here, why did they bring me here? I don't know."

"You've lost it, my friend. It's total chaos, and everyone for himself!"

"Okay, can you speak to the prison governor, or someone responsible for all this?"

"How am I supposed to see the prison governor? Okay, okay, when the prison governor comes I'll tell him what you've said."

I heard the click of the lock, and the dormitory head stood up. I grabbed his hand: "Please don't forget to tell him!"

He nodded his head, and the door opened. *God, please let the food in!* The food came in. The dormitory head spoke to the jailer: "Sir, there's someone here wants to speak…"

17

The jailer quickly interrupted him: "He can say whatever he wants, I don't know anything! I'll send you the duty head!"

After about half an hour, there was another knock on the door and a handsome man appeared. "What's up, head?" he asked, in a thick mountain accent.

The dormitory head grabbed me by the shoulder and I stood up. "Tell him," he said to me. "Tell Mr. Abu Rami!"

In a hesitant and stuttering voice, I explained the situation to him. "Okay, so what am I supposed to do with you?" he replied in the same mountain accent. "A Christian? So what? You might have been assisting the Muslim Brotherhood, for example; you might have sold them arms, for example; and that way you'd be even worse than them, for example!" Then he turned to the jailer and told him to shut the door.

Before the jailer could shut the door, Abu Rami turned to the people in the dormitory and shouted at them: "Pimps! You're not Muslim Brothers, you're the Devil's Brothers! Show us how clever you are! There's a Christian among you, look—work with him, and lead him to the true religion. You're only good for killing and destroying the country!" He slammed the steel door shut but quickly opened it again with a broad smile on his face. All eyes were on him. "Dogs… pimps… if you succeed in making him a Muslim, don't forget to enroll him in the Muslim Brotherhood, so that locking him up will have been worthwhile!"

Then he slammed the door shut.

The third period of lying down began.

My neighbor at the back had a large, fat behind, which both cramped me and gave me some comfort. It was better than the people with prominent bones, which stuck into your body mercilessly when we squeezed together. My neighbor at the front was a young man in his twenties who didn't give any sign of being religious. I couldn't sleep after hearing what Abu Rami had to say. I still nurtured a considerable hope that someone would discover the mistake and immediately move to correct it, but after this conversation, the transfer to the Desert Prison, and the seemingly endless confusion, I was overcome with despair and fear of an unknown fate.

Two or three hours, I don't know, and finally I started to nod off… tiredness, exhaustion, sleep… then gradually I woke up. A feeling of depression. I woke up a little more, feeling as if my feet were tied together. They had swollen up from Ayyoub's cane. I woke up a little more… a warm, damp feeling was coming up my legs, together with a little pain. A movement. I started up, and woke completely. I raised my head and looked at the top of my leg.

My neighbor to the front, the young man, was holding my upper leg with both hands. He had put my big toe in his mouth and started to suck it! I kicked him and kicked him again, and his hands let go and he pulled his head away. I carried on kicking and the youth woke completely, looking at me with anger and contempt. "Why did you wake me up?" he asked angrily.

"What do you mean, why did you wake me up? Can't you see what you're doing?"

"Curse your name! You've ruined my dream!"

"You were having a dream? What sort of dream?"

"Yes, me and Maysun, the very moment I took of her and she took hold of me, and we started to… you woke me up!"

"And who's Maysun?"

"Maysun? Maysun's my fiancée."

"Sorry, excuse me, go back to sleep. But don't mix my toe up with Maysun's lips!"

I couldn't sleep after that. Questions, questions. What sort of world was this that I'd been shoved into? Was this just the beginning? And where would it lead? Could any writer, scene setter, or director have imagined a world like this? Questions followed by questions...

For thirteen years I never heard the grating of the key in the steel door without feeling that my heart was about to be ripped out. I couldn't get used to it.

The key grated at an unusual time. The moment the door opened, the dormitory head jumped up. It was Abu Rami, with a tall man in his fifties wearing white spectacles beside him, and about twenty wardens to the rear. "Where's the dormitory head?" asked the man with the glasses.

"Here, sir!"

"Take all these men outside two by two, calmly and in good order, so that just you and the second smuggler remain here. Where is the second smuggler?"

"Here, sir!"

"You stay here too!"

So we went out, two by two. It was dawn on April 24.

April 24

We walked with difficulty, stumbling along the corridors and steps. We were handcuffed behind our backs with iron chains, ankles bound to the ankle of another prisoner with an iron shackle. Our names had been entered on lists.

The man with the glasses left us standing for a few minutes and went off carrying the lists of names, then came back. He was certainly important, so why shouldn't I explain things to him? He came closer. "Can I have a word, sir?" I asked.

"Go and eat shit!"

And a resounding blow.

Thousands of bright stars appeared before my eyes. The dawn was spring-like. I staggered, and shut up.

They dragged us out of the building and I saw four trucks with metal cages. The prisoners called these trucks "meat trucks," perhaps because they looked like the trucks used to distribute slaughtered animals from the abattoirs to the butchers, or perhaps because prisoners were lined up in them like the animals in the real "meat trucks."

A metal ladder with three steps. We went up slowly because our feet were shackled and it was impossible to use one's hands. They sat us down on the floor of the truck until the truck was full; then the door was locked with a large key. Two security men sat outside the door. A wait, a longer wait, and then the trucks moved off together. We left the city and the trucks' speed picked up. We left the darkness behind us, and gradually the first threads of the silver dawn appeared before us.

Was it a journey from darkness to light? I hoped so.

I heard someone ask someone else: "How long before we get there?"

"Four or five hours, with God's help!"

"God, brother, I can't wait that long! I was asleep. They woke me up and then straight away outside. And now I'm completely hemmed in here. What am I supposed to do? My bladder will burst!"

"If you can't hold on, I'll undo the zipper on your pants, and you do it here in the truck!"

"What? Really? In front of all these people?"

"It doesn't matter, just be thankful there are no women among us!"

All eyes turned toward him as he addressed the entire group in a loud voice, and explained the problem. Some people muttered, while others said nothing. Some indicated agreement. The speaker turned his back toward the beleaguered man, and with his shackled hands gripped the zipper and undid it, then got out the man's […] and moved away. "Go on, relieve yourself, brother!" This operation was repeated four times before we reached the Desert Prison; five other men vomited in the pool of urine. The vomit was all the same color. My own neighbor, whose leg was chained to mine, seemed to be suffering from a stomach disorder, so that I was enveloped in a fine veil of smells from his intestines.

At eight in the morning we reached the Desert Prison. I had looked at my watch a lot on the way. More than one person advised me to hide it, but where? I left it on my wrist.

In front of the prison were dozens of military policemen. The door was a small one, but the eye was caught by a stone plaque over the door, with the following written in black relief: *In retaliation there is life for you, men possessed of minds!* [Qur'an 2:179] The security men opened the truck doors for us, and the same men who'd treated us roughly and harshly got us down from the trucks with a gentleness mingled with pity. One of them even said: "May God comfort you!" They talked in whispers in hushed tones among themselves and avoided looking at the military police, who were ranged around us in a sort of circle. I noticed that they all stood in roughly the same way: legs slightly apart, chest pulled back, left hands resting on their hips, right hands holding either a thick cane, or a piece of twisted cable made of electric wires, or a black rubber contraption like a belt. Later I found out that it was a fan-belt from a tank engine. They gave us and the security men a superior look that suggested contempt for the security men and a hidden warning to us. The way they moved implied some impatience at the slow pace of the handover and reception procedures. They shuffled the weight of their bodies from one foot to another, shaking their right hands in bored, angry movements. All were wearing smart military uniforms. The highest rank among them was a sergeant major, who was signing the handover lists.

I read somewhere that when men from one of the African tribes encountered a white European for the first time, they looked at each other in astonishment, wondering why the man had stripped the skin from his face. I wondered what force had flayed the faces of the military policemen I could see in front of me. How had they been flayed? Why? Where? I didn't know. But I could see that these false faces weren't like the faces of the rest of humanity, not like our families' and friends' faces. They had an inhuman sheen. Invisible, to be sure, but definitely there!

"God grant you health… You can go now, your task is finished!" said the military police adjutant to the man with glasses. They had already undone our chains. The prisoners instinctively clung to one another. The security men went away. The circle began to contract. Absolute silence.

"Come on, line them up, two by two, and get them inside!"

They let us in through the small door. Two by two, in a long line, and through to a courtyard with trees and wildflowers in the middle and around the sides. It was surrounded on all sides by rooms that overlooked it. The procession stopped in front of another adjutant, sitting behind another table, with more lists of names. More than a hundred military policemen swarmed around us. All the prisoners avoided looking directly at any of them. Our heads were slightly bowed and our shoulders flopped. It was an attitude of deference, humiliation, and subservience. How was it that all the prisoners had agreed on this way of standing, as if we had been used to standing like that before? I don't know. Each one of us seemed to be trying to hide inside himself.

My head itched from the neck up, and like anyone whose head itches, I stretched out my hand without thinking to scratch it. I heard a voice thunder: "See this, everyone! See the dog! He's scratching his head now as well!"

"Whaaat? Scratching his head?"

The hands snatched me out of the line, bouncing me back and forth as they hit and cuffed me. One cuff propelled me forward, then a slap brought me to a stop; my neck and face were on fire. I wished I could cry just for a little. The adjutant summoned me to register my name. There was no one left except me. He registered my name and I became an official inmate in this prison.

Once again they led me away. There was a small iron door, smaller than the first door, between two rooms. *Why did the doors become smaller the further on we walked?* From this door we emerged into a large yard: it was Yard 1, and was covered with asphalt (all the paths and yards were covered in coarse asphalt). The yard was surrounded by single-story buildings, numbered consecutively: Dormitory 3, Dormitory 4… Dormitory 7.

The doors were smaller, but in Yard 1 hell opened its widest doors, and we were its fuel!

Calmly and precisely they stood us beside each other, with two or three meters separating us, and the adjutant called out: "Come on, everyone strip completely… put your clothes over your right arm, and keep just your underpants on."

After everyone had taken off their clothes and stood there waiting, I noticed that I was the only one wearing briefs. I was overcome by a feeling of being out of place.

The adjutant's voice was quiet at first, but as time went on it gradually started to get louder and sharper. The sharper and louder it got, the more aware I became of an increasing nervousness and tension in the policemen's movements. The fear and consternation in the prisoners' hearts also increased; they lowered their eyes and their shoulders slumped further and further down. Two policemen carrying whips approached me. "Take your underpants down," said one, "and make two security motions!"

I dropped my underpants to the knee and looked at the policeman, wondering what he meant.

"Make two security motions, or else…!"

"What am I supposed to do, sir? What do you mean?"

"Squat down and get up again twice. You really are an ass!"

These movements were performed in case a prisoner had concealed a forbidden substance in his anus.

One of the policemen gave the other a smile and said in a quiet voice: "Heavens, that's a small one!" I looked at "it," at my thing, and yes, it was very small. Even "it" was feeling terrified and afraid, and had taken refuge inside its bag, where I could not hide!

Behind me was a large dormitory whose door was labeled Dormitory 5–6. From beside the door a waste pipe emerged and led across the ground, carrying dirty black water.

The search ended. It was conducted with surgical precision; even the folds of our clothes were checked. All coins and notes, anything metal, belts and shoelaces were all confiscated. I was barefoot now. Despite all this precision in the search, however, my wristwatch passed through. I hadn't bothered to hide it, but no one had taken any notice of it.

"Come on, you dogs! Everyone pick up their clothes!" the adjutant shouted. I picked up my clothes, put them over my left arm, and immediately undid my watch and slipped it into the inside pocket of my jacket, with another feeling of victory.

The "municipals"

This was a word peculiar to the prisons here. They were soldiers who'd been put in prison—men who'd absconded from military service, soldiers who'd committed crimes of murder, rape, or theft, drug addicts... All convicted soldiers, the dregs of the army, spent their period of punishment in military prisons. In prisons like this one, their duties included cleaning, distributing food, and other tasks—hence the term "municipals." In the Desert Prison these people also had other duties.

They assembled us on one side of the courtyard. We piled together carrying our clothes. The adjutant's voice began to get louder. On the other side of the yard stood the municipals. There were a lot of them, and some were carrying thick sticks, called *falaqas*, from which a heavy rope hung down, attached to the two ends. The adjutant turned to address the prisoners and shouted in a malicious-sounding tone: "Which of you are officers? Officers, come here!" Two prisoners stepped forward, one middle-aged, the other a younger man.

"What's your rank?"

"Brigadier general."

"Brigadier general?"

"Yes."

"And you, what's your rank?"

"First lieutenant."

"Hmm."

He turned again to the prisoners and in an even louder voice asked: "Anyone who's a doctor, engineer, or lawyer, leave the line!"

More than ten men stepped out of the line. "Stand here!" he shouted, and then turned to the prisoners again: "Anyone with a university degree... step out of the line!"

26

More than thirty people left the line, myself included. The adjutant moved away and stood beside the drain then shouted at the policeman: "Bring me the brigadier general!"

More than ten men swooped on the brigadier, and in a few moments he was in front of the adjutant.

"How are you, brigadier?"

"Praise be to God, to whom alone praise is due in adversity!"

"So, brigadier... aren't you thirsty?"

"No, thank you!"

"But we must let you drink. I mean, we are Arabs, and the Arabs are famous for their generosity. I mean, we must extend hospitality to you. Just out of duty, nothing else!"

After this piece of mocking sarcasm, the two were silent for a moment. The adjutant then jumped up. "Do you see this drain?" he shouted. "Lie down and drink from it till you've quenched your thirst!"

"No, I'm not drinking!"

The adjutant looked as though he'd received an electric shock. "What... what? You won't drink?" he shouted, with genuine amazement. He then turned to the military police. "Make him drink, make him drink any way you want, dogs! Move, let me see!"

The brigadier was barefoot and naked except for his under-pants. In a few moments his body was covered in red and blue lines, as more than a dozen men swooped down on him, thrusting him back and forth between them. Thick sticks, twisted ropes, and tank fan-belts rained down on him from every side. The brigadier started to resist from the very first moment, hitting the men he could see in front of him with his fist. He succeeded in striking one of them as he lashed out, desperately trying to seize one of them, but they continued to beat hard on his outstretched arms as he tried to grab them. As they became more aggressive, blood began to stream from all over his body. His pants were torn and the elastic split, leaving the brigadier completely naked. His buttocks were whiter than the rest of his body, so the streams of blood were more visible there, and his testicles shook with every blow. After a little, his arms flopped to his sides and began to quiver as well. "They've broken his arms!" I heard a voice behind me whisper. "God have mercy! This brigadier... he's an absolute madman!"

I didn't turn around to see where the voice was coming from. I was preoccupied with what was going on in front of me. As well as beating him, the men were trying to wrestle him to the ground, but the brigadier resisted, trying to slip out of their clutches. He was helped by the blood that was making his body slippery. They crowded around him, but whenever they succeeded in bending him a little, he leaped up and escaped from their clutches. After every movement, the ferocity of the blows would increase.

I saw a thick cudgel rise up behind the brigadier and come down with the speed of lightning. I heard the sound of it colliding with the brigadier's head. A sound like no other! Even the military policemen stopped beating, paralyzed for a few seconds by the sound... and the man wielding the cudgel stepped back two paces, his eyes frozen. The brigadier swiveled around ninety degrees as if wanting to turn to see his attacker. He took one step, but as he was on the point of lifting his other foot he crashed down in a heap onto the rough asphalt.

The silence was like a smooth white sheet extending into the spaces of Yard 1. It was broken by the adjutant's powerful voice. "God, you idiots! Drag him away and make him drink!" he shouted.

As the policemen dragged the brigadier away, one of them turned to the adjutant. "Sir, he's unconscious, how can he drink?" he asked.

"Put his head in the drain, he'll wake up then make him drink!"

They put the brigadier's head into the water in the drain, but he didn't wake up.

"Sir, he's maybe given you his life!"

"God grant him no mercy! Drag him into the middle of the yard and leave him there!"

They dragged him away by his arms as he lay on his back, his head lolling from side to side, blood mingling with sticky black and white patches on his face. A trail of dark red lines stretched over the rough asphalt from the drain to the middle of the yard, where the brigadier's corpse was laid out. "Now bring the wretched lieutenant to me here!" shouted the adjutant, the veins in his neck tense and prominent.

"So, you wretch!" he asked when the lieutenant stood before him. "Are you going to drink or not?"

"Okay, sir, okay, I'll drink!"

The lieutenant laid himself out on the asphalt in front of the drain and sunk his jaws into the drain water. The adjutant put his military boot on the head of the sprawled-out lieutenant and pressed down on it. "That's not enough," he said. "You have to drink and swallow!"

"Now take this dog to the welcoming ceremony," the adjutant continued, speaking to the policemen. "I want the reception to be complete!"

The lieutenant who had drunk and swallowed the filthy water, with its saliva, snot, urine and other filth, was thrown onto his back with astonishing speed. Two of the municipals put his feet in the falaqa rope, wrapped the rope around his ankles and raised his legs high.

His feet were sticking into the air as, in a well-rehearsed routine, three policemen arranged themselves in front of and around his feet in such a way that their whips could fall on his feet in perfect rhythm without any of the whips getting in the way of the others. The lieutenant's screams rang out as his body contorted itself, trying without success to escape. His screams and pleas for help spurred the adjutant into action, and he hurried over to him. Like a football player, the adjutant directed the front of his boot toward the lieutenant's head and kicked the ball.

The lieutenant screamed like an animal, howled like a wolf… This provoked the adjutant even more, and he crushed the lieutenant's mouth under the sole of his boot. As the policemen continued their work on the lieutenant's feet, the adjutant continued his work of crushing: head, chest, and stomach. There were kicks on the hip, and hysterical movements from the adjutant, who was shouting almost incomprehensibly: "Pimps! Scum! You work against the President! He made you a man, he made you a lieutenant in the army! And you work against him? Foreign agents! Spies! When the President has filled us with bread! And now you come to work against him, dogs! Agents of America, agents of Israel, sons of whores! Now you're pleading? And outside you were working like real men! Cowards! Are you screaming now, you scum?"

Against the rhythm of the adjutant's shouts, and the collective dance being danced on the lieutenant like a traditional *dabka*, the beatings of the policemen became more violent and vicious, even as the lieutenant's screams and appeals for help gradually subsided.

After a little the first lieutenant lay stretched out beside the brigadier. To this day I don't know what happened to him. Did he die or not? Had the prison administration received orders to kill the officers during the reception process?

Now came our turn. *May death come to you, you who forsake the prayer!* A phrase that I later heard so many times from the Islamists that I grew sick of it. But our turn had indeed come, the turn of anyone with a university degree: *licence*, baccalaureate, diploma, master's, doctorate... The doctors drank and swallowed the drain water; the engineers drank and swallowed the drain water; lawyers, university professors, even the film director drank and swallowed the drain water... yes, I drank and swallowed the drain water. The taste was indescribable. The strange thing was that none of those who drank it vomited. These people all had two things in common: a university degree and drinking drain water.

Then came more than thirty falaqas, each one carried by two municipals, with three men and three whips in front of them. And lots, lots of violence, pain and screaming.

Pain, weakness, violence, force, death.

My feet were swollen from the effects of Ayyoub's cane and I could hardly walk. When I walked over the rough asphalt in Yard 1, I was like someone walking on nails. The municipals lifted my legs up in the falaqa and the three whips lashed my swollen feet. A searing wave of pain swept through my inside, rising from my belly to explode in my chest. When the whips came down I couldn't breathe. My lungs suffered convulsions. They closed around the trapped air and stopped working. When the second wave of pain exploded in my chest, the air trapped in my lungs exploded, producing a scream of pain that I could feel escaping from my skull, from my eyes... I screamed and screamed, my legs nailed to the air. All my attempts to move them, to pull them away, failed. They were becoming detached from me, a mere source of pain, connected by a thread to the bottom of my abdomen and chest. Clashing waves of pain, a pain that started in the legs then spread upwards through the base of the abdomen to the chest before breaking in the head, producing a scream of pain, of terror and humiliation, strewing incredulity and incomprehension. More than thirty parallel, intersecting screams from more than thirty men, spreading through Yard 1.

31

At first, I sought refuge in God—I who had all my life prided myself on my atheism—but God could do nothing in the face of the force of the police. I grew angry and asked myself: "But where is God? Yard 1 is the best evidence for the nonexistence of a being called God!"

More than thirty screams of pain… of defeat… coming from the mouths of more than thirty cultured, educated men. More than thirty heads, every one full of ambitions, hopes and dreams. All were screaming. The howl of thirty wolves, the roar of more than thirty lions, would not be louder than the screams of these civilized people, could not be wilder or more animal-like.

My screams were lost in the midst of this forest of screams and the sound of whips landing on feet. The waves grew higher. I appealed to the Head of State. The beating grew more violent. I understood from them that I should not besmirch the name of His Excellency with my filthy mouth. I appealed to their Prophet: "For the sake of the Prophet!"

A blow to the head and the adjutant's thundering voice: "Yes, I'll fuck your mother, and the mother of Muhammad! Has any-one but Muhammad destroyed our house?"

I saw him moving away from me slowly and shouted: "Sir, please, your sister. Just a word!"

Waves of pain rising higher and higher, clashing together with more and more force. The adjutant moved further and further away. I shouted at the top of my voice: "Sir, I'm not a Muslim, I'm a Christian, I'm a Christian, sir, please, I'll kiss your hand, kiss your feet, I'm a Christian!"

The adjutant stood up, extremely slowly. He'd made out my voice amid all the other voices and heard it. He came back even more slowly, stood near me, and raised his right hand to the policemen, as if to say "Enough!"

My fate was now completely dependent on a word from the mouth of this adjutant, who hardly knew how to read.

"Are you a Christian or not?" he asked me, screwing up his eyes.

"Yes, sir, yes. May God forgive you and give you long life!"

"A Christian... turned into a Muslim Brother?"

"No, no, sir, I'm not Muslim Brotherhood!"

"Then why did they bring you here? Eh? For nothing? I mean, it's obvious, you dog! If these pimps deserve death once, you ought to die twice! Come on, you lot, a double ration for this dog! A Christian turned Muslim Brother!"

He went off and the three men increased the ration on my feet, as a fourth man brought his whip down on my naked thighs. The contractions grew worse with the pain. The flesh on the thighs is tender and is different from that on the soles of the feet. I choked on my screams then fell silent for a few moments to breathe in the air I would use to scream, a red veil quivering in front of my eyes, the level of pain unbearable.

Abandoned by the adjutant, I returned to God, for there was no one else except Him who could deliver me. In times of trouble and hopelessness a man returns to God. I returned to him, "secretly" hoping that he would deliver me from evil. I was very refined, with the most profound degree of faith and subservience.

"O Lord, deliver me. You are the Savior, deliver me from their hands!"

I spoke these words without saying them out loud. They revolved in my mind then quickly headed toward the heavens. My strength was ebbing, and my ability to scream was fading. The pain was becoming sharp as the edge of a sword blade. I could see the whips being lifted on high; I waited for them. If these whips came down on my body, I would certainly die. I had no strength left to endure more pain. Death… I returned to God: "Please God, let me die, let me die, spare me this torture." I developed a death wish; I genuinely desired death. But even death I couldn't attain.

The whips rose and fell. A red veil descended. The sky was pink, the pain became less, the screams became quieter. A gentle wave of tingling and numbness spread down from my feet to the other parts of my body. The numbness increased, and a wave of welcome relaxation swept over me. The whips rose and fell. Delicious pain. I felt my tense body relax, then I lost consciousness.

November 16

Since morning a cacophony of loudspeakers had been flooding the prison and its surroundings with patriotic songs and chants, glorifying the Head of State, attributing to him wisdom, courage, and numerous other qualities, for he is the Redeemer, the Great Leader, the Teacher, the Inspirer… proclaiming his universal virtues to every citizen, for were it not for him, the sun would not rise, and it is he who gives us air to breathe and water to drink…

The prisoners were all standing in orderly rows in the yards. For the first time since I came here they had allowed us to stand in the yard with our eyes open. They gave one of the prisoners a piece of paper, for him to shout out what was written on it, and for us to shout after him: "With our souls and blood we will redeem our beloved, adored leader!" Then they took us back to the dormitory. The ceremony had finished a short time ago.

I was feeling better now. More than six and a half months had gone by since I opened my eyes again to be confronted by a head that had been completely shaved. A bald man was leaning over me, trying to clean some of my injuries with a scrap of material that he had dampened with water. He saw I had regained consciousness, smiled at me and said: "Thank God you've woken up, I am Dr. Zahi.

Don't speak and don't move. Thank God you're okay, my brother, you're fated to have a new life, praise be to God most high!"

I couldn't speak or move. I needed three more days after regaining consciousness before I could speak, and more than a month before I could move. All this time, Dr. Zahi looked after me with the most meticulous care, compiling for me a sort of medical report and explaining to me in his delightful Eastern accent that my condition was serious for two reasons: first, one of my kidneys had been seriously damaged, so that I had been passing blood in my urine for a considerable time; and second, the area of skin on my body that had been damaged had reached an almost critical level—though the proportions varied according to the part of the body concerned. The skin on the back had almost completely disintegrated, as well as a portion of my belly, the front part of my thighs, and both the soles and upper part of my feet. The skin on my left foot had peeled off completely on the top and the bones were visible.

Zahi told me that I had been unconscious for six days, hovering between life and death. Salt was the only sterilizing agent available, so "Sheikh" Zahi—as he liked to be called, voluntarily dispensing with the title of doctor—had treated me with salt, as well as giving me water to drink, with a little diluted jam dissolved in the water.

He explained my medical situation to me, and informed me that according to the information that had reached them from the other dormitories, our intake was comprised of ninety-one individuals, of whom three had been killed in Yard 1 during the reception process and had not been admitted to the dormitories; ten others had died as a result of their serious injuries during the period when I was unconscious; two of the batch had been permanently paralyzed as a result of serious injury to their spines, and one had become blind after receiving a blow from a whip that had gouged out his eyes. After Zahi had finished conveying this information he said: "Thank God you are okay, thank God, my brother! And even though prayers are forbidden, you can make two prostrations in secret for the sake of God!"

Shaving

Nine days after I regained consciousness the dormitory head stood up in the morning and addressed everyone in the room:

"My brothers, today it is our turn to be shaved, so be patient and strong, God will help us! Pick up anyone who is sick and carry on blankets anyone who can't walk properly, each blanket to be held by four fedayeen. Be as quick as possible, speed is better, and God give us strength!"

He opened the door and everyone stood up. Four people picked me up. "Don't be afraid, brother, don't be afraid!" said one of them zealously. "We'll shield you with our bodies." There were two rows of policemen on each side of the door, with about two meters between one policeman and the next; each policeman carried a whip. As soon as a prisoner reached the door he would start to run, only to be met by the whips belonging to the right-hand row of policemen in front of him and pursued from behind by the left-hand row. Anyone who stumbled or fell could well die, for he would have broken the harmonious rhythm of the beating. The row behind him would stop and all the whips would converge on him. If he had a strong constitution and could get up, despite the dozens of whips raining down on him, he would be alright. A weak man, though, would be left stuck on the floor beneath the whips forever.

About three hundred prisoners from our dormitory rushed out, received a few quick, burning blows then lined up in the yard with their faces to the wall and eyes closed. They put the sick ones, including myself, in the middle of the yard. There were a lot of policemen and a lot of municipals holding razors for shaving the chin, as well as machines for shaving the hair off completely. It was completely sordid!

This was my first experience of shaving, which I would repeat many times in the days to come. From the first very time, however—as a result of my position as a sick man thrown into the middle of the yard, who could observe everything going on there despite his eyes being closed—my mind was struck by a number of human questions. The municipals were prisoners like us, and humiliated just like us; it was true that they were criminals—murderers, thieves, and perverts—but they suffered just like us from the appalling prison conditions, and politics meant nothing to them… so where did all this savage beating by the municipals come from, doled out to the prisoners with such terrible force during their shaving?

I was constantly asking myself, with amazement, whether it was comprehensible that a man should be so wicked. And this gratuitous vileness! Shaving the chin was a sort of operation to dissect or plough up the face, accompanied by cursing and spitting. Some people would take great pleasure in coughing before spitting on the prisoner's face, so that the spit would be accompanied by snot. The municipals' spit would stick to the prisoner's face and it was forbidden to wipe it off.

Shaving the head… with every pull of the machine over the head, after the municipals had shaken off the shaved off hair, they would hit the same machine hard on the shaved area, to the accompaniment of curses and whistles between the teeth: "You pimp, you son of a pimp, where did you get all these lice?" "You there, you queer, how come your head's a lice farm?" And with every blow from the machine, either the blood would swell up, or else a small circle would appear on the head where the blow had struck.

Coming from the same villages, towns, and even quarters, a lot of prisoners knew many of the municipals. But the same questions persisted: Why? Why were they so foul? What were the psychological motivations involved? Was it cruelty and sadism—either deeply rooted or incidental—which could be transmitted like an infection? Or was it the herd instinct? I wished I could have had the opportunity to speak to one of them.

One of the municipals rounded off my shave with a powerful blow to my bare head. "You dog, you son of a dog! You've broken my back. Couldn't you stand up straight?"

They let us all back in to the dormitory between the two rows of policemen as the whips rained down hard on the shaven heads. I lay down in the corner reserved for the sick. Signs of joy and pleasure could be seen in all the prisoners: "That's another shave completed successfully... and we're still alive!"

The Dormitory

As I lay for more than a month in this corner, I had the opportunity to observe and understand many things about this large dormitory. It was fifteen meters long and about six meters wide. There was a black iron door, and at the top of the walls, next to the roof, there were small windows fitted with thick iron bars. The windows were no more than fifty centimeters wide and a meter high. The most important feature of the dormitory was the skylight, about four meters long and two meters wide, which was set in the middle of the roof. It too was equipped with solid iron bars. This skylight, which was called the *sharraqa*, allowed the guard standing on the dormitory roof, who was armed with a rifle, to observe everything going on inside the dormitory at every hour of night and day. Every dormitory in the Desert Prison had an armed military policeman watching over it.

The hours of the day here fell into two parts, never more. Twelve hours of compulsory sleep, and twelve hours of compulsory sitting. Every prisoner had just three military blankets, one of which he folded and spread on the ground to make a bed, before covering himself with the other two. Anyone who had clothes surplus to the ones he was wearing would fold them and make them into a pillow, or else he would use his shoes as a pillow. Anyone like me who possessed neither surplus clothes nor shoes slept without a pillow.

Every prisoner had to follow instructions. From six in the evening to six in the morning he had to lie down without moving; then from six in the morning until six in the evening he had to fold up the three blankets and sit on them without moving. Visits to the restroom took place in accordance with a strict regime, since whenever the police guard felt like looking into the dormitory, he had to see no more than one person on his feet there, and it was part of the responsibilities of the dormitory head (who was also a prisoner) to arrange all this.

In the event of any breach—if someone sleeping made an unusual movement, for example; if two people were chatting to each other during the night; if there was more than one person on his feet; or if someone was sitting in a way that the guard didn't like—the guard would shout to the dormitory head: "Headman! You ass!"

"Yes, sir!"

"Teach this dog!..."

And so the prisoner would be "noted."

Each guard was on duty for two hours. The number of prisoners "noted" varied according to the whim of the guard. Every guard would inform the guard that followed him of the number he had "noted," and in the morning the total was reported to the sergeant, who came to the yard with a large number of military policemen and municipals, and shouted: "Okay, headman, you wretch! You've got thirty-three men 'noted.' Get them out here so I can see them!"

The fedayeen would come out. The reward or punishment for being "noted" had become a fixed one: five hundred lashes.

Food

There were three meals a day. Each prisoner had two loaves of military bread. The food came in plastic containers, with dinner usually being lentil soup, and lunch burghul and potato broth. The potatoes were cooked in a tomato pulp without being washed or peeled, so there was always several centimeters of earth lying at the bottom of the container of stew. Breakfast was *lebne*—strained yogurt—or olives and sometimes boiled eggs.

The municipals would bring in the containers of food, put them down in front of the dormitories then go away. More than six hundred loaves of bread, about ten plastic containers full of burghul, and the same number of broth, all stacked up in front of the dormitory.

Three times a day the black iron door would be opened to let the food in, and each time the fedayeen would be standing behind the door. As soon as the door was opened, they would all in the twinkling of an eye be at the food, which they would carry off with the speed of lightning. One *fedayi* for each container of burghul, and two to carry the container of broth; the bread would be piled up on the blankets, each blanket carried by four people. For the whole of the time it took for the food to be brought in, the policemen's whips would be working hard; every policeman was a specialist in devising new forms of torment.

In front of the precious container of lentil soup, the sergeant grabbed the fedayi who'd carried the dish in. "Leave the container on the floor, you whore!" he said. The prisoner left the container and stood there. "Now dip your hands in the soup and let's see…" His hands emerged from the soup with the skin peeling. Then the sergeant forced him to carry the container into the dormitory with his peeling hands. Every few days one or more people would be killed as the food was brought into the dormitories.

The fedayeen

There were people of all ages here: men of eighty, and youths no more than fifteen years old; sick people, weak people, and people with disabilities, either actual or as a result of torture. The fedayeen were a group of strong and physically fit young men who had volunteered to undertake important tasks requiring speed and the strength to carry things, like bringing the food into the dormitory; or, if a sick or elderly man had been "noted" by the guards, then one of the fedayeen would take the place of the sick man and receive the five hundred lashes. No one knew which dormitory in the jail it was that first devised this "fedayeen brigade," but at a certain point it became clear that every dormitory in the prison had one. In subsequent years the police discovered this. One day the guards were amusing themselves watching a dormitory and "noting" the inmates, when the number of prisoners who'd been "noted" exceeded the number of the members of the fedayeen brigade. Some of the fedayeen insisted on going out a second time to receive another five hundred lashes. The policemen immediately discovered fresh bruises and marks of beating on their feet, but despite that they did nothing about it.

"We're a blueprint for martyrdom," I heard one of the fedayeen say to his colleague. They were sincere in their quest for martyrdom, and the fedayeen brigades saved many lives. Their actions were characterized by great sincerity and an abandon that sprang from deep faith.

On another occasion I heard one of them utter a private prayer after the communal prayer he'd performed while remaining sitting: "God, verily you are able to do anything, grant me martyrdom in your illustrious name, and take me to your paradise, where are the best of prophets and believers."

Some of them undertook their duties in silence with great humility, but in others I observed a tone of arrogance and superiority when they spoke.

The bath

Six of us in the dormitory were sick and unable to go to the bath. In addition to myself, I had a colleague from the same intake who had remained unconscious for the whole of the time I was unable to move, and there were also four paralytics—two paralyzed as children, the third during reception, and the fourth paralyzed as a result of the "parachute" torture. Three of our intake had come into this dormitory. One died after two days. I regained consciousness after six days, while the third remained hovering between life and death for two months, after which he regained consciousness and recovered.

The bath was compulsory for everyone except those who could not move, especially as "Cleanliness is a Part of Faith" was inscribed on the door. The dormitory went to the bath twice during the month when I could not move, taking off all their clothes except for their underpants. After my partial recovery, when I was able to move again, I went with the rest of the dormitory to the bathroom.

The underpants I was wearing when I arrived had either been torn during the reception process or lost. After six days of unconsciousness I woke up to find myself wearing underpants that reached my knees, with my own clothes piled up beside me.

In these underpants I stood in line in the dormitory waiting to go to the bathroom. Everyone was on edge, everyone was scared. We stood behind the black door enveloped in prayers and supplications to God. Behind me two people were talking about the prison gates, all black and all made of iron. One of them was telling the other about a female prisoner called Tarifa who had promised herself—as a result of the many provocations that the black gates had caused her—that after she got out of prison she would bring a carpenter to remove all the doors of her house. She never wanted to see closed doors again. The door opened, and we ran out, two by two. On either side of us were policemen holding whips, which rose and fell on people at random. Everyone was barefoot. My feet hadn't healed properly yet. From Yard 6 we crossed three more yards until we reached the bathhouse, a rectangular building that contained several cubicles—a leftover from the French occupation. They let us in two at a time to a cubicle with no door, and handed out military soap with a blow to the head. Everyone had a slab of soap. There were shouts and curses, and in the midst of it all a lot of emphasis on not using the bathhouse as an opportunity to bugger one another. After all, they knew that we were all homosexuals and that we did all sorts of things to each other...

The temperature of the water falling from the shower was impossibly hot, and the place was full of steam. We could hardly bear the heat of the water on our bodies, and came out after just a minute—give or take a few seconds—as the whips fell again. There was a different rhythm to their whipping on our wet bodies, which stung hard as we ran back to the dormitory bearing only the marks of our beating.

A short time later, when the prison became overfull, the bathhouse would be closed and turned into a dormitory for Communist detainees.

Dr. Zahi continued to treat me and the other patients. Apart from the wound on the top of my left foot, all my injuries had almost healed. But the bones in the instep were protruding after the skin had been ripped off them, and Dr. Zahi was afraid of other complications; on one occasion he brought someone else with him, whom he introduced as a specialist in skin conditions. This doctor told me that in our dormitory alone there were twenty-three doctors with differing specialties.

My colleague from the same intake resisted death for more than two months, at the end of which (also as a result of Zahi's care and attention) his health started to improve. He gradually emerged from his state of unconsciousness, and when he was able to move his head, looked in my direction and registered an expression of great surprise at the sight. For a few minutes he seemed completely nonplussed, until Zahi, who was beside him, asked him if he had seen a dinosaur! But he merely fidgeted and didn't reply.

During the first couple of months, I had built up relationships with some of the other prisoners. I had a good relationship with Zahi and several times we sat talking together about prison and freedom. He shared with me several of his medical and family concerns and even revealed to me his fear that an epidemic might spread inside the prison, and how in the absence of medicines and medical procedures any epidemic would prove fatal. I asked him once when he had been imprisoned and brought to the Desert Prison.

"Immediately after the massacre," he replied.

"Which massacre do you mean?"

"Oh come on! Do you really mean you haven't heard of the massacre, my brother?"

"No, never. I wasn't in the country, I was in France."

He then related to me the details of what had happened in what is known as the Desert Prison massacre. There were about a thousand

Islamist prisoners in this jail. One scorching June day, helicopters landed, full of heavily armed soldiers led by the President's brother. They got out of the helicopters in the prison yards and machine-gunned the prisoners in their dormitories. Then they rounded up a number of them in the yards and butchered them all. Zahi came to the prison immediately after the massacre. Blood, human hair, and pieces of flesh and brains were still stuck to the walls and the floor of the dormitory where he'd been admitted.

Zahi paused for a moment in his account, looked gloomily up through the sharraqa and went on: "God have mercy on them all, they were all martyred, they were heroes of the first order. God's mercy be upon them! Imagine, my brother... during the massacre, imagine how many Muslim Brothers managed to attack the armed soldiers and snatch their arms. They knew they were going to die anyway, so why shouldn't they resist? So they carried on resisting with these weapons until they were either martyred or their am-munition ran out. The soldiers incurred substantial losses. God's mercy be upon them. It's strange that you've never heard of this massacre, my brother!"

During those two months no one asked about my religion. It didn't occur to anyone that I might be anything but a Muslim, especially as my name didn't give me away. After the experience I'd had in the intelligence center I didn't tell anyone, especially if it could be taken out of context. My colleague's shock when he saw me changed all that, and by two days later the whole dormitory had found out that I was a Christian, an atheist, and a spy! The results were immediately apparent. I was completely ostracized by everyone. No one would greet me, and if I said good morning to anyone, he would look in the opposite direction—contrary to the instructions of their Prophet, who said: "Return a greeting with a better one!" On the third day after the shock Zahi pretended that he wanted to examine my foot. "You being a Christian isn't a problem," he said, inspecting the foot closely. "That makes you one of the 'People of the Book.' But for you to be a spy for the regime, it just doesn't add up. You were going to be tortured to death, but these dogs don't kill their spies! But tell me, is it true that you announced in front of everyone at the intelligence center that you were an atheist?"

"It's true, doctor. But I said it to escape torture and prison!"

"That's not a sufficient excuse, but I think you're a good man, and for this reason I'm saying to you... be careful... be very careful! There is a group of extremists in this dormitory who think that it is their duty to kill unbelievers 'wherever they may be.' And you're known to everybody as an unbeliever. And another thing, please don't try to speak to me. I can't behave differently to the rest of them!"

"Thank you, doctor, for everything."

"No need to thank someone for doing their duty."

A week went by without any significant developments. Then one day I walked out of the lavatory limping, to be immediately surrounded by about a dozen men, all young, in their early twenties. "Stand there, you... you wretch... you unbeliever, this is the end of you, you dog!" one of them said, the words grating between his teeth. I was stunned. I stood motionless, my feet frozen to the ground, and for a few fractions of a second I looked into the eyes that were staring back at me, overflowing with hatred and malice, bursting with insistence and determination. The circle tightened around me. Total surrender, or rather, a sort of mental paralysis overtook me.

Throughout the preceding period I had been continually afraid: afraid of the secret service, afraid of the military police, afraid of the grating of the key in the dormitory door, afraid of beatings, pain, and death. But now—when I could see death staring at me through the eyes that surrounded me—was I afraid? I don't know, I was just like stone, a piece of wood bereft of sentiment and feelings, with no thoughts, no reactions. Total paralysis, total submission.

A heavy, leaden silence descended on the small space in front of the lavatory. It was a place that the guard on the roof couldn't see from the sharraqa in the roof. They approached me slowly, with extremely small steps, as they moved toward the center of the circle that had formed around me. Had they decided to torture me by prolonging my life of fear and terror? Were they afraid of my reactions? Had they not yet resolved on my death? I didn't know. Suddenly the silence was shattered. The human circle around me was broken as an elderly man leaped forward and put his arms around me. "Anyone that attacks this person has attacked me!" he said in a hoarse but calm voice, turning to those surrounding me. He said it in formal classical Arabic, taking the aggressors by surprise. They stopped. "Sheikh Mahmoud, Sheikh Mahmoud, we respect you, but what has this to do with you?" asked one of them. "You are a religious sheikh, and should be with us in putting an end to unbelief and unbelievers!"

"No, I am not with you! God most high said: 'Do not kill a soul that God has made sacrosanct except justly!'"

"But this man is an unbeliever, Sheikh Mahmoud!"

"God alone knows what is in men's souls and the secrets of their hearts!"

"But he's a Christian, and a spy!"

"Converse with them in a civilized way and do not entertain suspicions of people!"

Everyone in the dormitory was observing what was happening, though only a small group collected around us. I imagined that most of them were Sheikh Mahmoud's supporters. Suddenly I saw Dr. Zahi beside me. Sheikh Mahmoud turned to him. "Zahi, take this man to his place!" he ordered him. Dr. Zahi pulled me away, dragging me by the shoulder, and the circle around us opened up without any resistance. "Sit down in your place and don't say a word!" he said, leading me to my bed.

The dormitory head's place was beside the door. In that way he could always be ready to speak to the policeman when the door opened. They'd put my bed on the other side of the door in place of the person who'd been occupying it earlier. It seems they'd refused to have me among them. The door was on my left. The person on my right, who was my only neighbor, had moved his bed more than a quarter of a meter away from me despite the overcrowding and limited space, and no one had objected.

I was now completely ostracized, and continually under threat. I sat on my bed in a state of depression, avoiding looking in any particular direction. As the days passed, a shell began to grow around me, made up of two walls. One wall was formed of their hatred for me. I was swimming in a sea of hatred, loathing and revulsion, trying as hard as I could not to drown. The second wall was made up of my fear of them. I opened a window in the hard wall of the shell and began to spy on the dormitory from the inside, the only thing that I could do.

December 31

Today was New Year's Eve. Where would Suzanne have been spending the day? I hadn't being paying any attention to dates. The days here were all alike. But I heard the dormitory head remark to some of the prisoners that today was the Christian New Year and that tomorrow would be a Thursday, and that with luck the tyrants would stay awake, behave badly and disturb the peace until the morning, after which they would sleep. That meant that the helicopter wouldn't come tomorrow. No trials and no executions. After that, I listened to the sounds outside the dormitory. Some of the police seemed to be celebrating the New Year in their rooms. The phrase *A Party in Hell* went through my mind. Was it the title of a film? Or the title of a novel? A play? It didn't matter. My longing for Suzanne during the eight previous months had been almost wild.

And my family, where were they now? What were they doing? How would they be explaining my absence all this time? What had they done to find out where I was, or where and why I had disappeared…? My mother and father lived here and had been expecting me back. But I hadn't arrived home, so where was I? This must be their main concern. My father was a retired officer and had acquaintances, as did my uncle. My uncle also had some influence, as did other relatives. Why had they so far made no move to get me out of this hell? But how did I know they hadn't? Surely, they must all be making some effort by now.

These thoughts gave me some hope. But I needed someone to talk to about all these things, to question, and to share my concerns. I looked around me, only to be met by expressionless faces. More than half a year had passed since they had boycotted me. Just a few words from the dormitory head in case of necessity, and a few surreptitious words from Zahi. My lips were sealed, and only opened to put in food. I felt that my tongue had started to become rusty. Could a man forget how to speak if he didn't speak for a long time? I had to speak, even if only to myself. Let them say I was mad!

I couldn't touch anything of theirs, or their bodies. Once I was walking to the washbasins and my hand touched someone's hand, and he went back and washed to purify himself. If I used the water tap the person after me would wash it with soap seven times, because I was simply "unclean." Once I heard someone tell someone else that it wasn't enough to wash the tap with soap seven times, but that we ought to have some earth, for the Prophet (may God bless him and grant him peace!) said: "If a dog defiles a vessel, wash it seven times, once with earth."

The person distributing food would put my food in front of the bed and avoid touching my blanket or looking at me. They all would keep silent in front of me. But despite that I was able to discover a good deal about their inner lives and how they lived and coped inside the prison.

Prayer

Prayer was strictly forbidden by order of the prison governor. The punishment for being caught committing the crime of prayer was death. Despite that, they did not miss a single prayer time. There is a "prayer of fear" or something of the sort in Islam, but they had modified it so that people prayed sitting in their places, or in some other position, without the normal bowings or prostrations. The prison administration knew this too, and made sure that it was reported to the prison governor, who repeated it in front of the communist prisoners.

The way the prison governor talked was always like a lecture or a formal address. "These dogs," he told the communists, "these Muslim Brothers, it was only yesterday that I spent more than half an hour explaining to them and trying to make them understand that nationalism was more important than religion. But would you believe it? Today they are back there praying again! These people are very strange! Why are their minds so closed?"

Communication

All the dormitories were connected to each other, each dormitory being adjacent to two others, on the left and the right, and sometimes also one at the rear. This greatly facilitated communication between the prisoners, which was done by tapping on the wall. One tap on the wall, two taps, a strong tap, a weak tap—the same code as telegrams transmitted using Morse code. Everything that happened inside the prison, new intakes, who'd died, the number and names of those executed, news from outside the prison as conveyed by recently arrived prisoners—all this was transmitted through the dormitories using Morse code. Every dormitory had a group who specialized in transmitting and receiving the codes, and these were supported by a group of memorizers.

The memorizing started with the beginning of the "trial," as the Islamists called it. The older sheikhs would sit and recite chapters and verses of the Qur'an to a group of youths, and the youths would carry on repeating them until they had memorized them. In this way, a mechanism for memorization was generated. There was no one in the dormitory who hadn't memorized the Qur'an from beginning to end. With each new intake a new cycle began. Later, the process developed in a different direction. A group of young men would be selected who, in addition to memorizing the Qur'an and the *hadith*s of the Prophet Muhammad, would memorize what might be described as the prison "register," comprising the names of everyone connected with the Islamist movements who had been admitted to the prison. In our dormitory there was a young man, not yet twenty, who had memorized more than thirty thousand names—the name of the prisoner, the name of his city, town or village, the date of his admission to prison, and his fate. Some of them specialized in executions and murders; they called everyone killed or executed in prison a martyr, and this was the register of martyrs. They also memorized the name, family address, and date of execution or murder.

I liked this procedure and started to train myself to do it. After I'd acquired the necessary proficiency, I decided to write this diary. I would write a sentence in my mind, then repeat it, memorize it, then write it out again, and memorize it. By the end of the day I would have written and memorized the main events of the day. I discovered that this was a good way to keep the mind sharp and pass the long time in prison. The following morning, I would recite everything I'd memorized the previous day.

I later discovered that what saved my life was that the other prisoners weren't a single group. As well as the fundamentalists who had sentenced me to death, there was a political organization that didn't carry arms and hadn't taken part in military operations. Then there was the Islamic Liberation Group—a pacifist grouping that included Sheikh Mahmoud and Zahi, who saved my life—as well as a large number of disparate Sufi groups, and others. Although these groups appeared similar to each other, they actually differed to such an extent that they would accuse each other of heresy, and would indulge in violent beatings and physical fist fights without mercy. They were so cruel that some members of the extremist group would relate how they had concluded their military training with a practical demonstration, during which they had killed some garbage men in the early morning while they were cleaning the streets. This was merely training, or a "baptism of blood." These same men could turn into extremely gentle people, who would cry when a new arrival related how the security services tortured a small child in front of its parents in order to get them to confess, or how a girl had been raped in front of her father to humiliate him and force him to reveal any information he possessed.

Their bravery in the face of torture and death was legendary, especially with the fedayeen brigades. I saw some of them genuinely rejoicing as they went to their executions. I don't believe that such bravery could be found anywhere else or in any other human group. There was a lot of cowardice as well, but cowardice does not attract the same attention as bravery. For in this situation cowardice and fear appear natural, while bravery seems exceptional. But here, when cowardice was excessive, it was traced back to lack of faith in God.

Like a tortoise that has sensed danger and retreated inside its shell, I sat in my own shell, secretly watching and observing, recording, and waiting for release.

August 31

Two summers and one winter had passed since my arrival here in the midst of this vast desert. Here there were not four seasons but only two—summer and winter—and we didn't know which one was crueler than the other. In summer, winter seemed like a mercy, while in winter we felt the opposite.

We were now at the height of summer. The weather was scorching and there was no air to breathe. The atmosphere was so heavy that it required a great effort to suck it into our lungs, and this made us sweat a lot. I heard someone who already knew the area say that the temperature outside sometimes reached 50°C or even 60°C and that it was at least 45°C in the shade inside the dormitory. "Damn it, are we prisoners in an oven?" someone asked with a groan.

Some older prisoners had a fight. The dormitory head knocked on the door and informed the policeman that someone had died, so they opened the door. "Where's the body? Come on, get it outside!" said the policeman, his voice almost running with the temperature.

The dormitory head had somehow managed to keep some plastic food containers inside the dormitory. In the early morning, before people had woken up, the "day service" would fill the containers with water. All the prisoners were in their underpants, covering just their private parts between the waist and the knee. Four of them would occupy the small area in front of the lavatories, and four members of the "day service" would pour water over the heads and bodies of the first four. This service was organized as a rota by the prisoners themselves, but I was exempt from all categories of duties. The first to bathe would then quickly leave, dripping with water, and another four would come in, and so on.

Six blankets soaked in water, each held by two of the "duty" standing at equal intervals inside the dormitory, were shaken to circulate the air and moisten the atmosphere, like fans. This was an ordinary summer's day.

By contrast, the winter's day was a sort of shrunken day. Everyone had threadbare clothes, which offered no protection against a bitter desert cold that ate away at the bones and made the joints stiff. I had just three blankets, worn out by time and used by hundreds of prisoners before me. I wore my smart Parisian suit, with its jacket and trousers—the police had confiscated the tie. The suit jacket was still in good condition, but the trousers were ripped at the knees and the rear; the zipper had broken and the buttons had come off. I wore it night and day for days at a time. I had pulled out some threads from the blanket, twisted them together and made them into a belt to hold up the trousers instead of the buttons and zipper. I'd seen someone else do this, so I tried it myself. There were no needles or thread here. I had two pairs of underpants. One of the new arrivals in the dormitory had a very rich family, who'd been able to visit him while he was in the security office, after paying the equivalent of a small fortune as a bribe to the officer responsible. They'd been advised to take a lot of clothes for their son. He brought with him more than a hundred sets of underpants, my share of which was a single pair, which the dormitory head gave me, saying:

"Take these, so that you have a spare!"

The desert cold was more severe than any other cold. I had lived through some very cold days in France when the temperature dropped below zero, but that seemed like a civilized cold, while the cold here was rude and relentless. The problem of lice was also worse in the winter. The only solution for the lice—which were widespread throughout the dormitories—was to sit down, take all your clothes off, and start searching for them in the folds of your clothes. Everyone here did that, and I followed suit after my skin had begun to itch, though I couldn't produce the sound like "tchah!" that other people made between their teeth whenever they crushed one between their thumbnails.

Every day after breakfast everyone took off their clothes and started to examine them, looking for lice. I too took hold of a louse and crushed it between my nails. It was disturbing to find so many lice. "Where can all these lice have come from?" someone wondered angrily. "Every day we rid our clothes of them; every day we perform our ablutions five times; we wash our bodies with soap and cold water most days; we wash our clothes, we wash our blankets, and the next day we see more and more lice! Damn it, could someone actually be spraying the dormitories with lice?"

September 10

For the first time, a discussion was going on in the dormitory about something other than things mentioned in the Qur'an or the traditions of the Prophet. It was a long discussion, with more than ten people taking part, including two disabled men. All discussions, arguments, even fights were conducted in a quiet voice, for fear of being overheard by the police. The subject of the discussion was Islamic civilization and Western civilization. It was started by a chance remark made by a doctor who had studied in Europe about freedom and the ideals of Western democracy. The discussion went on a long time and ended with one of the disabled men saying: "You say Western civilization! Look around you, my friend! I'm disabled from the 'German chair'; here's Muhammad Ali, disabled as well by a bullet made in Russia that lodged in his spine; this prison was built by France; and the handcuffs they put around my wrists have 'Made in Spain' written on them. The officer who arrested me was carrying a Belgian revolver, and the officers who supervised the investigation and torture were trained in America, Britain, and Russia… These are the products of Western civilization. If you add to all this, the vast quantity of debauchery, depravity, and moral corruption, then there you have Western civilization in all its glory in front of your eyes."

In a tired voice, and the tone of someone wanting to put an end to a pointless conversation without acknowledging his opponent's arguments, the doctor replied: "There are a lot of accusations there… I don't say that we should imitate the West or adopt its negative aspects, but the West also has science, medicine, and agricultural and industrial development. And on top of all that, and more important than everything, people there have freedom and respect. If we want to progress, we need to learn a lot from them, especially respect for people and respect for their freedom. There is nothing wrong with that."

December 25

I couldn't sleep. At six o'clock I pulled the blanket over me as usual, and stretched myself out. At half past midnight my sides had started to hurt and I'd grown tired of lying down, so I sat up and wrapped myself in my blankets. Five minutes later, the guard's voice came through the skylight:

"Dormitory head, you ass!"

"Yes, sir!"

"Note down that idiot who's sitting up beside you for me!"

"Yes, sir!"

So he "noted" me. I lay down immediately. Tomorrow morning, my breakfast would be five hundred lashes on my feet with the tank fan belt! The foot that had been injured had healed completely, leaving a long scar, but it always hurt on cold days so I wrapped it up more than the other one. I dreamed of a pair of woollen socks... one of my little dreams. What would be the fate of this poor foot when it received five hundred lashes? I couldn't sleep till morning. Then the door opened and the policeman shouted to the dormitory head to let out the people who had been "noted." I jumped up, but the dormitory head quickly said: "Stay where you are, don't move, one of the lads has taken your place!"

I was astonished. One of the fedayeen, one of the fundamentalists who had tried to kill me because I was an unbeliever, was now sacrificing himself for me and taking five hundred lashes on my behalf! For almost a year and a half, I hadn't spoken a single word. I looked at the dormitory head in astonishment. Two words fell from my lips involuntarily: "But... why?" The dormitory head didn't reply, but cut me off with a wave of his hand. His gesture was full of loathing and contempt.

The people who'd been lashed came back from their drubbing, running barefoot over the rough asphalt. More than one of them gave me a look of hatred and contempt from the corner of his eye. So why?

I needed a considerable time before I was able to arrive at a plausible conjecture: namely, that as I was a spy, they were anxious I should have no contact with any of the police, and thus be able to act as an informer.

The same day, it was our dormitory's turn for the "break."

The Break

In other prisons, the "break" is a short period of time in which the prisoner is let out from his dormitory to a courtyard with fresh air and some sports facilities in it, so that he can do some physical exercise, take the sun, and get a tan... absorb all the air, sunshine, and exercise that he needs, in other words. Here, before the "break," before the police opened the door, the prisoners in the dormitory would have been formed into a twisting line, one behind the other. Then the row slowly emerged, heads bent down and eyes closed, each prisoner holding on to the clothes of the one in front of him. The yard would be packed with police and municipals around the sides, and the row would move quickly or slowly depending on the mood and inclination of the sergeant.

Tuesday and Thursday were different from the other days of the week here. Executions were held on these two days. When we went out for the "break" on Tuesdays or Thursdays there were more beatings and torture than on other days, and the beatings during the "break" were usually on the head.

"Why are you raising your head, you dog?"

And the whip would fall on the head.

"And you, you son of a whore! Why are you opening your eyes under there?"

And the whip would fall on the head.

There was less torture during the summer. The heat of the sun, which penetrated our brains, made the policemen feel lazy and reluctant to move. But in winter the torture was intense.

Sometimes, while the line was moving around, the policemen would gather around the sergeants, and conversations would take place that we couldn't hear. Then suddenly the idea of using us to entertain themselves would take their fancy and the sergeant would shout: "You wretch, you, you, tall boy! Tallest one in the line, come here!" So one of the municipals would run and drag over the tallest prisoner, who was more than two meters tall, while the sergeant sat on a concrete block that looked like a chair, puffing out his chest and pulling his head backwards and upwards, one leg on top of the other. "Hey, you wretch! Are you a human being or a giraffe?"

The men gathered around him would laugh loudly, as the sergeant continued: "Come on, you! Run around the yard five times and make a noise like a giraffe! Come on, quickly, look smart about it!" The prisoner ran around, making various noises, though no one actually knew what a giraffe sounded like, even the sergeant himself, I think. At all events, the prisoner ran around five times, then stopped, and the sergeant said: "You wretch! Come on, now you're going to bray like a donkey!" The tall prisoner brayed, and the policemen laughed. "Come on, you wretch! Now you're going to bark like a dog!" The tall prisoner barked, the policemen laughed, and the sergeant shook with laughter. "You wretch!" he said. "Ha, ha, that's great, very good! You really are like a dog!"

Then he turned to the line of prisoners making their way along with bowed heads and closed eyes, and shouted: "You wretch, you, you! Shortest one in the row! Come here!"

One of the municipals ran up, dragging the shortest one in the row. A young boy of not more than fifteen, a little over a meter and a half tall, stood in front of the sergeant, who laughed and said: "You wretch! Midget, stand in front of this tall dog!" The short prisoner stood in front of the tall one and the guard shouted: "You wretch! The tall one! Go on, howl and take a bite out of the dog in front of you, take a piece out of his shoulder! And when you've taken the piece out... a thousand lashes!" The tall man howled three or four times in a row then went up to the short man and bent over him, placing his jaws over his shoulder. The short man screamed with pain and screwed himself up as he was bitten. "You wretch! The tall one! Where's the piece of flesh? Policemen! Let him have it!" The police rained down their whips on the tall prisoner, bringing him down to the level of his shorter colleague as he fell to his knees, tottering. Then the sergeant shouted: "Enough!" The police stopped beating. "Wretch, the tall one! Get up and stay standing!"

The tall prisoner stood up. "Wretch, the short one! Stand behind him!" The short prisoner went back behind the tall one. "Now then, both of you, take off your clothes!" They both took off their clothes and stayed there in just their pants. "Wretch, the short one! Take down his pants!"

The short prisoner dropped down the tall one's pants to the knees. "Take down your own pants as well!" The short prisoner dropped his own pants as well. "Now then, get closer, fuck him! Do what you do to each other every night, you queers! Come on, closer, fuck him!"

The short prisoner hesitated, and the tall prisoner's buttocks tightened and quivered, as the sergeant gestured to one of the policemen, who came over and brought his whip down on the short prisoner's back. The short one held on to the tall one from behind, and the tall one shuddered. The short prisoner's limp member hardly reached the tall one's knees. The sergeant and the other policemen laughed.

The line moved on, with bowed heads and closed eyes. Despite that, everyone could see, everyone could hear. And the anger and humiliation piled up.

The sergeant ordered them to change places, so that the tall prisoner was behind the short one. His limp, shriveled member reached halfway up the back of the short one. The laughter continued...

The line moved on, with bowed heads and closed eyes.

Another "break," another day, another sergeant, other policemen, other municipals, the same prisoners, a few more, a few less.

The sergeant sat on the same concrete block, one leg over the other, shouting as he looked at the line moving along, with bowed heads and closed eyes.

"Bring me that idiot… the fat one!"

They brought a fat man in his forties. The guard established his name, the name of his city, how long he had spent in jail, and other details. Then he asked him: "Are you married or single?"

"Married, sir!"

"You know how much your wife costs now? I'm telling you, she's become a whore. You've been in prison three years, and she's with someone new every day."

The prisoner, with bowed head and closed eyes, said nothing, as the guard went on: "Why are you silent? Say something! Or are you ashamed to say that you're married to a whore in front of these young men? What, are pimps ashamed as well?"

The days went by, the sergeants changed, but the methods stayed the same. "Your wife's a whore" became "your sister's a whore," if the prisoner wasn't married, or even "your mother's a whore," or "your daughter's a whore" if the prisoner had girls.

I wondered: was this just a diversion or a habit of thought? Was the driving factor behind such a concentration on this topic the sergeants' sexual hang-ups and "Eastern" complexes, which they rid themselves of through the power they wielded over the prisoners? Or was it an acquired way of behaving, intended to crush and humiliate a man through the woman—whether she be wife, sister, mother, or any other female relative—as representing the highest values of honor that a Muslim could have? With us Easterners in general, a woman's honor means not having sex outside marriage, and any different behavior on her part may damage and bring shame on the family as a whole.

It was impossible to find out the names of the policemen or sergeants, though the prisoners gave them names of their own. These names were either based on some distinctive characteristic of the person concerned, like "one-eyed," or "four-ways"—for a guard who shook so uncontrollably as he walked that it seemed the various parts of his body were each moving in a different direction. Or else the name would depend on some piece of clothing, like the guard called "Abu Shahata," who always appeared wearing wooden shoes. Usually, though, the name would be related to an expression that the sergeant was constantly repeating; there was one guard known as "You wretch," one known as "Son of a whore!", one called "Donkey," and so on. So a prisoner might ask his friend on his return from punishment: "Who's in the yard today?" "Son of a whore!," his friend would reply, meaning the sergeant who was always repeating this expression.

February 22

In the early morning, before the food had been brought in, the police would open the door to the dormitory and come in like a hundred raging bulls invading the place. They would shout, curse, and lash with their whips. "Face to the wall, face to the wall!" they would shout between their lashes and curses. As soon as the first policeman came in like this, the prisoners leaped up and turned their faces to the wall. I stood up, not knowing what to do... I felt the whip come down on my cheek and wrap itself around my neck from the back, as the policeman shouted: "Face to the wall!" I turned my face around and froze, as a shaft of pain made its way down from my face to my neck. After about five minutes, silence reigned then the voice of a policeman could be heard shouting at the top of his voice: "Attention! In your places, get ready!" All the policemen stamped their feet on the ground, and the line moved forward. Then, in an even louder voice: "The dormitory's ready, lieutenant colonel, sir!"

It was the prison governor. He started to walk from one end of the dormitory to the other between two rows of policemen who were standing at the ready, military style. My curiosity got the better of me and without thinking about it I sneaked a look at the lieutenant colonel out of the corner of my eye. I could see him; he was a young man of around thirty with fair hair, who both walked and talked rather tensely. He spoke as if he was talking to himself, and I couldn't understand either his words or the connection between them.

"I'm ruined! I'll send her to hell! A thousand criminals in exchange for a single hair!" Then he shouted in a strangulated voice: "Dogs! Criminals! You still don't know me properly! By God, I'll slaughter you like sheep!" "Out of the way!" he shouted to a group of policemen standing between him and the prisoners. The sound of revolver shots, one after the other. I cowered when I heard them and lowered my head to my chest. Then, with astonishing speed, the lieutenant colonel left, dragging behind him a line of policemen, and the door shut.

Fourteen shots and fourteen dead. That was the lieutenant colonel's entire supply of ammunition, so it appeared. The doctors, including Zahi, ran to the corner of the dormitory where the dead lay, and examined them all. All had died instantly, from a single bullet to the back of the head. They dragged the bodies to the middle of the dormitory and a pool of fresh blood formed. Some people sat around the blood crying, but most were stunned and motionless, the doctors in a state of bewilderment, not knowing what to do. One of the fedayeen stood up and said: "There is

63

no power and no strength save in God. We are God's and to God do we return. May the mercy of God be upon them, they have departed first and we shall follow later. O God, give them rest in your spacious gardens: these are martyrs in the cause of elevating your word, the word of truth, so grant them mercy, O merciful, compassionate one!" He was silent for a moment then continued, directing his words to everyone: "Come, brothers, let us perform our duty."

They waited until the flow of blood from the corpses had stopped, then carried them and set them down near the door in front of me and the dormitory head. Among the dead was Sheikh Mahmoud, who had saved my life. I secretly prayed for him, and felt sorrow for them all, for their faces had become familiar to me, but my sorrow for Sheikh Mahmoud was the greatest.

They cleared the ground of blood, and cleaned all the blankets that had been soiled. There was then a discussion between two groups in front of the dormitory head. One group said that we should take all their clothes, because the living took precedence over the dead, but the other group opposed this view and thought it would be shameful. Finally, the view prevailed that those remaining alive needed the clothes, so a group was charged with removing the clothes and cleaning them. The corpses were taken out of the dormitory at night, naked except for their underpants.

Three years later, a new arrival would declare that the reason for this massacre was that the armed organization had sent a death threat to the major if he didn't improve the treatment of the Islamist prisoners. The major found this threat under the windshield wiper of his car as he was going to work one morning, so he proceeded to kill the people concerned and spread the news so that the organization would hear of it, accompanied by a counter-threat: "For a written note I killed fourteen individuals! If a hair of my own head or that of anyone who concerns me is touched, the equivalent will be one hundred. And if any harm befalls any of my relatives or any of them dies, I will not leave anyone alive."

There were no further threats.

Our dormitory was close to the rear door of the prison. Food came in through this door; the Russian truck would park at the rear and the municipals would proceed to unload the large pots of food. In the same truck and through the same door, the corpses would be carried away each day a little after midnight. By listening to the thud of the corpses against the floor of the truck, we could deduce the number of those who had died that day. On the day of the lieutenant colonel's visit, those of us who were awake counted twenty-three thuds. Through the efforts of the Morse teams in both directions everyone was informed of this, and the figure stuck in people's minds.

March 24

We walked, we turned.

I was walking in the line around the yard, with bowed head and closed eyes, clutching the pajama cord of the person in front of me, as he pulled me behind him. We walked, we turned, and sometimes I wondered: "What sort of being am I? Am I a person? An animal? A thing?"

I had a friend from my own district studying in France, who received from his family at the beginning of each month a sum of money enough to last him till the end of the month. Instead of making a budget and dividing the money over thirty days he would invite me to a splendid evening's entertainment or a posh restaurant. This evening would cost him about half his monthly allowance, so that in the final ten days of the month he would be borrowing from me and other friends in order to eat. I once asked him: "Why do you spend all this money on a single evening's entertainment so that you don't have a single cent left for the last third of the month?"

"During this once-a-month evening's entertainment, I feel that I'm a human being," he replied. "The people who work in that sort of hotel and restaurant are trained well to make you feel this way. Their speech, the way they serve you, their appearance... all these things make you feel that you are a respected person. My friend, I have a real hunger to feel other people respecting me. It doesn't matter that I go hungry for a few days each month, for this feeling that I am a human being lasts me a whole month."

I observed this friend on every occasion he invited me out for the evening after receiving the money dispatched to him by his family, and on each occasion I saw a man who was proud of himself, confident, walking beside me with pride. I also watched him on the three occasions that he had to consult our embassy in Paris, and on each occasion he begged and implored me to accompany him, despite the fact that he used all sort of flimsy excuses to try to postpone going until the very last minute. When he reached the embassy he was a changed man. He would go in hesitantly, with a quick glance behind him (perhaps he wanted to check that I was there). I would read in this glance of his an expression of fear and nervousness, and a plea for help.

He would come out quickly, dejected and silent, gesturing to me to walk quickly, and I would walk beside him in silence. The first and second times, he contented himself with spitting with a reverberating noise as soon as we were away from the embassy. The third time, he spoke: "Dogs! They want to turn me into a spy! A spy! Spy on who? They want me to spy on Yusuf! They threatened me with imprisonment and deportation. They said they had five prison cells in the embassy building, the dogs! Shit, shit!"

We walked, we turned around the yard.

Shutting the eyes makes hundreds of images leap into the mind.

At the beginning of my life I was addicted to studying. At home my name was "bookworm." I devoured all the novels and short stories I could lay my hands on. Then, when I shut my eyes, I would feel thousands of words and letters leap into my mind and collide—bang against the sides of my head, then fall to the ground, for others to take their place. I would sit huddled in the damp cellar of our shady house, which I had cleaned and arranged and turned into my favorite place, far from the family and the noise that went with it. Eyes shut and tired of reading, I would play the game of leaping words and letters. I am consumed by longing for a short spell in that corner.

In my adolescence and early youth, I fell in love with the cinema. I would leave one theater and go straight to another. Sometimes I would see three films in a single day, so I was known as the "cinema rat." I knew all the capital's cinemas well, and knew by heart the cinemas' programs for the coming weeks.

We walked, we turned, under the lashing of the whips, heads bowed, eyes closed, each one clinging on to the behind of the one in front. And we turned.

Bookworm, cinema rat, but now I felt I was a mule.

In many places in the countryside, before the spread of mechanical devices for pumping water from wells, they would extract the water from these wells using the force of a machine called a "mule." (In some places they called it a *dulab* and in other places a *gharraf*.) They tied the mule to a post and covered its eyes (to this day I don't know why they covered the mules' eyes) and it carried on walking and turning, turning around the well from morning to evening, a pointless exercise from the mule's point of view. And so we continued turning!

Now playing: A Western film depicting the life of a twenty-five-year-old nun, whose family had dedicated her to the monastic life. A girl with a pure soul, content and happy with the life of a nun, pure as ice, living in a convent on a faraway island. The events of the film move on, and pirates attack the island, and the virgin falls into the hands of a wicked, immoral pirate, who throws her to the ground and rapes her.

Scene: The pirate stands up with his huge body and moves away muttering... to a nun lying on the ground, with legs apart... the camera moves closer... lines of the virgin's blood flow down her thighs... she is unconscious.

We walked, we turned around the yard, tightly blindfolded, every moment expecting a blow or a kick... or a whip. Despite that, we sometimes forgot; our thoughts took us in all directions, as we dreamed of a day when we wouldn't hear the word "break," a day when we didn't walk or turn. Memories came back, overcoming all the nervous tension; they came back, and I was teased by the faces of family and friends, especially the women. My mother, my sister, Suzanne, all "my" women came back, and sometimes the memory of what remained painted a smile on my lips.

We walked, we turned.

In Arabic, *istinthār* means expelling snot through the nostrils, while *tanakhkhum* means excreting the mucus into the mouth itself.

As we walked and turned, a pudgy hand stretched out, gripped me by the arm and pulled me out of the line. I shut my eyes firmly, and bowed my head until it touched my chest. He continued to clutch my arm, while the other hand grabbed my lower jaw and jerked my head violently upwards. His voice gave out a hiss, mingled with a terrible hatred: "Lift your head, you dog, open your mouth, so I can see!"

I opened my mouth and he told me to open it wider, so I did. He cleared his throat hard, three times, and without my being able to see him, I sensed that his mouth had been filled with mucus. I felt his head draw closer to me, then he spat all the contents of his mouth into mine. In an instinctive reaction, my mouth tried to expel its new contents and I was seized by an involuntary need to vomit, but he was quicker than me and quicker than my mouth. He shut my mouth with one hand, while with the speed of lightning he stretched out the other toward my genitals, grabbed my testicles and squeezed them hard. The terrible wave of pain that came up from my testicles almost made me lose consciousness, and I stopped breathing for two or three seconds, enough for me to swallow his mucus and spit, and resume breathing. He continued to squeeze my testicles until he was satisfied that I had swallowed everything.

I carried on walking, I carried on turning, eyes closed, head bowed. The pain of the crushed testicles slowly abated, but little by little the sense that I was full of filth increased.

The nun recovered consciousness filled with a sense that she was unclean inside. She eventually went mad. Her feeling of uncleanness increased the more she washed.

We went back to the dormitory and I tried to vomit by any means possible, without success. I drank vast quantities of water but the sense that my inside was full of filth only increased.

I would leave prison and drink vast quantities of water, *arak*, wine, and whiskey, all sorts of hot and cold drinks, but I could never rid myself of the sense that the policeman's mucus was clinging to my intestines, to my gullet, refusing to come out.

March 30

Dr. Zahi's prognostications proved correct. About two years had passed since I came here. Isolated and forced to sit in my place, only leaving it for the "break" or to go to the toilet, I was unable to look at anyone directly, even though I didn't believe that they all wanted to kill me or had wanted to kill me. But I couldn't distinguish between those who wanted me dead and those who didn't. The important thing was that they all boycotted me and no one wanted me here among them, and nor did I want to be here. For the whole of this time I had been desperate for someone to talk to, to test my ability to speak again, but the power of hatred made me cling to the blanket and made the blanket cling to the ground.

Now that Dr. Zahi's prognostications had proved correct, I had started to sit in my place willingly, not wanting any contact with anyone, not wanting to speak to anyone.

It was meningitis. It had turned into an epidemic with incredible speed. It started about a month ago, one person at first, then another... then another. The prisoner doctors got together and studied the problem. By the time they had come to an agreed-upon conclusion, there were more than ten cases. The internal Morse system for communication between dormitories buzzed with queries and information, and it became clear that the situation was general throughout all the dormitories.

When the number of cases reached twenty—two had died, two lost their sight, and the rest were critical—the doctors demanded a general discussion in the dormitory. They spoke and explained the matter precisely and objectively, then asked the dormitory head to knock on the door, ask for the adjutant, and put him in the picture. The dormitory head refused this request and said that it would be impossible. One of the doctors replied that, in a few days' time, if no medicine was provided, everyone in this dormitory and probably in the whole prison would be affected. And in these sanitary conditions, with a total lack of medicine, being infected would certainly mean death or something like it. So, since we would die

70

anyway, let us ask for the adjutant and put him in the picture even if it was a one in a million chance.

"Doctor, doctor, do you have any doubt that these people want us dead? And do you expect that someone who wants to kill you would treat you? We've been here for years. Have you ever seen a doctor treat a patient in prison? Do you imagine that these people have a single grain of mercy or humanity? Or that they fear God? Leave us to die in God's mercy, and do not seek mercy from these wild beasts. Death is demanded by right of every Muslim man and woman, and death in these circumstances is a mercy from God."

I listened to the whole of this conversation in alarm. The dormitory head had one of the strongest personalities I had ever seen in my life. He had been an army officer, forceful, stern and unyielding.

The doctors did not give in. One of them turned to the dormitory head and said: "Yes, death is a right, we shall all die at our appointed time, but our religion commands us not to throw ourselves to destruction, and if you ask for the adjutant this may help save many Muslim souls, which is both your duty and ours. And if you cannot ask for the adjutant, let one of us ask for him instead of you," the doctor added, using words intended to embarrass him. The dormitory head leaped up—obviously needled—and said: "Okay, everyone, give me a couple of hours to think of the best way."

The gathering broke up and the doctors gave everyone several pieces of medical advice. I hurriedly found my suit jacket and ripped out one of the inside pockets, then unraveled a thread from the blanket and made a mask, which I put over my mouth and nose. Everyone looked at me with scorn, but within a couple of days everyone had masks.

After about a quarter of an hour, the dormitory head suddenly stood up. I looked at him. His eyes were red and it was clear that he had comprehended the extent of the insult that the doctor had directed at him. He stood firmly in front of the door, and knocked on it hard several times with clenched fist. The voice of the duty sergeant could be heard asking him from the yard: "What do you want, you wretch?"

"I want the adjutant, the matter's extremely urgent!"

"What? What? What? The adjutant just like that? What do you want from the adjutant, you wretch?"

The dormitory head grew angry and started to mutter: "For heaven's sake, am I asking to see the President of the Republic? He's only a piddling little adjutant… God curse these times!" Then he shouted at the top of his voice: "It's serious, extremely serious, the adjutant must come now, for your sakes, not for ours!"

After a quarter of an hour, the door opened and the adjutant demanded that the oaf of a dormitory head come out. The dormitory head explained to him the extent of the disease as he had heard it from the doctors, and finished by saying: "Sir, this disease is extremely infectious. The police may catch the infection from the prisoners and die. It's possible, God forbid, that you could die yourself! Anyway, it's our duty to inform you, and if you want to hear more, I'll call Dr. Samir!"

So they summoned Dr. Samir and he explained the matter in more detail to the adjutant, confirming what the dormitory head had said, that the infection might spread to the police. Then they let Dr. Samir and the dormitory head back in without punishment and closed the door. A quarter of an hour later they opened it again, and the adjutant and all the police were standing outside the dormitory. A doctor with the rank of second lieutenant, the prison military doctor, came in, and we then knew that there was actually a doctor in the prison! He stood at the door beside me and asked everyone to sit in their places and open their eyes. We weren't used to being spoken to like that. He asked all the doctors to stand up, and seemed astonished when he saw how many there were, though he tried to hide his astonishment. He asked them the basis of their diagnosis, so they enumerated their reasons to him. Then he went into the corner where the sick men were lying and took a quick look at them before retreating again to the door, where he stopped and turned around. He pointed to two of the younger doctors and asked them to come to him. When they came he asked them without turning around: "Do you recognize me?"

"Yes."

"Um…"

After the doctor had left and the policeman shut the door, some people went up to the two doctors and one of them explained: "This doctor was our colleague while we were studying, and we graduated together. He's from the coast, from the same sect as the President and his family. After graduation, we no longer saw him, he disappeared to his estate."

Less than twenty-four hours later, the doctor came back again, together with the adjutant, the policeman, and the municipals. He summoned Dr. Samir and said to him: "You have to treat all the patients in jail. Here is the necessary medicine, we've got large quantities of it. You'll have a sergeant and police personnel with you, who will need to see every drop of medicine that you use, and every syringe that you use you must hand over to the police, every cardboard box… are you ready?"

"Yes, ready."

So Dr. Samir started his rounds of the dormitories, with the policeman accompanying him, the municipals carrying the boxes of medicines, and a large box for everything that had been used up. He would go out in the morning, and return in the evening tired and exhausted. Despite that, the number of infections continued to increase, though actual fatalities decreased and became rarer. Today the first doctor, Dr. Zahi, was added to the list of those infected with the disease.

May 1

Zahi died.

It's not because I owed my life to him twice over, once for the medical treatment he gave me when I was on the point of death when first admitted, and again when he ordered Sheikh Mahmoud to snatch me from the hands of the fundamentalists, but rather because I loved this man, who never lost his smile, even in the darkest circumstances. His dialect was the lovely dialect of the Eastern Province, and you would see him anywhere he could extend the hand of assistance. He had a breadth of horizon and a breadth of culture that were rare in this place. I felt that he must be here by mistake—a place of such bigotry and extremism, of such narrow horizons and cultural shallowness.

I felt a deep sorrow I had never felt in my life before, a sorrow that made me forget my excessive caution, and which brought me out of my shell as soon as I heard the news. I forgot my wariness of them and of the illness. I walked over to where Zahi was lying as if I were walking in my sleep. I knelt down beside him, raised his hand to my brow, and burst into tears, weeping loudly. I wept bitter tears. Was it my grief for Zahi that had exploded like that? Or was it a simple explosion of the repression that had accumulated since I returned to my country? With his death, I felt I had lost the last support I had there and had become naked. Zahi was the only one I could look directly in the eye, though usually we would snatch only furtive glances. I felt there was a secret understanding between the two of us, and I often read in his eyes that he would never desert me.

Zahi was a man, a great man.

I wept and wept. Then someone kicked me. I lifted my head and through my tears saw one of "them." "Get up, you! Don't defile the martyrs!"

I got up, went back to my place, and retreated into my shell again. I wiped away my tears on the outside but left them flowing inside.

May 3

I mustn't go mad! That was my resolution from the start, but in spite of it I sometimes felt that I was on the edge of madness. At that point I would sing, but silently. I would sing in my mind, and always French songs, I never sang an Arabic song.

I wouldn't open my mouth at all, I wouldn't articulate a single letter. I would sit the whole day in a single place, leaving it just four or five times in the day to go to the wash-place and the lavatory, and only moving on days when we had a "break." I would sit, thinking and thinking. Once I thought: Can a man possibly stop thinking?

Dozens of times I went over the past in the minutest detail, a detail that I could not possibly have recalled even if I had lived a dozen lives outside this place. I would recall everything that was happy and delightful, everything that was beautiful outside.

I was now thirty years old. After obtaining my secondary certificate I had quit my studies, attracted by the prospect of commercial work and of making a quick buck with a friend of mine. Four years of unsuccessful commercial work, when my family bore the responsibility for smoothing things out, and after that to France and my studies there. Six years in France and now I was here.

I reviewed the past and dreamed of the future. It became a habit, creating these daydreams that I greatly enjoyed. I became addicted to daydreams. I would build a dream bit by bit, formulating the small and precise details, sketching them and correcting them. I would spend long hours, sitting or lying down, lost to the real world, living a beautiful reality in which everything was sweet, simple and easy. In every daydream there would always be a woman—every woman I'd ever passed or who'd passed me—and the cells of my body would be on fire. I would mingle the past with the present, recalling the most passionate moments and reconstruct them, inventing new situations. I would toss and turn, unable to sleep, waiting until the end of the night when I could go to the lavatory to masturbate. It was the only solution to be able to sleep. If anyone had asked me at that moment to sum up prison in a single phrase, I would have said: "Prison is a woman! Or rather, her searing absence."

I looked around me furtively. How did other people solve this problem, when some of them had never in their lives seen so much as the heel of a woman apart from their mother's? What did they think about? What did they dream of? Some of them were mere adolescents, with all the headstrong impetuosity of adolescent imaginations. They had plenty of wet dreams while sleeping—that I knew from my constant spying on them by night. One of them would be asleep, and suddenly he would quiver or emit a faint sound, after which he would wake up. Most of them would then say "I take refuge with God from Satan, the accursed," and get up to wash, because they had strict rules about cleanliness, and couldn't eat, drink, or pray unless they were completely pure and clean. Any sort of ejaculation, whether through bodily contact or a wet dream, required a complete washing of the body.

I was almost certain that the rumors of homosexual practices circulated by the police were pure fabrication, since even on a practical level such practices would be impossible.

I went back to my dreams and tossed and turned, not knowing how long it would last. I heard the movements of people waking up in the dormitory. I tried hard to sleep but it didn't come. I heard the noise of a helicopter.

The helicopter! When we heard the sound of the helicopter, everyone in the prison became tense or shaky, even the police and the municipals. Some people called the helicopter "death," or the "angel of death" who came down from heaven. One prisoner said that the angel of death sat in the front seat of the helicopter because they had made a pact with him.

The prison was several hundred kilometers from the capital, so the field court commission usually arrived by helicopter twice a week, on Monday and Thursday. This court commission might consist of three officers or it might be just one. After entering the room set aside for them they gave the prison administration two lists. The first list contained the names of those to be tried that day. The police would take this list and go around the dormitories calling out the names. Starting with the last dormitory in Yard 7, they would then begin to assemble them with the help of whips, shouts and curses, driving them with bowed heads and closed eyes to Yard Zero, where they were sat on the ground with their hands above their heads and their heads between their knees.

The first name to be called entered the courtroom with a hard blow to the neck at the door of the room. "Are you X, son of Y?" the officer asked.

"Yes, sir!"

"Take him out!"

The first prisoner's trial over, the second came in, then the third. In this way, the trial of more than a hundred persons might be concluded in two or three hours. Sometimes the trial proceedings were interrupted, as the officer asked the prisoner: "Are you X, son of Y?"

"Yes, sir!"

"You son of a dog, you took part in blowing up the cooperative?"

"No, sir, by God! I've had nothing to do with anything!"

"You son of a dog, you deny it as well? Police!"

The police came into the room. "Put him in the tire until he confesses!"

The torture party started in front of the courtroom. Beatings and shouting began, making things difficult for the court commission; work stopped and the officials drank an Arab coffee; then after a little everything became quiet again and the police brought the prisoner back in, staggering:

"What? Is he still being obstinate?"

"No, sir! I confess everything!"

"Sentenced to death, take him out!"

Most prisoners' trials with the "field court" took no longer than a single minute; most prisoners didn't see the judge or "officer," and most of them never found out the verdicts issued on them, which decided their fates. This court had two sorts of competences: it had the right to deliver sentences of execution and carry out as many as it liked, and to imprison anyone it liked for as long as it liked. But it did not have to right to release an innocent man. It was well known here that the first and second dormitories were known even to the police as the "innocent dormitories." The same court had over many years delivered innocent verdicts on prisoners arrested by mistake who were actually still children, with ages ranging from eleven to fifteen, but they all remained in prison without being released. The prisoners in the "innocent dormitories" remained in prison for periods of between ten and fifteen years, and these children had reached manhood by the time they came out.

The second list of names was a list of those to be hanged on that same day. The police would take this list round all the dormitories as well, ordering those whose names were on the list to make themselves ready.

Today there were four people from our dormitory due to be executed. After they had been informed, the four prisoners got up and went to the wash area, where they washed themselves in accordance with Islamic practice. Then they all prayed in the normal way, bowing and prostrating themselves in full view of everyone. There was no fear in their prayer. Is there fear after death? After that they walked around the dormitory and bade everyone farewell with handshakes and kisses. "Forgive us, my friends! We beg you to forgive us our mistakes, pray to God for us, that He may take us in the wideness of His mercy and give us a good end."

I knew the four people well; they were all young men of about my age or older. A large proportion of those who were executed were young men, only a few more than forty.

Calm, a faint smile. I watched them carefully but surreptitiously: was their composure genuine or manufactured? I watched the hands, the corners of the lips, the eyes, but didn't notice anything to suggest fear or terror. They said their farewells and shook hands with everyone except me, standing beside the dormitory head. Then they took off all their clothes that were still in a decent state and usable by those who remained alive after them, and put on worn-out clothes that were good for nothing. They handed over the good clothes to the dormitory head for them to be distributed as he saw fit, then stood behind the door that would soon be opened for them to go out.

The executions took place opposite our dormitory. We had seen the gallows several times as we went out or returned from our "break." This was also where those who were to have their sentences carried out were assembled.

From time to time we could hear the sound of *Allah akbar!, God is most great!* emerging from the throats of several men at the same time; it seems that this was the group whose turn it was to be executed. In the past, the hairs on my body always used to stand on end whenever I heard these words being uttered opposite our dormitory.

At night, those still awake would compare the number that had been communicated through the Morse system with the number of sounds of corpses crashing to the floor of the truck.

"Exactly, forty-five martyrs!"

And on the two following days, people good at such things would memorize their names and addresses.

July 15

Now I had someone to talk to.

Just when the guard was on the roof near to the skylight, one of the prisoners stood up in the middle of the dormitory and put his hand on his cheek like someone holding a telephone receiver. "Hello, hello!" he shouted. "Give me the chief!" "The chief" was the nickname of the President's brother, who commanded one of the most powerful army units and was considered to be the President's successor.

No one said a word. All eyes were on either the guard or the prisoner, who continued to demand "the chief," sometimes using his first name. Within a few seconds, four people fell on him and dragged him with his mouth gagged from the middle of the dormitory to the wash place, where the guard couldn't see him. One of them came back and with a smile said to the dormitory head: "It seems that our brother has gone to pieces!"

There were a good many disabled, paralyzed, and insane people in the dormitory, as well as one dumb and three blind prisoners. The most conspicuous case of madness apart from Yusuf was the case of the doctor of geology—I don't know whether it was insanity or something else—a man in his fifties who had gone to America to study geology; been successful and gained his doctorate *summa cum laude*, then returned to his country. A few years after returning, he had assumed the management of a scientific institute. He was religiously inclined, performed all his religious obligations at the correct times, fasted and prayed, and went to Mecca on pilgrimage. When the furious struggle between the Islamists and the authorities flared up, these were precisely the charges against him. One day at dawn, the secret service dragged him away from his family. What happened after that, no one knew.

The geology professor would sit cross-legged on the ground with his face to the wall, then cover himself completely with his blanket, night and day, summer and winter. For years, many people tried to talk to him, to question him, but he didn't say a word, didn't open an eye. Someone lifted the blanket a little at the front and put food in his lap, and he would eat still covered with the blanket. He would go to the lavatory covered with the blanket, and every few days two people would hold him under the arms and lead him to the washrooms—he was very compliant—undress him and wash his body, then bring him back, covered again. His place was directly opposite mine.

■ ■ ■

We were hungry now, very hungry. Three months ago the quantity of food the prison administration gave us was drastically reduced. Each prisoner used to have two loaves of military bread every day, but now it was one loaf for every four prisoners. My daily allowance was a quarter of a loaf for three meals. Today my breakfast was three olives (that was my complete allowance), and a small spoonful of jam for supper. If there were eggs for breakfast, it was a boiled egg between three prisoners. The doctors advised everyone not to throw away the egg shells, but to crush them and eat them, as a calcium substitute.

After three months of starvation, everyone had pale faces and exhibited symptoms of weight loss. Everyone moved less and people who had been exercising in secret stopped doing so. The policemen watched, and continued their work as usual.

Yusuf sat on the bed opposite me, a small piece of bread in his right hand, with a little apricot jam on top of it. He handed it to me and said: "Take it, this is for you!"

"Thank you, Yusuf. But it's yours, you must eat it!"

"No, I'm full! You're a young man who'll be getting married tomorrow, you need to eat honey, the doctor said honey is good for you!" Then, without giving me a chance to continue, he went on: "So what is your wish?"

"I want to get out of here."

"Look, it's nice here. You know that I've got a red thorough-bred horse and clothes that are all white, whiter than white. Just wait a few days and you'll see your brother wearing clothes whiter than white and riding the red horse, and standing in the middle of Moscow. In Red Square!"

He paused for a little then went on in a slightly sharper tone: "By God, we'd like to demolish the walls of Moscow, we'd like to wipe away unbelief and the unbelievers!"

September 15

I was starving. More than five months had gone by since the start of the reduced rations, and the survival instinct had begun to spark quarrels among the prisoners about how the food was distributed. They remitted the matter to the most revered and respected among them, and there was much speculation about the reason for the small quantity of food.

"They want us to die of starvation!"

"Maybe the authorities intend to let us go but don't want us to be strong when we are released. We need to be sick so that we can't do anything outside!"

A lot of speculation, a lot of analyses, but the police were watching.

Today the policemen opened the door and ordered the food to be brought in. The fedayeen ran to let in the miserable quantities of food, and for the first time there were no whips and no blows. The adjutant appeared and stood at the dormitory door, with a red watermelon in his hand weighing around three kilos. "Come here!" he shouted to the dormitory head. The dormitory head hurried over to him. "Take this watermelon!" the adjutant shouted. "It's the dormitory's allocation." He paused for a moment then, after the dormitory head had taken the watermelon, went on: "I want to see how you're going to divide the watermelon between the prisoners!"

The dormitory head hesitated for a moment. Signs of confusion started to appear on his face at first, followed by signs of challenge and provocation—I had come to know him well because my place was close to his—as he bowed his head for a moment then turned to the inside of the dormitory and shouted at the top of his voice: "Sick people! This watermelon is for you!" And he gave it to one of the prisoners. The adjutant looked hard at him for two seconds, then took two steps backwards and slammed the door hard in the face of the dormitory head.

All the prisoners sat down. Everyone—even myself—felt a strong sense of pride that the dormitory head had defeated the adjutant. It was enough that he had made him angry. While everyone was immersed in conversation, I happened to glance to the left and could see the yard—Yard 6, the execution yard—in front of me there to the side. I examined the door, and suddenly came across an irregular hole, a little bigger than the size of a walnut. This hole had been made just now! I looked around me and found a piece of concrete on the edge of my bed. I picked it up and plugged the hole with it, filling it completely. The hole was at the level of my head when I was sitting.

When the adjutant had slammed the door hard, this piece of concrete had fallen down. It seems that it had cracked and made this hole. Now I could see everything that was going on in the yard whenever I wanted. I could spy on the world outside in the same way that I could spy inwards through the hole in my shell.

Yusuf, the "boss's madman," stopped visiting me, or perhaps they no longer allowed him to visit me. After his visits they paid me renewed attention, and a group of people took it upon themselves to stop him visiting me again. They would sit and watch him until they saw him heading in my direction, when one of them would call him or stand in his way and tease him.

"Hey, Yusuf! Don't you want to tell the boss something?"

"Yes, I want to tell him... but my telephone's disconnected!"

"Come here! I've got a telephone!"

Then the other prisoner would escort him to his place and talk to him until Yusuf had forgotten that he had been coming to me.

Hunger gnawed at my stomach.

September 20

Three days since I discovered the hole; three days that I hadn't been able to look through it. My heart beat faster whenever I thought about it. I'd been thinking the whole day how to conquer my fear of the police and, more important, my fear of the other prisoners. What would they do if they saw me looking through the hole?

Inspiration struck when I looked in front of me at the geology professor. Why shouldn't I do as he did? I could turn my face to the wall and cover my head with the blanket, in such a way that the blanket covered the hole as well; then I would be able to look freely without anyone noticing, and at the same time be spared the hostile glances, which had recently increased. But I would have to try the covering for two or three days before I dared to open the hole and look through it.

The lice were scratching my body. I'd not yet got used to them or learned to live with them.

The hunger was growing worse and worse.

September 30

I'd succeeded in getting them used to seeing me covered in a blanket. Two days ago a prisoner walked by behind me while I was covered up, and I heard him say to the dormitory head: "What's going on, Abu Muhammad? We used to have just one of them and now we have two. What's happened? Has this gentleman lost his marbles as well?"

"Leave it in the hands of God. Lord, we ask for you a good end!"

I was unable to look through the crack even once, because the police were in an extremely agitated state. There had been occasional periods when we felt the guards had relaxed their grip a little, but all of a sudden things would return to their previous state, and the iron grip would resume. At this point, people here and there would start to speculate about significant developments outside—that the regime had suffered serious losses; that its position had been weakened, and it might be about to fall; and that as a result of its inability to confront what was happening outside it was trying to compensate here by taking it out on the miserable prisoners, who were completely helpless.

October 6

Today was a full one.

Ever since morning the yard had been seething with the sounds of beatings, shouts, and screams. The dormitory door was opened and the fedayeen went out to bring in the food—to the accompaniment of beatings with canes and whips—when one of the fedayeen received a blow from a stick that knocked him to the ground. This was the last time he ever fell. He stayed there outside on his own in front of the policemen, until after a little the sergeant shouted: "Come on, you dogs! Come here and take him inside!"

So he went back to the dormitory carried by others instead of carrying the food.

The doctors received him in the dormitory, where more than an hour later he breathed his last and surrendered his spirit, after giving his last instructions to his friend in a trembling voice: "Give my greetings to my father, if God grants you release. Tell him about me, and say to him that he can be proud of his son!"

One of the doctors came up to the dormitory head, the sorrow visible on his face: "May your life be long, Abu Muhammad, a new day and a new martyr. God have mercy on him, they left not a place on his body without beating it... so many injuries... even his testicles were crushed!"

"God have mercy upon him, get the young men to prepare him for burial, so that we can knock on the door and take him out!"

The whole dormitory got down to the business of preparing the martyr for burial. All the talk was of the martyr, of what he had left behind, and of his final instructions. They said a silent prayer for him and moved him near the door, putting him down in the open space dividing me from Abu Muhammad, the dormitory head. "Bloody hell, what is this?" someone commented: "Are we to die one after the other like sheep?"

No one replied to him.

Abu Muhammad stood up and banged on the door with his clenched fist. A voice answered him from outside: "What do you want, you son of a whore? Why are you knocking at the door?"

"Sir, we have a martyr! Sorry, sorry, I mean we have a dead man!"

Abu Muhammad had thrown caution to the winds by repeating the word martyr in the dormitory. He realized his mistake and corrected himself, but it was too late. The little peephole in the steel door opened and the sergeant's head appeared. "Who said martyr, head man?" he inquired, completely calmly, directing his question at Abu Muhammad, who stood there.

"I did, sir!"

The sergeant closed the peephole and shouted to the policemen to open the door. In the few seconds that it took to open the door, Abu Muhammad turned to the others and said: "Forgive me, my friends! Pray for me! And if any of you would be so kind, go to my children and tell them how their father died!"

The door opened. There were a bunch of policemen in front of the door looking in, and a bunch of prisoners, Abu Muhammad at the head of them, looking out. "Come on, you son of a whore, get out!" shouted the sergeant. Abu Muhammad hurled himself into the midst of the guards and the sergeant shouted to the policemen to close the door. All the other prisoners, except for the elderly and the geology professor, were standing up. I sat down as well and covered myself with my blanket. Quickly and calmly I moved the concrete block just a little…. then a little more. I did not really realize or appreciate what I was doing. The police were immediately in front of our dormitory and the hole was a large one, large enough for any of the policemen to notice it. But I opened the hole and looked.

Abu Muhammad was a former officer and a real man. Some time ago, when some disturbances had occurred in the dormitory—as a result, in the first instance, of the limited food distribution—he felt that he had been wronged by someone, and for the next seven days he didn't touch a single morsel of food. Seven days without food after months of starvation. A group of elders, the most respected people in the dormitory, went to him to placate him and to apologize on behalf of everyone. They expressed the sincere hope that he would forget everything and said that they would not leave him until he had eaten. To which, Abu Muhammad replied: "Abu Muhammad cannot allow a morsel of food to humiliate him. If there is someone who has behaved or will behave dishonorably, the person will not be Abu Muhammad. Death, not humiliation."

After I had opened the hole, the first person I saw was Abu Muhammad. He had a thick stick in his hand that I was certain he had snatched from one of the policemen after surprising them with the manner of his exit. He was beating about with it right and left, surrounded by a circle of policemen and municipals. Then I saw a policeman stretched out on the ground. The circle tightened around Abu Muhammad and blows rained down on him from both sides and from behind. In pain, he turned and attacked, and the circle widened again. A real battle, even though it was unequal in numerical terms. On one side, there was a man who knew that he would die in any event, but had decided not to die a cheap and easy death, while on the other side there was a large group of people who were used to killing others with ease.

The numbers got the better of his bravery. After what I reckoned was about a quarter of an hour—during which the adjutant, the doctor and the prison governor had all arrived—Abu

Muhammad fell to the ground. There were now four people lying on the ground, three of them policemen, including the sergeant, the "son of a whore." I'd seen how Abu Muhammad had deliberately set out to attack him, despite the fact that the sergeant was a long way from him, and how Abu Muhammad's stick had come down on his head.

The doctor examined them all. One of the policemen was given urgent medical treatment, but the other policeman and the sergeant had died, as had Abu Muhammad. The doctor presented his conclusions to the prison director, who turned to the adjutant, instructing him to assemble all the police and municipals in the prison, and for all available armed guards to take up positions on the roofs above the Yard 6 dormitories. I knew that the spectacle hadn't ended yet, but I closed the hole firmly and drew aside the blanket.

Among the things I can never forget are the bravery of the general in the first yard and the bravery of Abu Muhammad in Yard 6. Like everyone else in the prison, I wondered: How, or why, can it happen that officers should be in prison like this, to be killed here, when everyone knows that we are in a state of war? But I immediately suppressed this thought and wiped it from my mind.

The major, the prison governor, regarded what had happened both as a mutiny and as constituting a serious precedent that needed to be countered as harshly and forcefully as possible, so as to be a lesson to everyone. There were about three hundred prisoners, surrounded on the outside of the square by considerably more guards and municipals, and dozens of armed guards on the roofs.

"Don't leave anyone in the dormitories!"

They assembled us in the middle of the yard, putting the elderly at the end of the line near the dormitory. The prison governor then gave a lecture, half of which consisted of oaths, and the other half of threats and menaces—threats that he carried out. "I don't want anyone to go back into the dormitory walking," he said to his adjutant. "The fit ones can go back crawling on their stomachs."

Some prisoners would later call this day "torture day" while others would call it "Abu Muhammad's day."

The torture continued from just before noon until after sunset. The most painful thing was the sight of the paralyzed prisoners being beaten and trying to move, trying to escape the blows... and staying where they were.

We crawled and shuffled back inside. Anyone who was unable to drag himself or someone else was hurled back inside the dormitory by the municipals. We started to tend and wash our wounds, searching for scraps of rags to bandage them. We were consumed by hunger but slept nonetheless.

October 7

In the morning, everyone looked at everyone else, and anyone who could, tried to comfort his neighbor. The tally was three dead, passed away during the night. My own injuries were minor, and posed no danger.

The sergeant arrived with some policemen. Everyone who could do so stood up. I discovered that Abu Hussein, who was the person who distributed the food and kept everyone happy, had moved his bed during the night to Abu Muhammad's place.

The adjutant took two steps forward and surveyed the whole dormitory, with a smile at the corner of his mouth. He looked at Abu Hussein, then looked at me, and waved his hand in my direction. "You'll be dormitory head," he said.

I didn't reply. The adjutant also said nothing and stepped back, wanting to leave. Abu Hussein made a movement, pretending to be afraid, then raised his hand and said: "Sir, a word, please!"

"What is it?"

"Sir, this man you're appointing as dormitory head, sir, he's mad!"

The adjutant turned to me and asked: "You, are you mad?"

I didn't reply, I didn't know how to reply. "Okay," said the sergeant. "So *you'll* be dormitory head!"

"As you wish, sir… but we've got three corpses."

"Corpses? Or martyrs?"

"Corpses, sir, corpses!"

"Just say they died, you ass!"

"They died, sir, they died!"

"Take them out then, dammit!"

He shut the door. So Abu Hussein became dormitory head. He calmly came up to me and said: "I know you're not a spy. I made you out to be mad because needs must."

Here was another one of them making me feel secure beside him.

February 24

It was freezing cold and the hunger was wearing us down.

More than ten months had passed since we started on hunger rations. A quarter of a loaf, which I divided into three parts, struggling and struggling against the desire to consume it all at once. Ten months during which not a single prisoner managed to feel full. Everyone looked extremely gaunt, with yellow faces and signs of malnutrition plainly apparent.

At first, everyone dealt with the problem with a certain sense of pride and self-esteem, but little by little as the situation continued, instinctive modes of behavior began to raise their heads, for prison is essentially a world of small things, of petty trifles. Two elderly university professors, highly respected people, quarrelled and exchanged insults. The whole affair, which ended in a boycott, had started like this:

"My friend, how many times have I told you not to wear my wooden clogs."

"And what does it matter if I wear them? Will it make them lose their value?"

"It wears them out, it wears them out! Just don't wear them, that's all! I've told you a hundred times. Or don't you understand what I'm saying?"

"Not understand? Do you think I'm an ass like yourself?"

"Me an ass? You and your father and your whole family are the asses, and you're the biggest ass of all!"

Things might have ended in the two professors coming to blows if someone else hadn't intervened.

Not a day went by without an argument or worse, the sole subject of which was food.

"Why did you give me a portion of bread smaller than other people's?"

"Why are you giving X a whole spoonful of lebne when I barely got half a spoonful?"

"My ration of three olives isn't enough, and besides, they're small ones, while other people's are fat."

A month ago the doctors met with Abu Hussein, the dormitory head. One of the doctors explained to him that as a result of their examinations and observations they had strong reasons for believing that a number of prisoners had developed tuberculosis, and that if the present situation continued, it threatened to lead to a medical disaster. They asked him to report this to the prison administration. After discussion, it was decided to adopt the late Abu Muhammad's plan of action. They informed all the dormitories of what was going on through the Morse system, and it then became clear that all the dormitories had cases of TB. When the adjutant governor arrived in answer to a request, Abu Hussein explained the situation to him and added:

"Sir, the doctors are certain that it is TB, and as you know, sir, this is an extremely infectious disease. You and we are all in it together. The prisoners can become infected and get ill, but so too—God forbid—can the police!"

Treatment was begun. Penicillin, arginine…

■ ■ ■

For several months I had been continuously watching and spying on the prison yard through the peephole. I had memorized the faces of all the policemen, and watched the executions. Eight gallows. Every Tuesday and Thursday, I would hear the policemen talking, sometimes quite distinctly, while people here were wondering why we no longer heard shouts of *Allah akbar!* when the executions were carried out. Now I discovered the secret. After the condemned men had left the dormitory, the policemen would shut the door and seal the mouths of the condemned men with broad tape. It was as if a shout of *Allah akbar!* from the condemned men before their execution would pose a challenge and a provocation to the field court and prison administration, so they stopped the shout with tape.

The gallows were not fixed. They were not like the ordinary gallows that a condemned man is led up to. These gallows were lowered toward the man condemned to death then tilted by the stronger municipals until the rope reached the condemned man's neck. They then tightened the rope securely around his neck before pulling on the gallows from the rear, so that the condemned man was raised up on the gallows with his feet hanging in the air. Then, after he had breathed his last, they lowered him to the ground. Then came the second and third batches. Most people I saw executed were calm, but I also saw several cases where both human weakness and a lust for life were apparent. Some people lost control of their sphincters, which made the policemen extremely angry, for the stench was unbearable. They would curse and beat the person concerned. Other people would cry, and try to speak to plead for their lives, but the broad tape prevented them. One young prisoner was able to escape and run into Yard 6, which was an extremely large yard divided into two sections. Escape was impossible, but the policemen and municipals were forced to run after him for several minutes until they caught him and stood him under the gallows. He sat down on the ground then two municipals put his neck in the noose. A few moments later he was twisting his legs in the air.

MARCH 20

The treatment of the cases of TB continued, together with the rounds of the doctor undertaking the treatment, Dr. Samir. Two complete months had passed but the number of cases had seen a continual increase. According to Dr. Samir, the number of cases in the prison had reached 1,300, though there had been very few fatalities. Everyone here attributed the successful treatment of the meningitis and tuberculosis to the prison doctor, and everyone was praising his humanity until twenty days ago, when a Morse message was received, composed of just a few words:

"The prison doctor has killed two colleagues in his own cohort."

The message came from the seventh dormitory. Three days later another message was received:

"The prison doctor has killed three colleagues in his cohort."

This message came from Dormitory 24.

Abu Hussein, who in addition to being intelligent was a very dynamic person, sensed danger and summoned the two doctors, who were colleagues of the prison doctor. He spoke with them at considerable length, and questioned them about a number of things. His great fear was that the prison doctor would kill all the colleagues in his group, including these two doctors. Abu Hussein used all his intelligence and cunning to stop them becoming too fearful, but at the same time he didn't want to lie to them. It was a long discussion, the most important point being when Abu Hussein told them: "I don't want to make light of the matter and lie to you. It seems that your colleague has started there and it is possible that he may finish here. I pray to God I may be wrong, but it's possible (God forbid!) that your turn may be coming. And if so, can I or anyone else do anything now?"

The two doctors said nothing for a short period, after which they spoke by turn: "There is nothing we or you can do, Abu Hussein, except to say: 'God is our judge and the best of helpers. The hour will come when we shall all stand before God, and oh, woe to that hour'!"

"But tell me why he should be doing this? Is it revenge? And on whom?"

"Honestly, Abu Hussein, we don't know much about him. All we and all our colleagues know is that when he entered university he was extremely poor, a shy, simple country boy. His colleagues from the city may have acted superior to him, and some of them may have treated him with contempt. Everyone knew that he came from the same family as the President and he didn't hide the fact. He studied medicine at the expense of the state, and it was said that he worked as an informer for the security services. Everyone from the city avoided him. The story was—and it has some sense to it—that he was in love with a female colleague from the city. Until his third year of university his love remained an unspoken one, for he didn't dare to approach her or convey his feelings to her. Then in the third year he was alone with her in one of the laboratories and used the opportunity to take hold of her hand and confess his love to her, saying that he worshipped her, et cetera, et cetera...

"The reaction of the girl—who came from a conservative city family known for its wealth and influence—was extremely forceful and was probably the cause of everything that happened subsequently. She rejected him contemptuously and complained to the university administration, then informed her family of what had happened. He was punished by the university, but the family's reaction was even harsher. Three of the student's brothers prowled around the college for a full three days with their sister. It was obvious to everyone that they were concealing weapons underneath their clothes. They were looking for him with the intention of killing him, so the girl said later, but he was nowhere to be found: he had disappeared and no longer came into college.

"A week later he came into college as if nothing had happened. The girl's brothers had withdrawn, and the university's punishment was suspended. 'He brought his relatives in the secret service, used them as go-betweens, and kissed hands until my family let him off,' as the girl would later explain to other people.

"He pursued his studies in isolation, mixing only with one or two students from his own region. After this episode, everyone treated him with contempt, and some of his fellow students occasionally made barbed comments to his face.

"But I swear by God, Abu Hussein, my brother, this group of ours never paid any attention whatever to these matters. There were more than twenty-five of us young men in a single class who believed in God and attended religious lessons in the mosque after work. That is why we are here now. How many brothers were arrested and how many escaped, I don't know, but God helped everyone."

"Hmm…" I said to myself, "There must be a woman in there somewhere! This person feels shame, but if he kills the witnesses to his shame, will the shame be wiped away? Stupid…"

But I believed that this explanation, despite its force, was not sufficient. I believed there was another reason that no one knew!

Today, March 20, one day before the spring festival, these two doctors had an appointment with their colleague. The policemen let the two doctors out and closed the door. I hurried over to my blanket and the spyhole. I saw the two doctors being led by the policemen to the prison doctor, who was standing about four or five meters from the dormitory. He was standing with his hands clasped over his chest, smiling. He welcomed them then turned to the policemen and gave them an order: "Go away and stay beside the municipals!"

There were seven enormous municipals in the middle of the yard. The policemen took up their positions beside them. I could hear the conversation only with difficulty. "Now then," said the prison doctor, "you may well be saying, 'Praise be to God, who can change men's fortunes!' Yes, and I can say the same! I want to ask you something: which one of you would like to give me his sister as a wife?"

Neither of the doctors replied. Their heads bent a little lower, as the prison doctor went on: "Why don't you say something? What's the matter, 'Adnan? Couldn't I marry your sister in accordance with the *sunna* of God and the Prophet? Is marriage some sort of shame?"

"But I don't have a sister, thank God!"

At this point the prison doctor said something to 'Adnan that I didn't hear. There was a short period of silence before he turned to the other doctor and said: "Very well, colleague Salim, don't you have a sister either?"

"Yes, I have a sister!"

"Okay, let me marry her according to the *sunna* of God and the Prophet!"

"Marriage is a serious matter, and at the moment we're not in a position to discuss things like that. Anyway, the long and the short of it is that I'm not her guardian!"

"That's a sort of cop-out..." Then he moved closer to him and said in a louder voice: "Or do you think that we're not good enough for you—that you're rich and important people, and we're peasants, eh?"

He moved still closer to him, waved his hand in front of his face, then gnashed his teeth and screamed at him at the top of his voice: "Look, you! Open your eyes and come here. You see this boot? My boots are better than you and your sister and your family—better than your tribe and the whole of your sect! You filthy dog!"

Then he turned to where the municipals were standing and shouted: "You lot! Come here, take them to the middle of the yard!"

The municipals dragged the doctors off, followed by the prison doctor, shouting: "These are superior people... high up, that is, high up! And now we're about to lift them a little higher! Come on, let's see!" I could see but not hear the middle of the square. 'Adnan lay on his back as seven municipals took hold of him by his legs, his arms, his hips, and under his head. This was the "parachute" torture. The "parachute" meant one of three things. Either multiple fractures in different parts of the body, especially the pelvis; permanent paralysis, if the fracture was of the spinal column; or, as a third possibility, death—especially if the head came down before the rest of the body. This usually happened if the municipal holding the head was not as strong as the others.

The municipals lifted 'Adnan up, face upwards and back parallel to the asphalt surface, rocked him a little, then shouted at the top of their voices: "Come on, one two, three!" They threw him up, and there was an enormous bang on the ground. 'Adnan gave a horrific cry of pain and did not move. The prison doctor waited for a little, then with his back to 'Adnan and the others lit a cigarette. He was looking toward the door of our dormitory. He drew on his cigarette and blew the smoke out, then turned and gave a signal to the municipals, who came forward and once more lifted 'Adnan. One, two, three… and this time there was no scream.

He pointed toward Salim, mumbling something that I couldn't hear. Salim came forward and bent over 'Adnan, then straightened up and said something to the prison doctor, who leaped up and gave him a slap on the face. I could hear the slap even sitting inside the dormitory. The prison doctor began to scream and wave his hands around, and Salim was given the same treatment as 'Adnan.

They left them lying in the middle of the yard for ever. Then the prison doctor left the yard, surrounded by his retinue. In total, the prison doctor had killed fourteen of his own cohort. If any, or even just one, of these doctors knew the reasons that had prompted their colleague to kill them, he took the secret with him to the grave, for the killer would never speak, and the subject remained a matter of speculation inside the prison. No one knew the real truth.

May 6

As a result of the long rounds he made inside the prison, Dr. Samir was able to establish certain things that no one else had been able to. He knew how the prison was divided up, and how the yards and dormitories were arranged. He acquired an enormous amount of knowledge about the residents of each dormitory, and was able to convey news between the various dormitories. There might be a group of brothers from a single family who had been arrested together but no longer knew anything about each other. He would ask about them and reassure them that the others were there in dormitory number so and so. The most important thing was that he acquired the privilege of being able to speak to the police with his eyes open. As a result of their constant contact, the police were used to his striking up a conversation with them, which was impossible for other people.

Last Monday, the helicopter came. The field court personnel decamped to the room allocated them, and handed over the two lists to the prison administration—one list of those to be tried, and one list of those to be executed. I sat in front of the peephole covered in a blanket to spy on the police and the execution process, which had become quite routine for me. As usual, the prisoners due to be executed arrived and the usual procedures were all followed. The gallows were prepared then the municipals readied themselves and set the first batch of eight people under the gallows. It only remained to lower the gallows and the ropes, when someone whose mouth had not yet been taped shouted out: "Sir, please, we haven't been tried yet!"

The guard, who was standing in front of him with the tape in his hand, rained down blows and curses on the man—who was not permitted to address them first—but his shouts reached the adjutant standing at the end of the gallows. "Leave him, leave him!" the adjutant shouted. Then he went up to the prisoner and asked him: "What do you mean?"

"Sir, we're not condemned men, we haven't been to court yet!"

"What are you talking about?"

The adjutant turned to the duty sergeant and demanded the list. It seemed there had been a simple administrative error. The sergeants had made a mistake and taken the prisoners who were supposed to be executed to the court and brought the prisoners who were supposed to go to court to be executed. All the prisoners who'd been brought to the gallows knew they were there by mistake but only one person had dared alert the police to the error. The adjutant reprimanded the sergeant and the mistake was corrected.

About a month after the death of the two doctors 'Adnan and Salim, Dr. Samir returned from his rounds, went into the dormitory, greeted everyone, then stood there for a little before sitting down beside Abu Hussein. After the usual pleasantries, Abu Hussein asked: "What's up, doctor? I can see that you've something on your mind!"

"Yes, Abu Hussein," the doctor replied. "I want your advice!"

The doctor explained to Abu Hussein that nothing he was doing was producing any tangible results and that every day the situation of the TB patients was becoming worse and worse. *"I'm like someone trying to harvest water..."* Medicine alone was not enough, for the root of the problem lay in the food that the patients were consuming. "As you can see, Abu Hussein, people are hungry and if the prison food doesn't improve it's impossible for anyone to recover from this illness; on the contrary, the illness will become even worse, and the number of patients will increase. I'm seriously thinking of asking to be relieved of this work."

Other people also had their say, and the discussion went on a long time. Finally, Abu Hussein brought the discussion to a close by reminding Dr. Samir of his responsibilities before God as well as his human duty, and asked to him to turn his despair into a starting point to improve conditions.

"So what am I to do?" the doctor asked.

"Ask for the prison doctor, explain things to him, and ask him to improve the food."

"The prison doctor? That executioner?"

"Yes, that executioner. Do what you have to and leave the rest to God!"

Next morning, the policemen and municipals opened the door as usual, loaded with medicines, but the doctor didn't go out. Instead, he said to the sergeant: "Before the rounds, I have to see the prison doctor. It's essential!"

The prison doctor arrived shortly afterwards, and Samir explained the problem to him, as one doctor to another. He ended by saying that any treatment would be useless if the nutritional situation remained as it was. "Leave the food problem to me for two or three days, while you continue with your treatment as usual!" replied the prison doctor.

How easily can too little become too much! A week after this conversation the policemen opened the door to bring in breakfast and there was a mountain of bread and boiled eggs. The fedayeen brought in the food and distributed it. Everyone had seven loaves and five boiled eggs. Who was going to eat all this?

The doctors pointed out that one had to eat in moderation, because after so much near-starvation, the stomach shouldn't become too full. The restriction of food had lasted almost a full year (the prisoners called it "starvation year") and it was a year that changed people a lot. I changed too, and I could feel the change clearly inside me. After the first few weeks of the starvation year, though, it became routine. To be hungry became a natural thing, no longer requiring much thought, though with the decrease in body weight a profound sensation of purity and clarity was growing inside me.

I recalled how at the start of adolescence my awareness of the human body in general and of my own body in particular gradually developed, and through friends' whispers in school and street

I learned how to achieve that explosion of pleasure that sweeps through the whole body. I went into the bathroom at home and started to apply what I had learned from my friends. I almost fainted with pleasure, fear and surprise, but after only a few minutes I was overcome by a feeling of guilt, a feeling of pollution. I had lost my purity and innocence for ever. From that time this feeling had clung to me like my shadow, until I experienced the starvation year, when I felt this sense of guilt and pollution had gradually begun to leave me and I was returning to the simplicity and innocence of childhood. The thing that annoyed me most was that I was unable to share what I was feeling with anyone else. My sense of the return of innocence was a happiness that went with the privations of hunger.

Even my dreams changed. My daydreams before the starvation year had almost all been focused on women, but during this year most of them were redirected toward food. I started to conjure up some of the dishes that I loved, and I would dream of meals full of meat and gravy. And although I could deal with the results of my sexual daydreams I couldn't do anything about the needs left behind by daydreams of food!

Dr. Samir became a hero to the whole prison, but with genuine humility he said to Abu Hussein: "It's all down to you, Abu Hussein!"

They examined me today and confirmed that I did not have TB.

July 14

Over the previous period they had had considerable success in getting on top of the TB, and deaths from the disease eased. Dr. Samir estimated that around two thousand people were being treated for it. Another doctor started to help him on his rounds. Food now became a big problem. In the first few days when food was available freely, the prisoners began to try to horde everything they could, for fear of a return to the days of hunger. But the food supply continued at a rate two or three times in excess of the need or capacity of people to consume it. There wasn't a spare niche in the dormitory (which was in any event crammed full) that the prisoners didn't fill up with dry bread, so that moving about within the dormitory became difficult, then impossible. In this prison there was no trash receptacle, and it was absolutely forbidden to remove any trash from any of the dormitories.

The prisoners complained to Abu Hussein: "Abu Hussein, find a solution for us, see the adjutant in the hope that they can at least relieve us of the stale bread."

When Abu Hussein asked Dr. Samir to speak to the adjutant about the problem, Samir spoke to him the very same day: "Sir, we've accumulated a lot of dry bread. Could you possibly let the prisoners take it out of the dormitory, because it's more than we need. And maybe someone else could use it. If there are any sheep around, it might be good fodder for the sheep."

The adjutant replied firmly: "What, doctor? You've started to go on too much! Do you think we're shepherds? In any case, the prison regulations are quite clear: 'It is forbidden to remove even the smallest quantity of rubbish from the dormitories!' That's the first thing. The second is that you asked us to increase the food. We increased it, so everything that is in the room, you have to eat!"

This led to further argument in the dormitory. The place felt oppressive, and the dry bread attracted huge numbers of ants, cockroaches, and rats. The question was, how could we get rid of all this bread? The answer came from Abu Hussein: "My friends, to cut the answer short, in my opinion there's only one answer: we soak the bread in water in batches, marinate it till it becomes liquid then get rid of it through the latrines."

All hell broke loose in the dormitory. "That's forbidden!" someone said. "That's not what believers should do! God's bounty, and we flush it away down the lavatory!"

"That's not acceptable, by God! Bring back the year of starvation!"

"That's right! Better for the starvation year to last ten years than for someone to throw bread down the lavatory!"

"Oh merciful God, what have we come to?"

During the previous years—right up to the starvation year, in fact—I had noticed the great reverence attached to bread. Everyone had been very careful that no piece of bread should fall onto the floor. If anyone happened to see a piece of bread lying on the floor, he would pick it up respectfully, shake it, then kiss it and put it on his brow, and either eat it or put it somewhere up high. Bread held a sacred place in their eyes. But now Abu Hussein was daring to suggest that they should throw bread down the lavatory, and people were greatly perturbed.

To be honest, the solution proposed by Abu Hussein had already occurred to me as I listened to their discussions. But after I'd seen how upset the whole dormitory was, I said "Thank God I'm forbidden to speak. If I'd been the one to have put forward this proposal, they'd have killed me for sure!"

Abu Hussein confronted their agitation with complete calm. He sat in his place, didn't argue or speak, and left them for another day.

Every day meant around a thousand surplus loaves of bread. Everyone had to walk between the mountains of bread, and reaching the wash-places or the lavatories became extremely difficult. The following day, there was a new discussion but Abu Hussein didn't take part in it, despite the fact that everyone was waiting for him to participate and give his opinion. People became exasperated at his silence until someone addressed him directly: "Hey, Abu Hussein!

You seem to be saying nothing! Don't you have an opinion about the problem, seeing that you are dormitory head?"

"Of course I've got an opinion! But before everything else I have to speak to the sheikhs… if only sheikh A and sheikh B could be here with me for a bit!"

He then enumerated the names of five sheikhs, who in practice represented all the factions and orientations to be found in the dormitory. I had come to know them all well through my constant spying. Each one of them was the most learned and respected of his group. Abu Hussein talked at length, starting his exposition by expounding a group of Qur'an verses and sayings of the Prophet Muhammad. Then he described the present situation and the dangers. He ended his speech by saying: "Yes, we all know that this is a blessing of God which we have to respect, but we mustn't forget that mankind is more important. Man is created in the image of God and therefore has a higher value than anything else on the face of the earth. He has ennobled us human beings… and then again, has not our religion taught us that 'necessity makes the forbidden acceptable'"?

His logic was impeccable; this man was a fox, with an outstanding leadership personality. He paused for a moment then said: "And finally, my good people… What's the best thing to do? It seems to me it's a no-brainer, as the saying goes! This blessing— either we take it all out of the dormitory, which is impossible; or we eat it all, which is also impossible; or we get rid of it down the lavatory. And don't forget that the lavatory is the only outlet through the ground we have here!"

One of the sheikhs asked him: "Okay, so what are *we* supposed to do, Abu Hussein?"

"A *fatwa*… You're the sheikhs in this dormitory, get together and pronounce a fatwa, not just for this dormitory but for them all!"

So a fatwa was issued by a majority of four to one, to include the whole of the prison. Our dormitory organized the way to get rid of the surplus food. Each day twenty people in turn had one single task: to soak the bread and flush it down the lavatory, together with any other substances, such as rice, burghul, potatoes, and eggs. Another sort of crisis arose, but it was less serious. A person had to wait a long time for his turn to go into the lavatory and relieve himself!

September 29

Yusuf, the "boss's madman," came back to visit me. For about a month, my position in the dormitory had improved slightly, but I was afraid that they would prevent him from visiting me.

I woke in the early morning an hour or two before usual to the groans of a man in obvious pain. His bed was near to mine. He had a hand on his belly and was writhing in agony, desperately trying to hide his moans. I looked around me... I was the only person to have been woken by his moans of distress. He looked directly at me, the first time that our eyes had met, and his look held the cry for help of a man in great pain. I was desperate to help him, but how? I looked around me in confusion. Although he had left a space of more than twenty-five centimeters between his bed and mine, he was very near. I wanted to ask him what was up and what he wanted, but I didn't know how to. At the same time, he turned his face away in the opposite direction, for several long minutes... Several prisoners woke and came up to him, and he asked them to bring him a doctor. A doctor came, examined him, and asked him what was the matter.

"Stomach ache, doctor, a bad stomach ache! My guts are in pieces, and the pain is unbearable! Am I going to die, doctor?"

Within an hour, three doctors had held a meeting with Abu Hussein, the dormitory head: "Acute appendicitis, which might rupture at any time. If he's not given immediate treatment and a surgical operation to remove the appendix, it will certainly rupture and the patient will die!"

Abu Hussein looked at the doctors then turned to the patient. "OK, and the solution?" he wondered, as if talking to himself. "We have to find a solution. I think there's only one solution, if I'm to have a clear conscience. We knock on the door and ask for the prison doctor, that's the only thing I can do. But do you suppose they'll answer us? Come on then, let's knock on the door and whatever happens, will happen! You can only die once! And God hasn't made anything worse than a monkey! What do you say?"

"As you wish, Abu Hussein!"

Abu Hussein knocked on the door. The policemen and municipals were distributing breakfast in the yard, when the voice of the sergeant, Abu Shahata, could be heard shouting, "Who's the dog that's knocking on the door?"

Abu Hussein told him the number of the dormitory and that Dr. Samir wanted the prison doctor on an important matter. Samir was taken by surprise but stood beside Abu Hussein awaiting the prison doctor.

"My God, doctor! How your name occurred to me, I don't know!" said Abu Hussein to Samir. "Maybe inspiration from on high. They've got to know you so maybe they'll listen to you!"

The TB was in its last stages. Dr. Samir was still continuing to treat dozens of cases that he had labeled as incurable, and so was in constant communication with the policemen. It took more than an hour for the doctor to arrive, for it was still early. My neighbor was racked with pain, trying to suppress his moans. Then the door opened and in front of him there appeared the doctor, the adjutant, and some policemen. The doctor asked Samir why he had been summoned and Samir explained things to him, but the prison doctor didn't say a word; he just turned his back and walked away. The adjutant gave Samir a long look. "You're making all this fuss just for an inflamed appendix?" he said. "It's true this dog's got appendicitis, but you're not worth anything yourself, and I've had that feeling for quite some time! Get out!"

Dr. Samir left the dormitory. "Who knocked on the door? What shit?" inquired the adjutant, addressing his words to Abu Hussein.

"I knocked on the door, sir!"

"Go outside as well, you dog, son of a bitch!"

Abu Hussein went outside as well, and the door shut. For half an hour we could hear the two of them shouting. When the helicopter arrived, the beating stopped and they sent them back into the dormitory.

"For God's sake, doctor, don't blame me! I brought this punishment on you, it's me that got you into this mess!"

Dr. Samir laughed, almost skipping as he walked, and patted Abu Hussein on the shoulder.

"It's nothing, Abu Hussein, it's nothing! Just a few lashes! I'll just make a note of them and, God willing, settle up when we get out. In front of Umm Hussein, that is. The important thing now is what do we do with the sick man?"

He posed this question to the whole dormitory, and there were several suggestions, comments and questions: "For hell's sake, I need to understand, why did they treat us for TB, but they won't treat us for appendicitis?"

"Brother, we need to understand properly: the appendix is one person—small change, that is—it makes no difference to them if he dies, but TB is a collective thing—that is, it affects everyone, and if everyone here dies, that's not in the interest of this sodding government, because we're just like hostages for them, and it uses the hostages to put pressure on those outside!"

The discussion and argument lasted no more than ten minutes. Meanwhile, a middle-aged doctor with white hair, small, sparkling eyes and handsome features came forward and sat down on Abu Hussein's bed. "You know that I'm a surgeon, don't you, Abu Hussein," he said. "I'm happy to do the operation to remove the sick man's appendix, but I need a few things, and the sick man will also need to confirm in front of everyone that the operation is at his own risk."

Without answering, Abu Hussein took the doctor by the hand and dragged him over to the sick man. After they had moved from my left to my right side, they sat down beside him. "Tell him what you need from him!" said Abu Hussein to the doctor.

"Look here, my friend, I'll be frank with you, you've got acute appendicitis, and if we don't operate quickly, it will rupture and you'll die. We've got a chance to operate, but in these conditions let me say that the chances of success are less than fifty percent. So now you have to make a choice in public between certain death and likely death!" The sick man chose the likely death and publicly absolved the doctor of all responsibility. Then the doctor informed Abu Hussein of what was needed for the operation: "We've got clean cloth, alcohol, salt, and antibiotics, which Samir can filch from the policemen. We've got sewing needles, thread, and fire. But what we need is some metal things that we can turn into scalpels!"

When all these things appeared, it became clear that I had been quite unobservant and that my spying had registered only what appeared on the surface. The interior of the dormitory had been dressed with rough concrete, which everyone used to pare their nails (there were no nail scissors in the prison). The concrete was used as a file, and all sorts of things were made or improvised on it. Sewing needles were made from small pieces of bone. Someone would hold the bone and start to scrape it on the wall, for a day, two days, or more… until it took on the shape of a needle. Then, using a nail, which would also have been filed against the wall, someone, with extraordinary patience, would open a hole in the needle. A nail here was regarded as a treasure, and it became clear that there were dozens of nails in the dormitory. Sewing was an easy matter; they would unravel a piece of cloth, and calmly and patiently re-sew the fine threads according to need. I noticed then that most of the clothes being worn were in tatters. How had it not occurred to me to wonder how they patched their clothes? I knew that my own trousers were frayed on the knees and legs and were in urgent need of repair.

Alcohol: some of the doctors, or perhaps it was a joint decision of them all, had fermented jam in plastic containers (how had they got hold of them?), and the liquid had turned to alcohol—maybe only weak, but still alcohol.

Abu Hussein then issued a general appeal to the dormitory: "Anyone who has a piece of metal of whatever shape or kind, please bring it!"

Metal appeared, nails, a one-lira coin with the Head of State's head on it, four empty sardine cans, metal wires, and a gold wedding ring. I put my hand into the inside pocket of my jacket and felt my watch. I took hold of it. I had to give it to them. But to whom? Would they accept it? Or would they throw it in my face as being defiled, as coming from an unclean person? My watch would be very useful for this purpose, for the metal chain was made up of several fine metal pieces which it would be easy to turn into sharp instruments. So too was the back cover, and even the glass if need be. I hesitated for several minutes. Several people were standing around, each of them holding a piece of metal which they were filing according to the doctor's instructions. A blanket was spread out in front of the lavatories where the guard on the roof couldn't see anything, and the sick man was laid out on the blanket, moaning all the time. The surgeon was having a discussion with a group of doctors in the middle of the dormitory.

I made up my mind. I would put the watch surreptitiously somewhere where they could find it easily. But wouldn't they ask whose it was? Would I be able to answer that it was mine? I didn't think so... If Yusuf, the "boss's madman," had visited me at that moment, I would have given it to him.

Whatever would happen, would happen. I stood up, walked over to the surgeon, and without a word handed him the watch. Everyone was astonished, and remained silent. The surgeon looked me directly in the eye. His warm, honey-colored eyes registered a hint of surprise. "Thank you," he said, as he slowly stretched his hand out and took the watch from me. Then, turning the watch over in his hands, he turned to the other doctors, and said: "Now we can begin. This watch will be very useful for us!"

I went back to my place and sat down, feeling a little elated and more contented. I tried to remember the impact of the word "thank-you" after all these years. One of "them" was thanking me, speaking directly to me and looking me straight in the eye, rather than avoiding looking at me out of repulsion or anger.

The doctor distributed the pieces of the watch and chain among some of the prisoners, who busied themselves with the chiseling and scraping process. Suddenly the key grated in the door, and the names of nine persons in our dormitory were announced, three for execution and six for trial. Preparations for the operation were suspended for more than an hour, during which the condemned men performed their ablutions, said their prayers, and bade farewell to the others, then took off their good clothes and put on worn ones. The door opened, and they went out.

"O God, make good our end, and may God's mercy be upon them!" said the surgeon, directing his words to the doctors and the colleagues who were making preparations. "Now let us continue our work, my friends, for the sick man can no longer bear any more!" The preparation of the instruments was completed, and the doctor made his way with a number of others to where the patient was lying in agony in front of the wash-place. I was gripped by curiosity, wanting to see the operation, and I said to myself that I had a right to see it. I slowly walked inside and went in to the lavatory. There were about ten people busy with the preparations. I left the lavatory and stood to one side. No one noticed me and I began to watch.

There was a plastic bag full of fat. They had apparently been collecting the congealed fat from on top of the food, cleansing it of impurities then putting it in a bag. They filled a sardine tin with the fat and stuck a piece of cloth in it after twisting it hard. Then someone got out a box of matches and lit the wick. *Where had the matches come from?* The fire took hold with a lot of smoke. Then they put another sardine tin full of water on top of the fire, with the instruments in it. At the same time, they blew into the smoke rising from the fat, trying to disperse it as far as possible so that it wouldn't go up to the roof where the guard could smell it. After a little the water boiled and the surgical instruments were sterilized.

Meanwhile, the surgeon had washed the patient's belly with soap and water, then brought some moist salt, which he rubbed on the same spot. He washed his hands thoroughly and insisted on putting on a mask before operating. The tone of his voice changed as he started to issue his orders: "We don't have any anesthetics, so you will have to put up with the pain and not move at all!"

"Come here, you four, hold him tightly, one at each corner!"

The surgeon took the instruments out of the sardine tin and started testing them one by one. He chose the scalpel made from my watch case, tried it on his thumbnails then said: "Come on my friend, in God is our strength! Hold him tight, guys, and don't let him move at all!"

He put the scalpel on the patient's belly—"*In the name of God, the merciful, the compassionate...*"—and made an incision about twelve centimeters long. "Oh, mother!" the sick man screamed, but he didn't move.

The operation ended. The doctor had worked with astonishing speed. After sewing up the wound, he wiped it and cleaned it, then opened several antibiotic tablets and spread the powder over the wound, followed by a clean piece of cloth, which he tied tightly.

"God willing, you'll be all right, my friend! Carry him to his bed!"

I went back to my own bed and found pajama trousers and two pieces of cloth with a bone needle and thread on top of them. I picked them up and looked around me but no one had noticed me. Who had put these things there? I recognized the trousers; they belonged to someone who had been executed today, but who had put them on my bed?

After a little I realized that they had given me these things. Were they a reward? Did this mean that I was no longer a spy and an unbeliever? I turned to Abu Hussein and held up the things in front of his face. "They're for you, they're yours, so long as they are on your bed," he said, before I could utter a word myself. I felt that his harsh tone was put on. From that day on, I felt that my situation improved a little. I patched my trousers front and back, and started to wear the pajama trousers when I washed my own trousers. And Yusuf, the "boss's madman," started to visit me again without hindrance.

By now, a month after the operation, the man had recovered and started to walk normally. But he was to be hanged about a year later.

January 1

Yesterday was New Year's Eve. Most people outside this place would be celebrating the occasion until morning, but here I think I was the only person to whom the day meant anything. Everyone went to sleep at the start of the evening. It was freezing cold. I put on my pajamas, with my pants and jacket over them, and wrapped myself in blankets, but it was no use. My feet were frozen, as were my nose and ears. I wrapped myself up well and covered my head. This cursed desert cold… cold as the edge of a blade!

I tried to escape from the cold into my dreams and invented a sort of New Year's party, tiring myself a little as I chose the guests and venue. I was the undisputed star of the party, and the table was full of food and drink, music and dancing. There was an atmosphere of jokes and hilarity. Outside, the ice fell as I stood behind the window, watching the pine trees crowned in white. Surrounded by warmth inside the house, I felt joy and tiredness at the same time. A comfortable bed, with coverings soft to the touch.

It was impossible, impossible to dream of warmth in the midst of this cold. I pulled back the cover a little, rubbed my hands together, blew on them, and rubbed my feet hard to make the blood flow. At midnight I heard voices in the yard in front of our dormitory. I covered myself with the blanket and looked through the peephole. The yard was lit up as usual. All the yards, roofs, dormitories, and prison walls were lit continuously night and day. There was a large group of policemen in the yard making a lot of noise… laughter, shouts and curses. I looked carefully. The adjutant in the middle of the yard was surrounded by a group of sergeants.

I felt a commotion inside the dormitory and looked out from under the blanket. Everyone had woken up. Some people were uttering religious expressions like "In the name of God" or "There is no power or might except in God!" while others were repeating phrases like "O Kindly One! O Protector! God make this night to pass well!" I looked at the yard again. The adjutant and the people with him moved a little closer to our dormitory (one of the largest dormitories on this yard) and asked the policemen to open the door and let the prisoners out into the yard. So we went out.

We went out barefoot and naked. They had even ordered us to take off our underpants. Then they lined us up in rows and told us to stand two paces away from each other and not take advantage of our nakedness to bugger each other!

A message had come via the Morse system from Yard 2 a few days before to the effect that the sergeant ("You queer!") had forced a prisoner to bugger his brother!

Why were the policemen so obsessed with this subject?

The policemen, sergeants, and the adjutant were all wearing military coats and had wrapped their heads in woolen scarves. The adjutant walked up and down in front of the line, while the policemen kept everyone in line: "At the ready, or else…!" "Bow your head!"

There was a breeze from the north—a light breeze but freezing cold, I think it was several degrees below zero. They soaked us with water from top to toe, and ordered us not to move. There were policemen walking around us and between the rows with sticks and whips in their hands.

The adjutant began a long speech. The way he stood, as well as most of his expressions and gestures, were a repetition and imitation of those of the prison governor himself. Three quarters of his address consisted of foul curses. He began by pinning on the prisoners the responsibility for their being still in prison while the whole world was celebrating. Indeed, if we hadn't been here at that moment, he also would be celebrating. The officers had gone away to celebrate and left all the responsibility on his shoulders. A man of historical significance. He finished his speech, pulled his chest in and left the yard without giving any instructions as to our fate. The sound of chattering teeth could be clearly heard, and everyone was shaking with cold. I could scarcely manage to stand upright. I think that everyone was asking the same question: "How is this all going to end? What are they going to do with us? It is the prelude to a new massacre? Will we be going back to 'our' dormitory?"

Not a word, not a shout, not a curse; total silence, broken only by the footsteps of the policemen walking around us. They had even slipped their hands carrying the whips and canes into their pockets, so that the whips hung down from their pockets.

The body... the numbness grew and spread, the pain grew deeper and all-enveloping. Teeth chattered. From the tongue to the rectum there was a single tremor; nose, ears, hands, and feet were all detached from the body. Tears fell with the cold and froze on the cheeks and corners of a trembling mouth. The question was: when would I fall to the ground?

Someone fell before me, stopping all the policemen in their tracks as he did so. Their hands came out of their pockets. Some of them raced to drag the fallen prisoner to the front of the line where the sergeants were gathered. "Come on," said one of them, "Warm him up!"

Whips rained down on every part of his frozen body. He tried to stand up but the whips raining down on him stopped him. Another person fell, and was dragged to the "warming" place, then another, and another...

I battled with myself for fear of falling. There was a total separation between the brain and the body. My brain was completely clear and conscious of everything happening around me, but my body was gradually becoming detached as it became frozen and numb. The tears mingled with the mucus running from my nose and I found it difficult to breathe. I didn't dare lift my hands to my nose, even if my hands had obeyed my wishes!

I fell. I fell without losing consciousness and they dragged me to the front of the line.

I had experienced all sorts of physical pain. But to collapse in the cold when you are soaking is something that cannot be described.

The party ended as dawn began to appear, and another person had collapsed and been revived by the policemen. We ran back into the dormitory to the accompaniment of the whips. We ran lightly and elegantly. I thought that I wouldn't be able to get up, but as soon as I heard the order to go in and saw the whips coming down, I leapt up. I have often wondered where this strength came from. Resistance?

This time I saw genuine joy on people's faces that they had escaped from an unknown fate that deep within themselves they greatly feared. But behind this joy a new layer of black hatred had piled up, made thicker as the pain and humiliation grew worse.

June 5

It used to be said that God created man with one mouth and two ears so that he would listen more than he talked. For myself, I had lacked a mouth for all these years but had dozens of ears.

Talk, talk, talk. Heaped-up pyramids of talk. I would turn one ear to the furthest corner of the dormitory to listen to them talking, while my other ear would be turned to the "Morse wall," awaiting messages from the other dormitories. I didn't move my eyes, only my ears. A third ear would turn to a group memorizing the Qur'an—I'd memorized a good portion of the Qur'an—, a fourth ear…, a fifth…

My lips were sealed. I yearned to speak, I longed to hear my own voice, but even when Yusuf was sitting with me I didn't speak, because he quite simply didn't give me the chance to ask him anything. As soon as he sat down he would start speaking. Sometimes the sentences would be coherent, but sometimes they were pure gibberish. They had no breaks or pauses, and usually when he got up to leave he would still be speaking.

Talk, talk, talk. Everyone talked and everyone listened. And because the talk was always in a whisper, or at least a quiet voice, when the whispers came together, they turned into something that was not exactly a hum or a rustle, a buzzing or a hiss, but a sort of combination of all these, which went into the ears and from there to the head, which at the end of the day changed into something like an empty bowl, something like a drum. I would tap my fingers on my head and hear a buzzing. Even after everyone had gone to sleep and there was no more noise, this muffled sound would continue buzzing in my ears, knocking on the walls of my head.

I would have one of my little dreams (all my dreams were now smaller!): I would dream of living just for a day in solitary confinement, in complete silence, with no sound, no hostile looks, no looks of contempt, and of sleeping soundly there. I would dream of taking a bath just once in the Turkish baths, with the masseur and bath attendant, surrounded by steam and showers of hot water. I would dream of standing on the sidewalk in front of a falafel stall, eating a sandwich and drinking *ayran*. I would dream of walking along a street quietly in the shade, walking like a man with no job and nothing to do, not going anywhere in particular, and not tied down to any particular time. I would dream of my mother waking me in the morning, as I teased her by refusing to wake up and covering my head in a blanket. I would dream of someone, anyone, saying good morning to me.

Talk, talk, talk. For ten days, all the talk had been around a single topic, the visit! For ten days, two of the prisoners in the dormitory had been putting their heads to the wall from which the messages usually came, listening to the taps and passing them on to four other people behind them: *f y (= "fi") a l m h j a* '—and so on until the message, the telegram, was complete: "In Dormitory 21 one of the brothers had a visit, his whole family came."

The first reaction was one of complete astonishment. When the message had been circulated to everyone, there was total silence, as everyone looked at everyone else. This was followed by sullen glances, as everyone remembered what they'd forgotten, or been forced to forget, most of the time. The dictionary of their lives had been reduced to just a few dozen words—beginning with lavatory, tap, purity, defilement, and ending with whip and the local words for the police. Reciting prayers and the Qur'an, despite the richness of their language, had also become mechanical, and no longer required any real thought.

Everyone now recalled that there was another life outside this place, beyond this restricted dictionary, and that actually this other life was real life, and their present situation just a passing aberration.

Their imaginations wandered to the place of family and loved ones, where women appeared as the dominant force—the woman as wife, mother, sister, daughter. A bitter, grey silence reigned, and insistent, burning questions began to be asked about the fate of people.

Time in prison was really two times, which gave rise to two contradictory sensations: time present, heavy and slow; and time past—the days, months, and years that had elapsed in prison— fleeting and insubstantial. You would suddenly wake up and ask yourself: "What? I've been in prison five years, seven years, ten years?" The fact is that I had been unaware of this time. O my God, how had all these years passed fast as lightning? You reflect, and you realize that this feeling comes from the fact that amid the crush of daily details you are seldom allowed the time to count the days and years. It is like being whipped. If you start to count the lashes you will certainly become weaker. Similarly, if you start to count the days and record them line by line on the wall, you will certainly become weaker... or mad!

After a few minutes Abu Hussein broke the silence, called one of the Morse group over, and asked him to contact Dormitory 21 to inquire about the visit—how it had come about, whether visits were now open to all, whether they needed contacts or bribes, how the guards had dealt with it, and whether the family had brought things, etc? The answer came that they didn't know anything about the mechanics of the visit but there were a lot of things—clothes, food, and money—involved, and the prisoner had gone to meet his visitors and come back without anyone beating him.

Three days later the prison governor gave a speech in which he spoke of his humanity and mercy, and of how his heart was consumed with pain when he saw his fellow countrymen in this state. "Anyone who receives a visit," he went on, "should ask his family to inform any other prisoners' families they know so that they can try to arrange visits by the same method." But what was the method? No one knew, and no one dared to ask. It was the first time he had addressed us with our eyes open and our heads not bowed to the ground.

Today there was a visit to someone in our dormitory called Abu 'Abdullah. They summoned him by his full name, all three parts of it. (It was rare for anyone's full name to be known here, for everyone called everyone else "Abu...": Abu Hussein, Abu 'Abdullah, Abu 'Ali, Abu Ahmad...). The guards asked Abu 'Abdullah to put on new clothes, and there was great competition to dress him in the best clothes in the dormitory. He went off, and came back more than half an hour later, panting, bruised, and dripping with sweat; he stood in the middle of the dormitory, then turned around and looked at everyone, though it seemed he could see no one. The dormitory door was still open and the municipals were bringing things in in plastic containers. After the guards had closed the door, someone said to someone else: "Good God! Good God! Eighty-five containers!"

Abu 'Abdullah received congratulations from everyone, still standing as if in a trance.

"Congratulations, Abu 'Abdullah, congratulations on the visit!"

"God bless you, may you have the same good fortune!"

"Congratulations, Abu 'Abdullah! How are the family?"

"Praise be to God, they are well and send greetings to everyone!"

Abu 'Abdullah broke the chain of congratulations and suddenly turned to Abu Hussein. "A kilo of gold, a kilo of gold, Abu Hussein! God is your support, a kilo of gold!"

Abu Hussein was taken by surprise and gave Abu 'Abdullah a searching look. After weighing things up for a moment, he asked: "I hope things are okay, Abu 'Abdullah, but what is this about a kilo of gold?"

"The visit, Abu Hussein, the visit. Every visit costs a kilo of gold!"

Several voices were raised beside that of Abu Hussein: "What? A kilo of gold for each visit?" they asked.

"Yes, a kilo of gold. I asked my family and they told me my mother had to go to the prison governor's mother and take a kilo of gold with her then the prison governor's mother would give her the paper for the visit!"

Abu Hussein tried to comfort Abu 'Abdullah: "So what, Abu 'Abdullah! A kilo of gold is nothing! The important thing is you saw your family and they saw you and were reassured about you.

I mean, that's worth all the money in the whole world. God curse gold and the father of gold. Money is dirty in the hands, it comes and goes, the important thing is you and your health and your family. Gold isn't important, the important thing is the man that produces the gold."

"Yes, that's true, yes, that's true, Abu Hussein!"

That day I had such a headache that I felt drunk, so drunk that my eyes clouded over.

The municipals brought the containers as far as the dormitory door, then the fedayeen went out and took the containers from them (without any beatings!) then emptied them inside the dormitory and handed them back to the municipals. Lots of clothes, especially underclothes (summer and winter weight), as if someone had told the family what we needed, and lots and lots of vegetables and fruit that could be eaten raw.

What excited me was the cucumbers, the green cucumbers, whose mingled smells wafted toward my nose. Three containers of cucumbers, which they emptied in the middle of the dormitory not far from me, forming a small green mountain, with a small red mountain of tomatoes beside it. The smell of the cucumbers filled the dormitory and everyone was happy. Abu 'Abdullah was surprised at the effect of the visit. Without thinking or even being conscious of it I went and sat beside the heap of green cucumbers. I leaned down and inhaled deeply. It was the smell of nature, the smell of life, its greenness was the greenness of life itself. I took hold of one, held it close to my nose and inhaled deeply. I shut my eyes and I think that all my features were smiling.

It was like an earthquake. My whole being shook. I opened my eyes and there was a forest of eyes staring at me. I took no notice but threw the cucumber back on the heap and walked over to my bed, stretched out and covered my head, and cried silently. I stayed under the blanket for several hours, not wanting to see anyone, not wanting to see anything. Crying had relaxed me a little, and it wasn't long before I fell asleep. I woke in the afternoon, lifted the blanket and sat up. In front of me was a varied collection of things. Half a cucumber, half a tomato, a loaf of ordinary bread, a piece of fine baklava, some halves of fruit, but the most important things were the clothes. Sports pajamas, woolen winter underpants, summer pants, woolen socks. And then shoes!

All these years, since they'd taken my shoes at intelligence headquarters, I hadn't worn anything on my feet. A thick layer of dead skin, split and crusted, had formed all over the bottom of my feet, but now here were some wooden clogs! I looked around me, and it was clear that I'd received the same as all the other prisoners, no more and no less. (They all hated me, they all despised me, some of them wanted to kill me, that was all true, but in vital matters they were fair to me.) I took the things, arranged them like a pillow, and ate, but I didn't want to eat the half cucumber.

June 6

Yesterday was a holiday. I couldn't sleep until late, but I woke up as usual in the morning. I was surprised to find two portions of "half cucumbers" beside my own piece. That made three halves. I worked out that two people must have forgone their cucumber rations for me, thinking that I must like cucumbers! They didn't know that with their smell and color the cucumbers had restored life, with all its burdens, to a soul that had forgotten life!

Two of "them" were being sympathetic to me, though they didn't dare show their sympathy.

I felt a little more relaxed and contented in myself. I looked around me. Could I work out who they were? All the faces were closed, all the eyes were dull.

MARCH 8

They let us out into the yard today as usual. They stood us in front of our dormitory, and similarly with the other dormitories. The prison radio had been blaring out songs praising the Head of State since morning, singing of his wisdom, bravery, and heroic deeds. They gave one of the prisoners a piece of paper on which were written various slogans for him to chant and for us to repeat after him: "We'll give our blood and our hearts for the President, down with the Muslim Brotherhood, down with the agents of imperialism…" The prisoners shouted extremely loudly, and saw no harm in shouting against themselves, or at least they didn't give any indication of reluctance to do so.

These celebrations took place two or three times a year. The celebrations this year were different, however, in that the prisoners today couldn't stop scratching and itching their bodies. It was scabies. Between one clap and the next, between one shout and another, the prisoners put out their hands to scratch their bodies.

The scabies had begun about five months previously. I'd escaped TB and meningitis but I was one of the first to catch scabies, which quickly spread through the whole prison. The odd thing was that all contact between the different dormitories was strictly forbidden, so how could an infection that started in just one dormitory spread through the entire prison? Even stranger was that the level of cleanliness here was good, for the prisoners generally paid great attention to cleanliness, especially their bodies and clothes, because it was a religious requirement for purity and for prayer. So how could things like lice and scabies spread so comprehensively?

The scabies started suddenly with a few people, including myself. It first appeared between the fingers, then spread to other body cavities. As it spread through the body, it was a torment as painful as fire. Every day that went by the number of sufferers increased. It was clear from the beginning that all preventative measures would be useless. Whatever precautions a healthy person might take would be in vain.

From the very first day the situation was defined by Dr. Ghassan, who was a member of the American Board for Skin Diseases. This doctor had several publications to his name and was considered a world authority in his field. He was also a highly respected person in the prison. He didn't interfere in anything that didn't concern him, and was way above any trivial concerns. He was the final medical authority for all the doctors in the dormitory. He examined the first cases of the disease, got up quietly and went to see Abu Hussein. He stood between my bed and Abu Hussein's and greeted him: "Peace be with you, Abu Hussein!"

Abu Hussein jumped up respectfully and returned the greeting: "And on you be peace, and the mercy and blessings of God! Come on, doctor, sit down."

Dr. Ghassan sat down and explained the situation completely calmly to Abu Hussein. He finished his account by saying: "This scabies is highly infectious, and in a few days we shall all be infected if we don't treat it. It's easy to treat, my brother, Abu Hussein. Take precautions, but keep me away from that idiot the prison doctor! I can't stand talking to him, not even a word! Understand?"

Abu Hussein nodded his head in agreement, at which point the doctor stood up and immediately went to his bed, which he normally never left. In fact, he was never seen sitting with anyone. This was the first time he had ever sat down on another prisoner's bed, and this was out of necessity. As he was leaving he turned toward me, took two steps forward, then stopped, walked over to me, and sat on my bed: "Peace be with you, my brother!" he said.

I was so surprised I don't know how I managed to reply, and when I did, it was in a voice that I myself had never heard before:

"And on you be peace, and the mercy and blessings of God!"

"Could you possibly stretch out your hands, my brother, so that I can examine them!"

I stretched out my hands in a mechanical way. He took them, separated the fingers then turned to Abu Hussein and said, as though continuing a conversation that had been interrupted: "See, Abu Hussein. This man's your neighbor and he's infected too! I saw him scratching as I was walking, and I knew that he was infected."

"There is no might or power save through God! God help us to bear all these trials, God grant us not a light burden but give us a strong back, O Lord, you hear and answer!"

After Abu Hussein had finished his prayer, the doctor responded: "Amen," then turned to me. "Try not to scratch, my friend!" he said. "However much your body itches, try not to scratch. And until God grants you release and there is some medicine provided, always try to wash your hands with soap and water. I pray to God to heal you, but do not fear. This is an irritating disease, but it is not dangerous."

Then he left.

※ ※ ※

Four months had elapsed since the start of the disease and Abu Hussein had kept trying to prevent its spreading.

As for me, I had recovered about four months after the start of my illness. How? I don't know. I was the only case to recover. I simply followed Dr. Ghassan's advice. Every half hour I would go to the wash-place, wash every affected part of my body thoroughly with soap and water, then scrape off the soft, moist soap, put it on the affected places, and leave it to the following day. I never scratched my body. When I went to bed I would fetch my clean trousers, take hold of them by each end, and continue winding them in both directions until the trousers became like a chain. In this way I could be certain that I wouldn't scratch even when I was asleep. The disease disappeared as suddenly as it had appeared. After I was sure I'd recovered I took the opportunity of speaking to Dr. Ghassan to give him the news, but he just nodded his head.

The scabies infection progressed at a rapid rate. I heard Dr. Ghassan talking to a group of doctors in the presence of Abu Hussein. He was using a lot of Latin medical terms that I didn't understand. After enumerating the various types of scabies, he concluded by saying that in the whole of medical history no cases like those being seen here had been recorded. He mentioned that in the worst cases of scabies the patient would have around 300 pustules, while here cases involving more than 3,000 pustules had been recorded, covering the whole body. This was one of the reasons for the scabies fatalities. He drew attention to a serious case where the disease had spread inside the buttocks and around the opening of the rectum, as a result of heavy scratching in that area, and this had led to the occurrence of numerous lesions, as numerous as the pustules around the opening of the rectum. As a result of the pustules being so close together, the lesions had coalesced after the blood had clotted, which had led to a blockage in the rectum, and then to death, as a result of the impossibility of cleansing the impurities from the body. He hoped it might be possible to bring someone from an advanced institute for medical research to observe these unusual cases first hand.

Dr. Ghassan asked Abu Hussein to form a nursing team whose task would be to bandage the hands of the patients who were in-fected with scabies in the rectum, to stop them from scratching themselves. Then he asked him to redouble his efforts with the prison administration.

For five days now, as well as this morning, Abu Hussein had

been deep in thought. Suddenly he leaped up and went over to Dr. Ghassan. He spoke to him for a short time, as the doctor nodded his head. Afterwards, Abu Hussein went around the whole dormitory, repeating: "My friends, anyone who has had a visit is invited to a meeting with me, four or five at a time."

There were about thirty people in our dormitory who had had visits, and because the family knew that this visit might be exceptional or even unique, they would try to supply "their" prisoner with everything he would need for a long time into the future— especially clothes and money. It was clear to me that the families of the Islamist prisoners were among the better off in society, so that the lowest sum given to a prisoner was 2,000 lira, while some received a good deal more than that. Our dormitory had therefore amassed several million lira with no opportunity to purchase anything. The visits went on for about six months. Some Qur'an reciters would count and memorize the number of visits so that they could work out how many kilos of gold the prison governor had acquired. At the final count, after the visits were stopped, the number had reached 665 kilos of gold.

The visits were stopped as a result of the prison governor being transferred and replaced by his adjutant. The end of the visits was not the only result of the prison governor's transfer, there was another consequence as well. A Morse telegram came from the first dormitories saying: "The new prison governor assembled all the policemen and sergeants working inside the prison and informed them that with effect from that day it was not permitted for ordinary guards and soldiers to take a prisoner's life unless a sergeant was present in the yard. Beating, torture, flaying, none of this was a problem, but killing was not permitted except in the presence of a sergeant." Everyone considered this an indication that the new governor was better and more humane than the old one.

The first group of five came to Abu Hussein, and after greetings, salaams, and courtesies—as though they were visiting him at home—he invited them to sit down. As they all scratched and itched, he immediately, without any preliminaries, launched into his subject:

"My friends, we need your charitable contributions, for God's sake!"

The five said nothing for a moment then one of them said: "Abu Hussein, our souls and our possessions are there for God's work, but first explain what you intend to do with the money, and the amount required. Don't we need to know?"

"Of course you need to know. But it doesn't need a lot of intelligence. God created wealth and gave it to us for us to spend it and buy things with it!"

"Okay, what do you want to buy?"

"I want to buy a doctor... a medical doctor!"

"A doctor?"

Everyone laughed.

"Yes, a doctor. I want to buy the prison doctor! There's no other way. You understand this country well, and from top to bottom everyone has his price. I don't think that this doctor's any different. They all have their price. Let's fill the pockets of this doctor so that he brings us medicine for the scabies and we can rid Muhammad's nation of this affliction!"

Everyone agreed. Further meetings followed and Abu Hussein collected a worthwhile sum. Then, when the sergeant opened the door, he demanded that the doctor come for an important matter.

The doctor was angry when the door was opened, and shouted in Abu Hussein's face: "If you've summoned me because of the scabies, I'll break your bones, you dog, I've told you a thousand times that we haven't got medicine for scabies. But let's see, what do you want?"

"Sir, for the sake of God! Have a little patience and listen to me for a bit. Sir, as you know, recently we've been having visits and we've amassed quite a bit of money. And as you can see, we don't need money here because it's forbidden to buy anything!"

Such was the bait that Abu Hussein threw to the doctor. The doctor began to nibble at the bait, turned to the policemen who surrounded him, and ordered them to move away. "Yes, okay," he said, "but what have I got to do with all this nonsense? Whether or not you've got money, what can I do for you?"

"Sir, do us this service, for God's sake. You're a man of great humanity and you've helped us a lot with no reward for yourself. Help us this time again. Buy us the medicine at our expense, even if it is on the black market. It doesn't matter if the medicine is expensive, we're ready to buy it at twice or even three times the normal price. A service for God's sake, sir..."

The doctor's tone suddenly changed from annoyance and anger to a gentler, more manipulative tone: "But you know that this medicine is extremely expensive?"

"That's okay, sir. However much it costs, just let it be enough for all these people, because they are all infected!"

"Okay, come over here for a moment!"

The doctor took Abu Hussein outside the dormitory and they spoke in low voices. The deal was done.

Two days later, the medicine arrived in cardboard boxes, and three days ago everyone, including myself, whether infected or not, began treatment with benzoate on the instructions of Dr. Ghassan and under his strict supervision. Using blankets, five cubicles were prepared, which people could go behind and start to rub their whole bodies with benzoate. During this short period, positive results began to appear. The other dormitories were informed, and they all made contracts with the doctor, who became a millionaire. Someone commented that if ever they asked the prison doctor how he became so rich, he would have to say that it was scabies that turned him from a scab into a millionaire.

You see, my brother, that sometimes evil can be good and useful!

July 23

Despite so many years having gone by, I had stayed squatting in my shell, peeping in and out, inside and outside the dormitory. As time went by, however, I had lost interest in many things as I already knew all about them.

I had memorized the Qur'an thoroughly and I had often repeated verses and long chapters of it spontaneously. I had memorized all the prayers, even the incidental ones, like the "Prayer of Fear," the "Funeral Prayer," and the "Prayers of Comfort." I had listened to the arguments of the various factions about legal ordinances, their modes of thought, their reactions, their aspirations, and their hopes. I no longer focused much of my attention on any of this when I looked out through the opening in my shell. In the same way, when I peeped out of the dormitory through the spyhole, the sight of the other dormitories' "breaks," punishments, and tortures, had all become normal and routine.

Despite this, I continued to look out through the spyhole every day in the expectation that something new or unusual might occur. And usually there was indeed something new, for torture—even if it is in some ways all the same and everyone has learned it in the same school—still retains some connection with the heart and soul of the individual. Every sergeant and every policeman added something peculiar to himself to the previously repeated actions, and created something new for us to add to the "create" column—a creative touch of torture!

More than a year ago, during one of the dormitories' "breaks," a sergeant was standing under the wall when a mouse passed in front of him and he squashed it under his military boot. The mouse was crushed and died. The sergeant took a paper handkerchief out of his pocket and picked the mouse up by its tail with the handkerchief. The he went up to the rows of prisoners turning around the yard, grabbed one of the prisoners at random and forced him to swallow the mouse, which he did. From that day on, the sergeants and ordinary policemen spent a significant part of their time catching mice, cockroaches, and tortoises, and forcing the prisoners to swallow them. They all did this now, but the innovation, the "creation," belonged to the first sergeant to do this.

Even the executions, although I was addicted to watching them, were no longer charged with the same degree of alarm and apprehension. The men condemned to death would be led to the gallows eight at a time, and after the broad strips of tape had been secured across their mouths, they would be chained, the gallows would be raised, their necks would bow, their bodies would go limp, then the first batch would be lowered and the second batch lifted up...

I would watch them all: policemen, municipals, and condemned men. The focus of my attention shifted from the actions themselves to their faces, emotions, and reactions—the fear, terror, anger, relief, joy, delight, or pleasure etched on their faces.

The beast

Everyone—his fellow municipals, all the policemen, and even the adjutant—called him "the beast." He was a young man of about twenty-five, perhaps no more than 160 centimeters tall, but his shoulders were probably more than 120 centimeters wide, and his waist perhaps 60 or 70 centimeters. From the front and rear he looked like a square, and from the side he looked like a box, with strapping muscles. I'd seen him once lift a prisoner above his head with one hand. He was extremely strong and he never missed an execution. Indeed, he always played a crucial part in them, and all the guards relied on him.

At one of the execution parties, after they'd taken down the first batch, put the ropes on the necks of the second batch and lifted them up, the bodies of seven of the eight condemned men went limp, but the eighth continued to struggle, as if he were refusing to die. His body performed contortions as it hung there. Everyone waited for a few minutes but his spirit was stubborn and refused to leave his body. He moved his legs, trying to lift his body upwards. As the waiting grew longer, everyone was overcome by a sensation of choking and shortness of breath. The adjutant touched the man's neck with his right hand and began to rub it, but the body hanging in the air continued to struggle. I started to pant underneath the blanket. The adjutant called out: "Beast, relieve us of this duty! Let him find his rest!"

The beast came forward, stood underneath him, took hold of his legs and started to pull him down. The prisoner who was hanging there was wearing, as usual, shabby, worn-out clothes, so when they pulled him down the clothes came off him, and the bottom half of the prisoner was exposed. The beast carried on pulling, and pulling, and finally succeeded. The prisoner died, but as soon as he had died it seems that his anal sphincter relaxed for the last time so that he spilled everything in his bowels over the beast (who was still pulling). A large quantity of liquid waste covered the beast's head, face, and chest. The beast retreated and started to look at everyone. The adjutant, who was the first to grasp the situation, burst out laughing and said: "You used to be called 'beast', but now your name will be 'dirty beast'!"

Everyone laughed a lot, and even I laughed out loud. From that day on the beast had two names. Colleagues who feared and respected his valor called him the beast, but the soldiers and sergeants, and those who weren't afraid of him, called him the shit.

Most of the soldiers and sergeants were regular troops who were doing their two and a half years' military service. The overwhelming majority of them came from the coast and the mountains. They had thick accents and their movements were uncouth and unsophisticated. It was impossible to find anyone from the large cities or the capital among them. The fact that they were called up meant that they changed regularly, for in a single year there were two sets of graduates from the military police academies. So every six months a new batch would arrive and the old batch would be released.

The last batch arrived four months ago. There were thirteen of them, three sergeants and ten ordinary troops. When they entered our yard my heart sank between my knees, for my younger brother Samir was marching at their head in military police uniform. But when they got closer I saw that it was just someone who was very like my brother. I called him Samir to myself, while the other prisoners called him "Crooked" because he always had his head leaning to the right.

At first the administration did not ask the new arrivals to perform any duties on the level of torture or executions. For about a month they were left to stand and watch what was happening. The new arrivals were always reluctant to take hold of the whip or the cane, and even after a month had gone by, when they started to involve them, their beatings would be light and uncertain. At executions, they would stand the new arrivals some way from the gallows. As soon as the hanging procedures began, they would move

135

closer to each other, their faces would turn pale, and some of them would shake and look away, while others would suffer convulsions in the stomach which would make them vomit. The adjutant and the older policemen would see all this and deal with it as if they had seen nothing. By the time of the second and third hanging parties, they would relax, take courage, and behave naturally like the rest of their colleagues.

I watched sergeant Samir—"Crooked"—all the time. When he attended his first execution party he vomited so violently that I thought he would empty his entire inside. He sat on the ground with his hands over his eyes till the executions were finished. Then two of his colleagues helped him up and led him out of the yard, supporting him under the armpits. The last execution party he attended was extremely lively. He had a stick more than a meter long in his hand, and teased his colleagues with a permanent grin on his face. When the final batch of executions was complete, he stood in front of one of the victims and started to rock him. He put the stick on the ground and assumed the attitude of a boxer, turning the suspended corpse into a sandbag, and directing punches toward it. "Beast, beast, come here!" he shouted to the beast.

The beast ran toward him. "Yes, sir!"

"See this dog, he was hanging by his neck a quarter of an hour and still didn't die. Pull him by the feet, give him some rest!"

The policemen and municipals who'd heard this conversation laughed as they recalled what had happened to the beast. For his part, the beast said nothing for a moment as he looked at Samir.

February 24

The winter had been very cold, with a lot of rain, more than usually falls in the desert. The edge was taken off the cold by extra clothing, particularly woolen socks.

This winter had passed like previous winters before it. For ten winters I had been sitting in the same place, between the same walls, with the same black door beside me. Many of the faces around me had changed. No one remained of the fedayeen squadron that saw to letting the food in and volunteered to receive punishments in place of the aged and infirm. They had been here when I arrived at the dormitory but now they had all gone, either hanged, murdered, or dead from disease. Abu Hussein, the current head of the dormitory, had developed white eyebrows, when previously there had been not a single white hair in them. And despite the fact that I saw everyone every day, I could detect the ravages of time and the effect of suffering on their faces when I recalled their faces ten years ago. What had happened to my own face, do you suppose?

Oh for a fragment of a mirror!

We knew nothing at all about what was happening in the world outside this dormitory. Even the latest arrivals did not come straight from life. Most of them had spent two, three, or four years in secret service detention centers. They were usually leaders of religious organizations and were made to stay in the security service HQs for investigation purposes. Despite that, the prisoners would continue quizzing them for several days about the latest news. Even two- or four-year-old news was considered new and fresh in comparison with ten-year-old news.

Among these new arrivals was Abu al-Qa'qa', one of the leaders of the fundamentalist group and, so I was given to understand, a hero of the military operations that the organization undertook against the government authorities. He was said to be the planner and executor of a series of daring operations that struck terror in the ranks of the security services. Later, however, a quiet rumor made its way through the dormitory, among people belonging to other organizations, to the effect that he had been extremely cowardly during the investigation; that his cooperation with the security services and his confessions to them had led to the arrest of the entire brigade under his command, which consisted of four hundred soldiers; and that they had all been executed. These soldiers were intent on revenge on him. They considered him a traitor and had sworn a collective oath "that if any of them left prison, the first duty he was required to undertake was the liquidation of Abu al-Qaʿqaʿ."

But none of them left prison.

When Abu al-Qaʿqaʿ arrived, the dormitory lost its calm and inner peace. The first thing that Abu al-Qaʿqaʿ did was to acquaint himself with the organization's members, who had become a minority in the dormitory as a result of the constant hemorrhaging of their ranks. There were only just forty of them. At first, he knew none of them, for not a single one of those in prison had been under his command. After he had acquainted himself with them he visited them one by one. For two days he went from bed to bed, and after that he started to hold meetings. At the first meeting with the first group he noticed that they were reticent toward him. Without anyone asking him, he started to tell the story of how he had been arrested and of the investigation. Most of what he said was in a rather formal Arabic:

"So the exchange of fire between them and us continued for about four hours. We were on the fourth floor and they had occupied all the rooftops and streets around our building. Our ammunition was beginning to get low. I had three colleagues with me, may God have mercy on them, may God's *fatiha* be on their souls, my brethren—all around recited the fatiha and wiped their faces—each one took one of the windows in the house, and I took the door, to prevent any of the criminals from going up or down the staircase, but after four hours they used RPGs on us. They threw the missiles in through a window. I myself was thrown onto the staircase and wasn't injured, but the three others,"—a short pause—"may God grant them paradise, Amen. At that point I decided to withdraw from the action, despite the siege, so I picked up five boxes and went down the stairs. I sent all the soldiers in front of me to hell, made my way into the street and ran, firing left and right until I was hit. There was a dog opposite me on the street who fired a hail of bullets at me, and I was hit three times, once in the thigh, but only in the flesh, it didn't touch the bone, then one grazed my head above my ear—that's where,"—he showed them a horizontal line above the ear with no hair on it—"and the third struck my chest above the right lung and came out of my back." He took off his shirt and we could see the place where the bullet had entered, just a small hollow, and the place where it had emerged, a larger hollow.

"I fell onto the ground and the gun came out of my hand. I reached out to grab a hand grenade, but could not reach it, for they were on top of me with their guns pointing at my head. They took me immediately to the security service station. They didn't bandage my wounds but immediately started an inquiry. I refused to answer any questions unless they took me to a hospital. The officer conducting the inquiry smiled and said: 'Give us your mustache and your chin, and we'll give you first aid!'

"They brought a thin, strong piece of string, which they inserted into a large needle. Then they inserted the needle into the place where the bullet had entered and drew it out through the place where the bullet had emerged, followed by the string itself. Then they drew out the string, tied it firmly, lifted me up and hung me up by the string, which started to tear my flesh. I felt as though I were being hanged. I lost consciousness several times, but they sprayed me with water to bring me round. They wanted quick information, but I refused to give them so much as my name. The pain was too much for a man to bear. It seems that the shoulder blade had got in the way of the string so that the whole of my body weight was on it and it had begun to slip out of joint. To this day, the position of my shoulder blade and arm is unnatural.

"This didn't last long, because in the meantime they had searched the apartment and found all our documents and registers. I had often warned the treasurer—may God have mercy on him and grant him forgiveness—not to keep any document, but they found a register in which he had entered the names of all the brothers and their expenses, the rent of the apartments they were living in, and the rental agreements for every apartment. By means of this register they arrested everyone during the night."

He was speaking all this time in an ordinary tone, which did not convey any hint of self-defense. It was as if he had not been accused at all. Suddenly, however, he moved on from the subject of his arrest and its consequences, and started on a powerful religious exposition about faith and strength, jihad and the need for it, the meanings of martyrdom, the next world, Paradise and what it contained. By the time the day was finished he had become a leader who could not be argued with, and the extremists gathered around him in force.

In the course of the following ten days he started on the other groups—especially the one to which Sheikh Mahmoud and Dr. Zahi belonged, which was a group opposed to the extremists. It did not believe in force or armed struggle but preferred peaceful means. He attacked them violently, ridiculing their views, and invited their elders to a public discussion and argument—because it was his duty to guide them to the right path. This provoked a violent and contemptuous reaction, and they refused any discussion with him. *"We do not need a person like you, who sold himself to the security services, to guide us."* The Sufis had the same reaction, when he accused them of being no more than ignorant dervishes, who had introduced heresies into Islam and neglected the cornerstone of Islamic jihad.

For about ten days, the dormitory was divided into two camps. On one side was Abu al-Qaʿqaʿ and his supporters, and on the other the rest of the dormitory. Abu al-Qaʿqaʿ easily managed to attract the opposition of everyone, not least because he continued to try to embarrass them and provoke them after they refused to enter a discussion with him about the essence and doctrines of Islam. He accused them of cowardice and demanded that prayers should be held in public, even in front of the prison administration. This demand was received by all with contempt, and even some of his own faction advised him to drop it. After that he demanded that the fedayeen should be made up of all organizations and should not be voluntary, because jihad was a duty prescribed for every Muslim. This was accepted by everyone, with the exception of his own group, who had in practice always been the mainstays of the fedayeen, because it would deprive them of the position and influence that they had enjoyed for a long time during the previous years. *"We undertake this work for God's sake, and our reward is from God, and we cannot compel anyone else to do it."*

Abu al-Qaʿqaʿ failed in everything, and succeeded only in attracting the hostility of everyone. He had been in the dormitory for just fifteen days when he thought he had found something he could use to embarrass everyone. I don't know which member of his faction it was who told him about me, but he then confronted everyone, asking: "How can you describe yourselves as Muslims when you allow an unbeliever, a spy, to live among you? And this despite the fact that God, may He be praised and exalted, said: 'Kill them wherever you find them!'" Then he demanded of everyone that they try me and bring down the punishment of God on me. And the punishment for unbelief and doubting the unity of God is death!

My life hung on the reaction of the other groups, who were all neutral, for the matter was of no concern to them, and they had no wish to create a problem with Abu al-Qa'qa' and his gang with unknown consequences. But the late Sheikh Mahmoud's group took a different view. Abu Hussein stood firm and unwavering as a mountain, and directing his words to Abu al-Qa'qa', made a speech in the middle of the dormitory (the question had ceased to be one of whispers and was now being discussed openly with raised voices): "In the first place, who are you to try people and hold them to account? This man"—pointing at me—"has been among us for several years and we have never observed anything bad about him. He is a man so wretched that he never speaks and no one knows what is in his heart. So by what right do you try him and hold him to account and want to kill him? You should know, Abu al-Qa'qa', that he has a Lord who will try him and hold him to account, just as He—not you—will try us all! Secondly, Abu al-Qa'qa', you should know that Sheikh Mahmoud, may God have mercy on him!, forbade anyone from harming this man; indeed, he took him under his wing and protected him. And we cannot allow anyone to harm someone who was protected by Sheikh Mahmoud. Thirdly, everyone, and particularly yourself, should know that any attempt to harm this person will be met with the most violent response from our side."

Abu al-Qa'qa' responded forcefully, relying on a selection of Qur'anic verses, hadiths of the Prophet, and episodes from Islamic history. Everyone in the dormitory nodded their heads in agreement and I thought that he would succeed in convincing everyone, but Abu Hussein took over the discussion and began to reply to him in a loud voice. He also quoted a selection of Qur'anic verses and hadiths, as well as the biography of the Prophet, in order to refute all the sources that Abu al-Qa'qa' had cited. Once again, everyone in the dormitory, even some of Abu al-Qa'qa''s own faction, were nodding their heads in agreement. Abu Hussein's argument was compelling, but Abu al-Qa'qa' did not want to concede defeat so he started to respond again. Then Abu Hussein replied, and they both seemed equally convincing to everyone.

There were several raised voices, and in the heat of the argument the policeman appeared on the roof above the skylight, and shouted: "What's this noise, dormitory head, you donkey?"

The guard recognized the two people who were standing up as Abu Hussein and Abu al-Qa'qa', and from the roof he informed the duty sergeant in the yard. They took the pair of them out for five hundred lashes each. From the moment they were taken out to when they reappeared, silence reigned in the dormitory, but as soon as the policeman shut the door they started their verbal battle again. Abu Hussein spoke first: "Fear the Lord, man, you're the cause of the punishment! Are you happy now?"

They resumed their verbal sparring. After more than an hour Abu Hussein said: "That's all I've got to say. Everyone sit down on his bed. We've got quite enough leaders here!"

"No one's claiming to be a leader... we just want to obey and apply God's commands, whether you like it or not!"

The atmosphere in the dormitory became a lot tenser. I thought that I should intervene, emerge from my shell, but how? Stand up and tell them my story? Refute all the charges that had been directed at me? To say that I was a Christian was not an accusation, because the true doctrines of Islam required them to treat Christians well. That I was a spy? I think this accusation had lost its force with the passage of time, for if I had been a spy I would not have waited more than ten years to put my espionage into practice. But how could I defend myself from the charge of unbelief and atheism? It was true that everyone who had heard me say I was an atheist was dead, but if they asked me about it in the course of my defense, would I be able to say that I was a believer? I didn't think so, but I couldn't come to a decision.

The atmosphere remained extremely tense. It seemed that Abu al-Qa'qa''s faction was up to something, for they were on their guard, but Abu Hussein's faction took a number of measures. Three of them sat on Abu Hussein's bed to my left the whole day long, and three others sat on the bed of my neighbor to the right. Then at night one of them would move his bed and sleep in front of me in the corridor at my feet, so that I would be surrounded by them. When I got up to go to the wash-place I noticed that two of the group would stand up and accompany me, apparently spontaneously, as if they were also going to the washroom by chance. So they were protecting me.

The situation continued like this for three days. On the fourth day a number of the fundamentalists contrived to pick a fist fight in front of the washrooms with one of the people guarding me. Within a few minutes the blood was flowing from his nose, and more than two hundred people had stood up and were fighting each other, so that it was no longer possible to know who was hitting whom, or who was trying to stop the fight. The fight lasted for several minutes, during which a lot of blood flowed. It was impossible to conceal such a commotion.

I was standing beside the door. Neither Abu Hussein nor Abu al-Qa'qa' took part, just their younger supporters. But when the policemen opened the door, the fight stopped of its own accord.

Abu Hussein tried to claim that some of the younger prisoners had been having a laugh. The sergeant screamed in his face, cursing him—"We didn't bring you in here to have a laugh!"—and ordered everyone out into the yard. So they went out. Whenever the sergeant saw someone with traces of blood on him, he turned to Abu Hussein and said: "Exercise? You slut! You told me it was exercise!"

The whole dormitory was punished severely. A policeman beat me with a square cable on the wound on my foot, which hurt me a lot. Then they let us back in and shut the door to the accompaniment of curses and oaths. I had forgotten the habit of speech, but at that moment I believed that if I did not speak I would choke. I steeled myself with the words of my father and uncle from my childhood about the need to be a man and accept responsibility. I walked into the middle of the dormitory and stood there. I could hardly stand from the pain. When they saw me gazing around at everyone in the dormitory they were silent. Two of my guards at once stood up and planted themselves at my side. I gestured to them to go back to their places. They hesitated but went back.

I was never an orator and I had never stood up to speak with hundreds of eyes staring at me. Nor had I ever claimed to be brave. On the contrary, the experience of arrest and imprisonment had at least shown me that I was more like a coward, but it was the pain, the intimidation, the torture, the forced abstinence from speaking... I turned my hands and eyes toward Abu al-Qaʿqaʾ and shouted in a loud voice—I myself did not recognize it: "Abu al-Qaʿqaʾ, do you want to kill me? Please, here I am, naked before you!" I don't know why I addressed him in such formal Arabic. "Please, but before you kill me, answer my questions, do you want to kill me by virtue of your being God's representative on earth? Can you prove that you are His representative? If you prove that, can you prove to me and others that He issued you with an order to kill me? I don't think so, and I can confidently state that you are not God's representative! Abu al-Qaʿqaʿ, you want to kill me to satisfy a lust for killing that you have. I hope that I am wrong in this, I hope that you are not a hateful, tortured person, I hope that you are not like the scorpion, which stings itself if it cannot find anyone else to sting. But I say, and I call everyone here to witness, that if killing me will solve the problem, then do it, send one of your followers to kill me, and I will redeem you with my blood."

I was silent for a little. Then I turned to the crowd of people and in a quieter tone said: "Listen, everyone, for more than ten years you have condemned me to silence, though I have listened to you a lot. Now listen to me for just a few minutes…"

I told them who I was, how I had come here, and defended myself against the three charges. When I reached the charge of heresy, I once again addressed Abu al-Qaʿqaʿ: "Abu al-Qaʿqaʿ, the question of belief or unbelief is a purely personal matter. You and all those like you must understand that. Faith is a private relationship between each person and his creator. You know that it is not difficult for me or anyone else to say: 'I bear witness that there is no God but God and that Muhammad is the messenger of God,' but if I were to say that, you and your followers would say that I was an atheist and had made the profession of faith out of fear. No, I am not afraid of you, and I will not be a hypocrite or a liar. If I just tell you that I am a Christian and hold to my religion, you will not be able to do anything about that, because your religion tells you to treat Christians well. But so that you won't be able to say I'm a coward, I will not even say this. Abu al-Qaʿqaʿ, listen to me, I am not afraid of you, and you are not my master! It is not for me to present you with an account sheet. If you are convinced that I have to be killed, then come on, get up and do not be afraid!"

At this point he fell silent. I remained standing, exchanging glances with Abu al-Qaʿqaʿ, trying hard not to let my eyes blink.

Then I was gripped from behind by Abu Hussein's hand and led to my bed. "Enough, say nothing, don't provoke him any more! I think the problem has been solved. God grant you forgiveness, but please say no more now!"

And in fact, as Abu Hussein had said, the problem was solved. Two days later, in fact, it was resolved decisively, for it was a Thursday, and Abu al-Qaʿqaʾ was led out to execution. The whole dormitory said the funeral prayer for him, asking for God's mercy on him. Abu Hussein made a comment, which he directed toward me: "May God have mercy on him. Nothing but mercy is right for the dead. Remember the good deeds of your dead! But, my brother, it is only twenty days that he spent here. It was like a whirlwind coming in to the dormitory. God have mercy on him! He turned the dormitory upside down. God have mercy on him! The longer one lives, the more one sees!"

My relationship with Abu Hussein improved and we started to exchange conversations. I said to myself, *if only Abu al-Qaʿqaʾ had come a long time ago.* Abu Hussein asked me about France and the life there, and especially about the women in France, and I would talk and talk. I would go into great detail, as I had a great hunger for speaking. I turned to him, teasing him a little: "What's up, Abu Hussein? I notice you're asking a lot about women, aren't you scared Umm Hussein might hear you?"

"Come on, brother, Umm Hussein is very dear to me, but she's an old woman now. If God separates us, then God willing I will marry a Frenchwoman. Tell me, are there Muslim women in France?"

"Yes, of course there are Muslim women."

"Praise be to God, praise be to God,"—he laughed—"you have guaranteed my future!"

Apart from Abu Hussein, there were just four doctors who had broken down the barrier erected around me. The four doctors were all graduates of European countries. One of them had graduated in France; he began to sit with me, and from the second sitting proposed that we speak in French.

I discovered that he had led life to the fullest and that he did not observe religious teachings except in Ramadan, when he would simply fast and pray. Apart from that, he had no connection with politics or religious organizations or anything else.

I asked him in French for an explanation: "Okay, if that's how it is, why did they arrest you?"

"If you can answer that question, so can I!"

Abu Hussein had no patience with these conversations in French: "Come on, give us a break! You've twisted your tongues quite enough! Speak Arabic so that we can understand you!"

The conversations in French almost made me dizzy, and gave me a headache. They had an effect inside me greater than that of seeing a cucumber for the first time. We would swap memories of places that we had both visited and knew well. So the relationship between us became very close for a time.

Once, as I was taking great pleasure in emphasizing the pronunciation of the French consonants—almost becoming intoxicated with it, in fact—he looked at me and startled me by asking: "Brother, since you are so... so sensible, I mean, why have you been covering yourself with a blanket like that mental case, the doctor of geology?"

I was silent for a little then told him about my big secret, the secret of the peephole.

I told him about it in French, but he answered in Arabic. He was wide-eyed, and his lower lip had dropped.

"Goodness! And we used to call you stupid!"

He asked if he could take a look through it, but I told him this would be impossible right now, as it would attract the attention of the others. Then after a little he suggested that we tell Abu Hussein, and I agreed.

Abu Hussein's reaction was similar to that of Dr. Nasim. Signs of astonishment spread across his face, and he used the same expression: "Goodness! By God, he's cleverer than he looks! And he hides it well! So you really are a spy, but spying *on* the police, not *for* the police!"

Two days later Abu Hussein told us he had decided to tell everyone in the dormitory about it, so that we could use the peephole freely, because everyone here was trustworthy. And so it came to pass.

With the exception of Abu Hussein and the doctors—with Dr. Nasim at their head—everyone continued to be reserved toward me. I knew that they had discussed the matter between themselves and arrived at the following conclusion: that what I had said with regard to rejecting the accusation of heresy was problematic and unconvincing, and that if I been a true believer, whether in Christianity or Islam, I would not have hesitated to proclaim it— for religion must be open. But against that, there was no longer any threat to my life, and in this way I gained the first of my basic rights as a human being—the right to life. I gained it from the anvil (the Muslim Brotherhood) but not from the hammer (the police), for any sergeant in the yard could still dispatch me to the other world with a blow from his stick.

OCTOBER 6

The last few months have passed quickly. Dr. Nasim (who really is like a *nasim*, a breeze) filled the hours of my long prison days. We were hardly ever apart. A short time after we had got to know each other, he made an agreement with my neighbor that they should change places. We would wake in the morning and without moving from under the blanket would resume an unfinished conversation from the previous day. We ate together, talked together, and made chess pieces from dough. This operation took more than twenty days. It was a beautiful chess set, for Nasim was a natural artist and poet, highly sensitive, who could look for beauty anywhere. His lifetime ambition was to teach plastic art but family pressure had made him study medicine. Despite that, he had abandoned medicine for a full year when he was in his fourth year and had shared a studio with another artist in Paris, until his father returned and compelled him to resume his medical studies. Despite that, he never ever abandoned drawing.

We would scrape off the burnt pieces from the bread, gather them together (including the black color), put a little gravy from the tomato sauce on them, then leave it all (including the red color) to thicken and dry for several days. We would make dough from the middle of the "military" bread, then Nasim would make chess pieces from the dough mixed with the coloring. Everyone who saw the pieces gasped in amazement. Then he started to make artistic shapes of his own design which were incredibly tasteful and beautiful.

We talked in French, we talked in Arabic, we played chess. We watched the yard through the spyhole, and after we had finished all that, if there was still a little time left, Nasim would take a piece of dough and start to shape it. In every shape that he fashioned you could feel a woman and the desire for her. Nasim lived a big love story, which was still etched into his emotions, and he spoke of it as the meaning of his life and also one of his biggest failures in life—the first of these failures being that he had studied medicine under pressure from his family and society.

I once asked him out of the blue, without any preliminaries: "Now… do you pray regularly?"

"Since being among these people, I have no longer prayed," he replied with complete simplicity.

"But what threw you in here among them?"

"It was my brother, my brother whom I couldn't stand and who couldn't stand me. An old-fashioned person, with narrow horizons. Even before I went to study in France, you could hear us every day shouting at each other as far as the street, and usually the reason was his attempts to interfere in my mother's and my sisters' dress. He wanted to make them wear black Islamic dress, but they would resist, and I would support them. More often than not, he and I would come to blows. He was a failure in academic terms.

"I went to France and stayed there for eight years. In the meantime, he had joined these people"—he pointed to the fundamentalist group—"and became urgently wanted by the security services, who arrested my father and mother. To escape from this dilemma, and to stave off the attention of the security services within the city, my father told them that he had fled to France to be with his brother. So I became a wanted man without my knowing it. I finished my studies and came back home, to be met at the airport by security men who wanted me to give up my brother to them, when I hadn't seen him for eight years."

"So here I am in front of you in this prison."

Nasim and I would take turns to spy through the peephole without a blanket. There were no more than five people who spied through the peephole, and it seems that everyone still considered my bed to be polluted, for spying through the peephole meant sitting on my bed.

Nasim and I, who were on continual watch, reported what we saw to Abu Hussein, who in turn reported it to everyone else.

Relations between the fundamentalists and the rest of the dormitory returned to a friendly state, especially as the fundamentalists were for the most part young and generally rather simple and goodhearted, so long as Abu al-Qaʿqaʾ, Saʿsaʾa or Abu Qarada didn't appear among them. They remained the most generous and ready to make sacrifices.

One Monday, I left the peephole entirely to Nasim so that he could observe the executions. He stayed close to the peephole, no longer speaking or moving.

Nasim would often use the expression "God damn!" when talking. Two hours after taking up position at the peephole, he leaped backwards, looked at me and said: "God damn, God damn!"

He looked at Abu Hussein: "God damn!"

He looked at the crowd: "God damn!"

Then, in a softer voice, after approaching me: "God damn! What is this? How could you bear these sights? Now then! Look, look, what on earth is going on!"

I looked through the peephole. There were eight corpses dangling from ropes, and several corpses on the ground. These eight corpses looked like the last batch of the day. The "beast," the municipals' colleague, was standing to the left of the second corpse, which was that of a fat man; he was holding a thick cane, which he used to rain down blows on the corpse, while the policemen watched him, laughing. With every blow of the cane that he brought down on the corpse, he shouted in a loud voice: "Long live the beloved President! We'd sacrifice ourselves for you, President!"—another blow of the cane on the corpse—"You dare to oppose the President"—another blow of the cane—"you queer! Our President is the best of presidents"—another blow of the cane—"move aside, you perverts!"—another blow of the cane—"we worship the President before God…"—another blow of the cane… the rhythm faltered… several more blows with the cane. I wondered whether he had exhausted the vocabulary he had memorized from being so often repeated on radio and TV and on the streets in state-organized marches; it certainly seemed so, as he began to turn to his private supply of words collected from the street.

He stopped the beating for a short time, but there was then a sharp blow to the head, during which I could hear the tinkle of bone. "You dog! You oppose the President?"—another blow of the cane—"The President's the most powerful person in the world,"—another blow—"the President will fuck your mothers,"—another blow—"the President's got the biggest cock in the whole world,"—another blow—"he'll fuck you and your sister one after the other!"—another blow with the stick. The beast paused for a moment panting, after which, with a series of hysterical movements, he placed one end of the cane between the buttocks of the corpse and shoved it forward. The whole body moved forward, as the beast continued pushing. The other end of the cane was between his hands as he levered it into the position of his penis and started to push the cane between the corpse's buttocks and shake it forward. "With our blood and souls, we will redeem you, Mr. President!" he shouted with every shake.

The cane stayed between the buttocks as the corpse continued to twitch, while the policemen laughed. Sergeant "Twister" came forward, guffawing. He took hold of the corpse from the front and held it firm for the beast. The beast continued to press the cane between the buttocks of the corpse, shouting: "With our blood and souls, we will redeem you, Mr. President!"

The Twister pushed from the front while the beast pushed with the cane from the rear. At the moment when the corpse's head escaped from the rope—seen from a distance it looked as though the corpse had cunningly moved its head to free itself of the rope—the corpse fell face down on the ground. The cane fell from the hand of the beast and stayed planted upright between the buttocks of the corpse. The beast leaped up and shouted a slogan he had often heard repeated on radio and television: "Down with colonialism, down with imperialism!"

"Down, down, down!" repeated Sergeant Twister after him.

"Long live our dear President!"

"Long live, long live!"

The cane stayed upright between the buttocks of the corpse, quivering.

"For ever, for ever, long live the President!"

With every repetition of the word "live" the cane quivered left and right.

October 20

My relationship with Nasim had become closer over the previous months. He was happy with me too. Nasim wasn't like the other people, he was open-minded, wasn't interested in politics, and he had never even thought of joining a religious organization, though in his life outside prison he performed his religious duties on special occasions. Once he said something to me that I had also been wondering about: "How did all those years go by when you and I were in the same place but we didn't get to know each other? And then afterwards, when we got to know each other, we became like twins! You are my soul mate, you really are!" I had the same feelings.

▦ ▦ ▦

The building workshops in the Desert Prison were still constructing new dormitories, despite the fact that the number of newcomers to the prison had decreased considerably in the last three years.

Prisoners... Who was the first prisoner in history? Who invented the prison? What did the first prisoner look like? Has there ever been a single prisoner in the whole world, at any time and in any prison, who spent a whole year or more in prison, only to emerge the same as before? What genius was it that had the idea of a prison? Was it God? It must have been. It is such a miracle as to be beyond the capacities of the human mind.

But, if God knew what prison was, why did He leave Satan free after he had disobeyed and not imprison him? I am sure Satan would have been bound to prostrate himself after spending several months—no, several weeks—not just in front of Adam but in front of Eve. Could God have made a mistake when he commanded the devil to bow down before Adam? Why didn't he order him to bow down before Eve? Would the devil have refused to bow down before Eve? But what if the devil had prostrated himself before Adam himself? Would the devil have become God's adjutant? Or his equal?

If I hadn't been a prisoner, how would ridiculous ideas like this have arisen?

New dormitories appeared in the prison. When were all the dormitories in this prison empty? People came in together or in successive waves. A few days and the dormitory quota was complete. A few dozen, a hundred, two hundred, three hundred or more! Everyone looked at everyone else. The faces were all the same. No one knew anyone. After a few minutes, people got to know each other. And this went on for years.

With the process of getting to know each other, a sorting process also began, as people met and mingled with each other. At first, groupings began on the political, organizational level—which was the reason for their entering prison. People who belonged to a single party, or a single organization, met each other, whether or not they had known each other previously. They became acquainted, formed a single group with a shared social life, and had their own meetings and their secrets—most if not all of them illusions.

They were just supporting each other. Each relied on the other, and this communal spirit formed for them an illusion of power, and hence of protection. To be protected by the group provided a sense of security. The process began extremely tensely, and reached the point of factionalism and hostility to others, but with time, those concerned began to relax, especially if the whole dormitory was of one organizational persuasion.

Among the lessons security officers receive—after the first lesson, which says "The first lesson of the security services is not to trust your colleagues!"—there are many more lessons, which may be right or wrong. In the text that includes how to deal with hostile organizations, however, there is a lesson which is always correct: "If you want the members of an organization to consume each other, put them in jail together!"

Frustration, aversion, hatred, disrespect for leaderships... then the close ties within the organizations begin to relax and to disintegrate, and people start to look at the environment beyond the frame of the single organization.

Days, weeks, months and years pass. New relationships spring up on a new basis, that of geography. People from one area, be it village, town, city, or even a wider area—the north, the east, or the coastal area—revive shared memories with an almost over-whelming longing as they recall familiar places: plains, valleys, mountains, streets, gardens, squares. Every day the intersections increase as they recall familiar public events and become better acquainted with one another. As knowledge increases, things previously thought to have been forgotten are unearthed through superficially innocent questions. For every individual, family or tribe has its positive features, just as it has things it is ashamed of and tries to forget, or make others forget. But it is prison that has its own laws—clear, simple, and shameless.

Someone asks a man from his own city whom he has got to know a question that may be innocent or in jest, like: "Are you a member of the family of *beys* that lives in a certain place?"

"Yes, I'm from those people's family!"

"Sorry, forgive me, but I heard a story, is it true that you acquired the status of *beys*, and your property and lands, because your grandmother was a friend of the Ottoman governor?"

"No, absolutely not, that's not true!"

The conversation ends and something sticks in the mind of the member of the *beys*' family, together with some displeasure. Someone else asks someone: "You're from the village of al-Haydariyya, but which family are you from?"

"I'm from the al-Baytar family."

"Al-Baytar! Tell me, I heard several years ago, that a woman from the al-Baytar family killed her husband with the help of her lover. Are you related to this woman at all?"

"The woman is my aunt, but the story isn't true, it's just an accusation!"

The conversation stops and something sticks in the mind of the al-Baytar family member, together with some displeasure. The questions multiply:

"Are you the son of so-and-so who stole the local council's chest?"

"Wasn't your mother so-and-so, who…?"

The conversations stop and many things stick in the mind, together with some displeasure. Days, weeks, months, years pass. New relationships spring up on a new basis: attitudes, hobbies, professions, those interested in literature, artists, teachers, doctors…

Days, weeks, months, and years pass. New relationships spring up on a new basis: taste, and social refinement.

A man distances himself and avoids his colleague in the organization or profession or area, because he makes noises with his mouth when he eats, and that is poor taste.

He distances himself and avoids him, because when he folds his blankets he folds them too vigorously and stirs up the dust for his neighbor. And that is poor taste. He distances himself and avoids him because when they have a conversation he doesn't leave enough space between their two heads. He gets too close to him when he speaks, and forces him to smell the foul odor from his mouth. And that is poor taste.

There are hundreds of problems that this enforced living together gives rise to among people who have not chosen each other, for they are from different backgrounds and walks of life, different upbringings, and different cultural levels.

The years have passed. One year kneeling on the breast of the one preceding it.

New relationships spring up on a new basis, and people draw further and further away from everything of a factional nature. The ashes of the dying years gradually cover the freshness of the memories about life outside. The "outside" retreats and people become immersed in the details of daily life in prison. The space occupied by these details grows larger in the prisoner's mind, at the expense of the "outside," which seems faraway and difficult to grasp. The thing that fades most is politics and its repercussions as a way of regulating a herd of people. The individual self returns, to grow at the expense of the collective self or the herd instinct. Things may go so far as to lead to a rupture or hostility toward the history that he himself helped to make. Another step and it reaches the stage of a sadistic flogging of the self. "Prison was necessary for us to discover the big lie we were living. What stupidity, what dream, brought us here?" he asks, his words tinged with bitterness.

New relationships spring up on a new basis. Mutual friendships are the penultimate stage. They begin as isolated cases at first, and do not develop into a phenomenon until the later stages. Even at this point they may not be absolutely public but they include the vast majority.

Two people similar to one other, two people different from one other… similarities and differences, despite being opposed in every respect, nevertheless form an appropriate basis, an appropriate ground for the growth of relations of mutual friendship.

After several years have passed, two people discover, through trial and error, and through continuous contact for twenty-four hours of every day, three hundred and sixty-five days of every year, that they are similar in certain things, in many things, in everything! They are attracted to each other, and a friendly relationship begins between the two of them.

After several years have passed, two people discover, through trial and error, and through continuous contact for twenty-four hours of every day, three hundred and sixty-five days of every year, that they are different in certain things, in many things, in everything! And just as a magnetic south pole is attracted to a north pole, they are attracted to one another. A friendly relationship begins between the two of them, which begins on a basis of equality, each party having the same rights and obligations. As the days pass, however, the two halves of the scales lose their balance, and as the first one rises, so the other one falls. One party begins to acquire and exhibit power, while the other relies more and more on his stronger friend for everything, so that he ends up as the gentler and more compliant party. The relation between the two continues on the basis of this sort of equation—strong and weak—for a long time. The strong one looks after the weaker one and extends his protection to him, enjoying this role immensely, while the weaker one, who enjoys the protection afforded to him under the wing of the stronger, is also extremely happy with his role.

For all these years, I had stayed snuggled within my shell, trying to observe, explain, and record everything happening in front of me in this collection of humanity. I observed, explained, and recorded many things. These pairings aroused my interest from their first beginnings, and I watched their development and transformations closely, explaining them in the context of the human need for company and society. Until, that is, a friendship of this sort grew up between Nasim and me because of the late Abu al-Qa'qa'. At the beginning of the attachment I was preoccupied by just one thing: that I should have someone to talk to!

It was only natural that I should gravitate with some force toward this person, who after more than ten years of complete boycott, was happy to sit on my bed and chat with me, then invite me to sit on his own bed. I had the feeling again that I was a human being with an existence that at least some people could respect—respect his person, his intelligence, and his views—and that this might be achievable with anyone who refused to boycott me and had a mind that was in the least bit open.

But Nasim was much more than that. Nasim was more than my dreams and hopes for a person to take me out of myself: his simplicity and refinement made me see him in front of me, pure and shining, as a white page shines under powerful lights. Within a few days he had entered my soul, squeezed it, crushed it, kneaded it with his soul and body. He was at one with it, and…

I was frightened, frightened, frightened!

Who was I? Was I? Was I… and…

Where was I going?

Both in my own country and in France I had known a lot of women. Some of them had been merely fleeting acquaintances (I may not even remember what they looked like now), while others (a lesser number) had carved into my emotions gaps that could not be closed. In these relationships I behaved completely naturally, like any ordinary man, and in the whole of my past I had never had any unnatural or deviant experiences. I had never observed in myself any inclination to indulge in sexual practices other than the ordinary ones between a man and a woman, nor had I ever noticed any homosexual leanings. On the contrary, I had a psychological aversion to them. Even during the period of adolescence, when young people play around with each other sexually in all sorts of ways, I did not indulge in any experiments of this sort. This may have been due to some of my own material circumstances. But now, what was happening to me? And how would all of this end?

The blazing emotions that I felt for Nasim I had never felt for any woman I had known in my life! We would sit together, talk together, play and eat together throughout the waking hours. He slept beside me and we would continue our conversations in whispers as we lay there. The pair of us were with each other all day, but despite that I still desperately longed for him.

He would leave me for short periods, to go to the lavatory or the washroom, for example, but his eyes would remain suspended over the stone washroom door until he came out, and from there exchanged a smile with me... and I relaxed. I knew nothing about his feelings, his emotions, or his ideas on the matter, but his effusiveness toward me, the warmth of the relationship, and his constant repetition of the phrase that I was his "soul mate" were all things that suggested he was either living in the same state as myself or else was extremely innocent.

The two scales in our relationship were fundamentally uneasily balanced. He was extremely gentle—even on the physical level his features were soft and slightly feminine—whereas I am rugged, with unkempt hair and severe, sharp features. As the relationship between us developed, I became more forceful and masculine, while his movements acquired more softness and fluidity—and were sometimes even flirtatious. I was now living out a frightening psychological battle between my intellect, with its harsh judgments, and my transient emotions and inclinations, which I sometimes felt were not subject to the commands or the prohibitions and inhibitions of the intellect. Should I discuss the matter with him openly? But why? What would be the point? Wouldn't that lead to this wonderful relationship of friendship being destroyed?

Touches between us—it sometimes happened that when we were deep in conversation or playing I would take his hand and feel a strange sense of peace and pleasure! And I would carry on holding it for longer than the situation required.

I turned once again to the dormitory, to observe and try to explain these widespread mutual friendships, but with new eyes—searching eyes, which tried to penetrate the thick outer wall of each of these relationships, then explore what was beneath the surface. But I didn't arrive at any useful information or conclusions in this respect. All the relationships were on the surface innocent. I was afraid, very afraid! Could the influences and effects of prison have changed my psychological makeup to make me travel in this direction? But my intellect absolutely refused this explanation. And my great fear… could that be a sign of health, if my feelings and emotions were signs of sickness? Or was this all just an illusion? Wasn't it possible that I was giving the matter more importance than it really deserved? Why shouldn't I let matters take their natural course, and let what may be, be.

This total and utter destruction of the human, this daily, constantly present death, wouldn't it lead to madness, or to the maddest and strangest of behavior and actions?

A large lump of saliva collected in my throat. Where should I throw it? Into whose face?

February 24

Lately I had noticed something else. Instead of my relationship with Nasim helping to draw me out of my shell, I had started letting him into it.

The dormitory continued in the same attitude toward me, namely an attitude of boycott. It was true that it was no longer a dangerous, hostile boycott, but had turned into a chilly, negative boycott; but little by little as my relationships became restricted to Nasim alone, the boycott tightened around him too. Some of the fundamentalists accused me of corrupting Nasim in his religion, saying it was quite likely Nasim had become an atheist as well. As evidence, they noted that Nasim had withdrawn from them and spent all his time with me speaking in the language of the unbelievers, and that we amused ourselves playing chess instead of reciting the name of God. When I brought this to Nasim's attention he said: "To hell with them a thousand times! Before they rejected me, I had rejected them from inside me."

He spoke at length and it became obvious to me that he did not like them. Sometimes he expressed his distaste for them. He described some of their behavior as backward and ignorant, and sometimes base.

I had believed that someone like Nasim (transparent and straightforward, a true artist, and extremely decent) could not know hatred, but in his conversations about them, I sometimes sensed some slivers of hatred piled up deep inside him. I spoke to him honesty of what I had noticed, and he didn't deny it or defend himself. "I don't know," he said. "A man doesn't notice his own situation. Maybe the basis for this hatred is my brother, that is 'their colleague'!" Nasim was constantly being astonished. He would see something or some incident repeated hundreds of times in front of him, but on each occasion he would exhibit the same degree of surprise and astonishment. And if it was something that he rejected, he would exhibit the same degree of protest and displeasure. The most important thing that distinguished him was his intelligence and refinement—his infinite refinement, and his aristocratic sensibility.

Now Nasim had gone for three days without eating, despite all my attempts to force him to do so.

■ ■ ■

There were two families in our dormitory, the first composed of four brothers, and the second made up of a father and three sons. At the start of the clashes between the religious movement and the authorities, and the beginning of the widespread sweeps and arrests, the three sons, who were all members of the organization, were able to escape and disappear from view. When the house was stormed, the security men found the father of the escapees alone. They led him off to the security services' detention center, where he remained under investigation for more than two months. They wanted him to show them where his sons were, when in fact he didn't actually know! After two months, they sent him to the capital, where they conducted further investigations, but without success. Finally, the officer got fed up with him and told him that they would keep him in prison as a hostage until he handed over his sons in person to the authorities.

The father remained there, with lots more people like himself. The prisoners jestingly called them "the hostage organization" or "the hostage party." The father stayed in the capital for several months, after which he was transferred with the others to the

Desert Prison, when the prisons and security service centers in the capital became too crowded.

Three years after the start of the father's incarceration, all his sons were in the Desert Prison. They were incarcerated one after the other. In the end, through Morse messages, they got to know each other's whereabouts. But despite the three brothers being imprisoned, the father was not set free.

After another three years, their turn came for the field court to examine their case. There were more than fifty people due to be tried on that day. A line four-deep, sitting on the floor. Each of them had to hold their hands clasped over their heads, with their heads between their knees, eyes closed.

The court called them by name. When a person's name was called, he leaped up and shouted "present!", and in less than a second he had to be in front of the court officials. In less than a minute or two his trial would be over. And in less than another second he had to go back to the place where he had been sitting.

It was in this atmosphere, and in spite of everything, that the father and the brothers saw each other and were able to pass their greetings to each other in a sort of chain. Then they were summoned one by one.

After their trials had finished, it seems that one of the officers noticed that all four had the same name, so the officials told the policemen to bring in the father and his sons. The court was composed of three officers, who were in a relaxed mood, together with the prison governor. They had distributed themselves throughout the room around a blazing heater, and it was quite warm in the room. They were drinking coffee, smoking, and exchanging jokes. At the moment when the four men entered the room, the prison governor was telling them a joke. The four men stood submissively at the closed door of the room, and none of those present paid them the least bit of attention, as they laughed raucously and swapped comments. After a few minutes one of the officers turned and looked hard at the four people. There was still an atmosphere of mirth as he spoke to the father: "Okay, *hajji*, you've all got the same name, are you related to each other?"

"Yes, sir, yes, these are my children and I'm their father!"

Another officer picked up the conversation. "Tell me, hajji, do you have any other sons!"

"No, sir, these are all the sons I have."

"That means the whole family is composed of criminals and agents!"

"No, sir! We're just ordinary people. God is sufficient for us and the best of protectors!"

The prison governor interrupted. "How old are you?" he asked the father.

"I don't know exactly, sir, but it's probably over seventy."

"Over seventy! And you've still got some tricks up your sleeve. You're still strong enough to beat and kill!"

"Sir, God protect you, we've never killed or beaten! We just got caught up in a fire that came too close!"

"It's not just a straightforward misfortune, old man! How long have you been in prison?"

"Maybe six or seven years, sir!"

"Okay, and after all these years aren't you missing your wife?"

"Sir, after all this, a man of my age only desires a just end!"

"Okay, I understand that. But apart from that, apart from that, don't you feel that there's anything you need?"

"Yes, sir! I'm an old man, and I find moving very difficult. If you could put my sons with me to look after me, you'd have done me a big favor!"

So the prison governor ordered his sons to be transferred to his dormitory.

At this point, the member of the court took over the conversation again: "Look, hajji, what do you expect the court's verdict to be?"

"Sir, God's mercy is vast, and you always judge fairly!"

"Right, listen to me! You are four people, one family! And we have sentenced three of you to death. Now you need to choose who will be executed and who is the one who must live!"

"God grant you a long life, sir, and extend the life of your children! If that's the situation, then As'ad must live and God take the other three of us!"

"And who is As'ad?"

"This is As'ad. Your servant, who kisses your hand, sir!"

"Why have you chosen As'ad, hajji?"

"Sir, I'm an old man, and I have had most of my life. Sa'd and Sa'id have been married for some time and have children of their own, who are still alive, but As'ad is still young and not yet married. Still in the flower of his youth, in fact! And it's forbidden to pluck flowers like that. Isn't that so, sir?"

"Yes, hajji, indeed! Policeman, policeman! Come here, take away this crowd and put them all in one dormitory!"

So all the members of the family went back to our dormitory. I'd heard this story and this discussion dozens of times during the previous two years, but five days ago—it being a Thursday—when the list of executions came and the policeman began to read it out, the names of those from our dormitory to be executed were Sa'd, Sa'id, and As'ad. The father was furious.

When the names were read out, As'ad was sleeping. Sa'id and Sa'd got up from their beds, made their way to As'ad's bed, and woke him up, calling him by name. When Sa'd called him, Sa'id was silent; then Sa'id called him and Sa'd was silent. "As'ad, my brother, As'ad, wake up, get up, come on, get up, brother, As'ad, get up! God has commanded and we cannot escape, As'ad, my brother!"

As'ad woke up, looked at his two brothers on either side of the bed, then sat up straight, and looked at them with an inquisitive expression. "What's up, my brother!" he asked, "What's happened?"

"No, it's nothing, just get up! Wake up! We have to get up, wash, perform our ablutions and pray, then after that we have to say goodbye to other people!"

As'ad's features contracted for a few moments, then he looked at his brothers and asked: "Me too, with you?"

"Yes, you are with us as well!"

"There is no power or strength save in God! God is sufficient and our best protector! We place our trust in God!"

Then all three headed for the wash-place, which had already emptied and been left for them alone.

Their seventy-year-old father leaped into the corridor separating the two parts of the dormitory, waving his hands in a gesture of incomprehension and disbelief. He went to the center of the dormitory, stood under the skylight from which the guard usually looked out and looked up to the heavens. With a strong but trembling voice, he said: "Oh Lord, Lord of the worlds, I have spent my whole life fasting, praying, and worshipping you. Oh Lord, I do not want to disbelieve! God forbid, I ask almighty God for forgiveness. But I want to ask one question: Why should it be like this?" Then turning to the others, he went on in a still louder voice, almost shouting: "Why like this? Lord of the worlds, why like this? You are powerful, you are the all-powerful! Why do you let these evildoers wreak havoc with us, why? What will you say? Will you say that God may move slowly but is never neglectful? And will words like that bring back my children? O God! Are you happy that As'ad, my twenty-five-year-old, should be executed at the hands of these evildoers? Tell me, answer me, why are you silent, you, you, I ask God almighty for forgiveness, O God, if you had three sons and they were all going to be executed in a single moment, what would you do? Eh? Very well, just answer this small question, you, Lord of the worlds, are You with us or with these evildoers? Up till now everything has said that you are with them, with the evildoers. I ask God almighty for forgiveness, I ask God almighty for forgiveness, Oh Lord, by your power and majesty, just As'ad, return to me just As'ad, do not let him die! I don't say all three, I just want As'ad, and you are powerful over everything!"

Silence and consternation settled over the dormitory, and Sa'd's father also fell silent. He sat on the floor, and put his head between his hands. After a little the three brothers returned. They said their final prayers and started to bid people farewell, but Abu Sa'd did not move from his place, his head still between his hands. The brothers finished saying their farewells, then came and stood in front of their father, who still had his face buried in his hands. When the brothers had taken their seats around him, Sa'd asked him: "Father, father, don't you want to say goodbye to us? Father, may God spare you, do not torment us at the end of our lives! I kiss your hands, my father!"

The father raised his head, gave them all a confused, devastated look, then lifted his hands toward them. The sons took hold of his hands and started to kiss them, then all four burst out in spontaneous weeping, which engulfed the whole of the dormitory. All the men started weeping and sobbing. As the expression of collective grief got louder and louder, Abu Hussein stood in the middle of the dormitory, and in a voice punctuated by sobs started to implore everyone to lower their voices. "For God's sake, my brothers, lower your voices, please! For God's sake!" The father released his hands from those of his sons and tried to embrace all three of them. The sons threw themselves into his arms. Their three heads met on his breast, and the father put his hands on their heads. All had their eyes closed and their tears were still flowing, but in silence.

The dormitory started to grow calm again. We all wiped away our tears, our gaze still directed toward the father and his sons. The father lifted his head a little, touched his hands on their shaved heads, and turned his eyes on the people who were staring at him. In a quiet but powerful voice he started to speak, like one talking to himself: "This is God's command! God's command, from which there is no escape. We are God's, and to God is our return! Never mind, do not fear, do not fear, my sons! Be brave! My heart and your mother's heart are with you! May God grant you peace in the next world! God's comfort and mine be with you! This death is a cup, the best of cups, and everyone must drink from it!"

He was silent for a moment then turned to the others and resumed his outburst: "Why like this? Why, my children? Why? My friends, these are my children, I have no others. As God is your protector, I have no others! As'ad! My friends, did any of you ever see anything like this? My children are all in front of me and will hang on the gallows! Will anyone tell me? Tell me, people, why me and my children? What sins have I committed under God's vault that he should punish me like this? Oh, my sons! If only I could have died a long time ago and not seen a sight like this! If only I could have died and not lived to see this day! Oh Lord, why?"

Three elderly men came forward to where the family sat in the middle of the dormitory. They took hold of the father under his arms, stood him up, and took turns to speak to him to reinforce his resolve, reminding him of the necessity of faith in the wisdom of God in the face of the worst of disasters. Then they led him gently to his bed. At the very moment he sat down on his bed, the key creaked in the door. The father leaped up but the men grabbed him and put him back in his place, urging him to be calm. As the door opened, everyone in the dormitory stood up and the three brothers walked toward the exit, as the guards shouted at them to hurry up. But when they reached the door they stopped and turned around, fixing their gazes for two or three seconds on their father, then went out and the door was shut behind them.

The father freed himself from the men's grip and ran with the nimbleness of a twenty-year-old, hands stretched in front of him toward the door, panting: "My children, my children! As'ad, come back, come back! There's been a mistake, come back, my son! Let me go in your place!" Abu Hussein caught him and embraced him, wrapping his arms around him hard, and with the help of the other men gently returned him to his place. They sat him down and sat around him to comfort him as he continued to stare at the door.

Ever since the three brothers had gone out, Nasim had been glued to the peephole watching, crying, and wiping away his tears that never stopped. The father got up again. Some people tried to stop him, but Abu Hussein gestured to them to leave him and told two of the younger ones to stand by the door as a precaution. When the father had left the crowd Abu Hussein said: "Leave him, leave him, my friends, his heart is broken, may God aid him and comfort him, leave him to do as he wants, but do not let him go near the door. It would be a great calamity and mountains would be needed to bear it! There is no power or might save in God!"

The father began walking quickly through the dormitory, from one end to the other, muttering unintelligibly, and gesturing in all directions. When he reached my bed he slowed a little, looked at Nasim, who was glued to the keyhole, then resumed walking. Abu Hussein sat down beside Nasim to ask him what was happening at the gallows, but Nasim did not reply. Abu Hussein looked at me. I was sitting behind Nasim and he seemed to be asking me to intervene. I put my hand on Nasim's shoulder and asked him to move back a little so that Abu Hussein could look through the peephole, but Nasim did not move back and pushed my hand off his shoulder nervously. His hand was shaking. At that moment, the father stood in front of my bed, looked at me, then got down on his knees in front of me and implored me: "Let me see them, for God's sake! For the sake of the Prophet! Let me see my children, my friends! Let me say farewell to them!"

Abu Hussein took him by the hand, stood him up, and walked with him through the dormitory, begging him to leave the matter in God's hands. "Cry, cry, hajji, and trust in God!"

"Abu Hussein, Abu Hussein, What should I cry, tears or blood?"

"God give you patience, God give us patience! We are God's and to Him do we return! God has given, and God has taken away."

Abu Hussein continued walking with the father for more than an hour. Everyone could hear their conversation, and little by little it seemed that the father was beginning to compose himself, until the moment when Nasim turned his head and looked inside. He had leaned his back against the wall and appeared shattered. He was looking at an odd angle and his look expressed nothing, but from it everyone knew that it was all over. I hurriedly closed the peephole before the father could look through it. He had stopped walking and was giving Nasim a terrified look. Then he put out his hand and in a searing voice shouted: "Oh, my sons!" He collapsed on the floor in front of Abu Hussein, and some younger prisoners helped carry him to his bed.

After a little, Abu Hussein turned to everyone in the dormitory, proposing that they recite the funeral prayers collectively and openly. At any other time, this idea would have seemed a stroke of madness and would have attracted strong opposition from most people, but at this moment everyone without exception supported it and agreed to it. For the first time in the more than eleven years that I had been here, more than three hundred people in the dormitory prayed a single prayer as one. I stood with them in the back row beside Nasim and Abu Hussein, who gave me a strange, wondering look. And I prayed. Then everyone went back to their places, muttering extra prayers of their own. There was an overwhelming feeling of sadness, though after this collective, open prayer, the sadness was mingled with a little self-satisfaction… an invisible feeling of victory.

Nasim sat on his bed after the prayer and from that moment until now has not spoken or eaten anything.

August 1

Today I had two wisdom teeth extracted and gained relief from the worst thing to which a prisoner here can be exposed—toothache.

My father, with his stern military mentality, had instilled in us some habits, under duress at first, which as time passed became habits that we could not get rid of. One of these was to brush one's teeth three times a day. I had become so used to this routine that it became impossible for me to sleep, however tired I was, unless I had brushed my teeth before settling down. It was now many years since I had seen a brush, and because everyone here was in the same position, it was natural for the teeth to decay and for suffering to set in. Toothache was, in fact, the worst thing that we were exposed to—worse than torture, death, and execution, because these were all temporary and finite, whereas toothache clings to a person night and day, preventing him from sleeping and not allowing him to rest for a single moment. Despite the interventions of the dentist prisoners, and despite the improvements in their techniques and methods as needs increased, they had only one cure and that was extraction.

It is well known how painful a tooth extraction by a dentist can be, despite the use of anesthetics. Even with the right equipment, the extraction can still be horribly painful. And here there were no anesthetics or equipment at all! All that the dentists could do was to make a strong cord by twisting together thin artificial nylon threads. The second thing was to identify the rotten tooth that needed removing.

There was a group in the dormitory, affectionately known as the "young sprouts," made up of eight people—or eight giants, rather—tall men, with enormous bodies and strapping muscles. They formed a single food group and naturally they consumed a double portion of food. After the dentist had identified the tooth that required extraction, came the turn of the young sprouts. One of them secured the rotten tooth with the strong cord, while another steadied the patient's head with both hands. Then the first one pulled hard. Only occasionally did the operation require more than one pull to extract the tooth suspended on the end of the thread. I didn't have my tooth pulled out like this. A few months ago the medical situation in the Desert Prison had improved, when the adjutant went around the prison dormitory and informed everyone that anyone who wanted to have a tooth extracted could do so using the prison dentist. Similarly, patients with routine illnesses could consult the prison doctor to purchase the medicines that they required. This improvement had begun two or three years ago, and was slow and gradual. It was a natural development because the number of new arrivals in the prison was less than before. Instead of the weekly batches being measured in the hundreds, they had begun to be numbered in the dozens then become fewer and fewer. The helicopter arrivals, and consequently the trials and executions, also became less frequent, and the police became less tense and overloaded. There were fewer cases of beating for beating's sake or killing for killing's sake. Beatings and killings were now carried out for a reason—usually for praying, for example, or when a prisoner could be seen opening his eyes during the "breaks."

Nasim's situation had deteriorated considerably. He had refused to eat or speak for five whole days after the execution of the three brothers. Then Abu Hussein and I came together to persuade him to take a little food. Despite that, he fell into a state of severe depression. He would not speak, no longer played chess, and gave up the artistic works he used to fashion from dough. About ten days later he was sitting beside me in total silence, when he slowly turned to me and asked in French: "Where do they bury the corpses of people who are killed or executed?"

"I don't know. I don't think that any of the prisoners know!"

"What do you think? Would Sa'd, Sa'id and As'ad's bodies already have decomposed?"

"Nasim, my brother, stop those black thoughts!"

"The policemen must dig a big pit then empty all the corpses into them and pile earth on top of them."

"Nasim, please! That's enough talk about this subject!"

"The worms must now be eating into the flesh of the three brothers. Worms in the eyes, worms in the belly, worms in the mouth, worms coming out of the nostrils, worms, worms..."

"Nasim, that's enough, I told you that's enough!"

After that he was silent, deep in his thoughts. All my efforts to bring him out of his silence met with failure. For several days he said nothing, then when he spoke it was to pose the big questions.

"What is life? What is the purpose of this life? Is it rational that life should be without purpose? Is it comprehensible that this life should have been created by God? What does God gain by creating a person like As'ad? God brought him into this life and he suffered a lot, then was executed. He died while he was still in the prime of life. He didn't even have enough time to prove whether he was a good or a bad man!"

The strange thing was that all his questionings and conversations about this subject were in French. My own feelings were more like a bereavement. He sunk into depression and introspection, while I plunged deeper and deeper into sadness and pain.

He stayed like that for about two months. Then, one morning, the policemen opened the dormitory door and before they could finish opening it as usual, Nasim jumped out like a coiled spring that had just been released. In less than a second he had got outside the dormitory, having kicked the door with his foot in order to completely open it.

At first, the policemen and municipals were taken by surprise. They had not recovered from the shock of the first surprise before they were overtaken by another, when they were attacked... The door was open and we were watching what was happening in the yard. Nasim was moving about, giving out wild shouts like a camel in heat. There were fewer than ten policemen and municipals around. I was astonished. What was this Herculean power that Nasim was exhibiting? Where had he learned these combat skills? He attacked one of them, leaping high in the air in front of him then bringing his fist down on the man's neck or nose and throwing him to the ground. Two policemen and a municipal were thrown to the ground in less than a minute. Some guards and municipals fled as quickly as possible, while others attacked Nasim to take hold of him. There was shouting and screaming in the yard, as the guards stationed on the rooftops peered down. They quickly grabbed their rifles, loaded them, then took up positions to fire, directing their weapons at Nasim. My heart sank between my feet. Would they open fire on him? But he was in close combat with the policemen.

One of the sergeants pounced on him from behind and grabbed him by the neck, trying to bring him down and secure him. The other policemen took courage and also attacked him, but as the sergeant held his neck from the rear Nasim began to quickly turn. He turned several times, his speed increasing with every turn. The sergeant's feet left the floor and he started to turn as Nasim's body turned. Suddenly Nasim stopped, grabbed the sergeant and flung him to the floor.

The black steel door to the yard was opened and police began to pour in. Nasim was now surrounded by dozens of people, so many that we could no longer see him. As their movements subsided, we were convinced that they had overpowered him.

One of the sergeants shouted "Hold him but don't beat him! The prison governor is coming!"

The prison governor—a tall man in his forties—arrived, flanked by his adjutant and a number of sergeants and policemen. He calmly walked over to where Nasim was lying on the ground. The door to our dormitory was still open, and we could see what was happening without turning our heads. The prison governor ordered Nasim to be brought before him. The group of policemen around Nasim dispersed and two of them stood him on his feet. Suddenly he started up and shook himself free from their clutches, shouting incomprehensibly as he approached the prison governor. A step or two, then a group of policemen jumped on him, surrounded him on all sides, and held him firm.

The prison governor had a conversation with his adjutant and the sergeants that we could not hear. One of the sergeants pointed the prison governor in the direction of our dormitory, and the governor walked through the door accompanied by his adjutant and some of the sergeants. He asked for Abu Hussein and spoke with him, then asked for a doctor from the dormitory and questioned him. He consulted briefly with the prison doctor, then asked again for the doctor from the dormitory to ask him what medicine he needed. Then, after giving an instruction for Nasim to be returned to the dormitory, he left without any fuss.

The prison governor's behavior was almost one of understanding and affection, the behavior of a shepherd. This extraordinary event prompted endless speculation, analyses, and explanations. After the door had been shut, Nasim stayed for about two hours pacing quickly up and down the dormitory in bursts. Each burst took about five minutes, after which he would stand and start the dabka, as he sang: *"Bye bye, exile, my country awaits us!"* Then he would resume his rapid pacing. He didn't look at anyone or in any particular place. When he walked or when he danced, he would look at a fixed spot in front of him and not turn his eyes away from it.

After these two hours, the small window in the door, the *talaqa*, was opened. The dormitory head was summoned, and very carefully the sergeant gave Abu Hussein three boxes of medicine, saying: "Here we are, medicine for the madman!" At that moment Nasim was immediately in front of the door. Hearing the expression the sergeant had used, he leaped up and darted toward the door like an arrow. The sergeant saw him dashing off and automatically rushed backwards, despite the door being closed. Nasim reached the door and put his hand through the window, trying to grab the sergeant, as he shouted: "Madman? You're the madman, you dog! Your father's mad, your mother's mad, you're an animal, you're all mad!"

I heard the voice of the sergeant outside, shouting at the soldier: "He's crackers, he's crackers! For heaven's sake, do we really need madmen?"

For the first time in about twelve years I saw the police scared. They fled into the yard to escape Nasim and I saw that they were terrified! It was the first time I had seen them on the receiving end of abuse rather than giving it out! Receiving it and not answering back! I wondered whether the overwhelming force that the police represented actually required madness, required a mad confrontation, to keep it in check?

Nasim refused to take the medicine from the doctor. The doctor then conferred with Abu Hussein, explaining to him that any patient with this condition would refuse to take the medicine and would have to be compelled to swallow the pills. He asked for the help of the group of "sprouts" to give him the medicine by force, for in these sorts of cases the patient possessed an enormous, unnatural strength and it would take four or five people to be able to hold him and force him to swallow the pills. Just before noon, Nasim took the pills, and immediately fell into a deep sleep. He woke after midnight. I was watching him and he gave me a faint smile without moving from where he was. "How are you, how are you doing?" he asked.

"I'm extremely well, how are *you*?"

"Okay, but tired. I want to sleep!"

Then he slept till morning. When he woke up, he behaved naturally, as if he hadn't experienced any problem or anything like that. That, at least, was the general view, though I did myself notice several changes—slight in themselves, but which at the same time had some deep significance. These observations formed during the following weeks and months. There was a constant smile hanging on his lips, a fake smile, or perhaps a smile mingled with a sadness in the depths of his soul, and he lost the capacity for astonishment that had been one of the main characteristics of his personality. He was no longer angered by the things that he disliked, and he continued his refusal to work with dough. The doctor entrusted to me as his friend and neighbor the task of giving him his medicine regularly, emphasizing the importance of my never forgetting the right times to give it to him, because any interruption in his taking it would surely lead to a return of his earlier state of extreme agitation and aggressiveness.

The friendship between us continued just as warmly as before, and we resumed our earlier shared daily life. Several days went by without his mentioning in conversation what had happened even once. Even the subject of the execution of the three brothers was never again mentioned. My own feelings toward him remained as they had been, unchanged, but I sensed that something inside Nasim had died. And I was very sad that this thing had died.

SEPTEMBER 25

The air was full of dust.

In six or seven months I would have completed my twelfth year in prison. I had taken to counting the days and months again, and in the experience of prisoners this was a bad sign. But wasn't I entitled to ask myself how long? Some people had been here several years longer than me. And were still here! If the children who had been tried and acquitted by the field court were still living in the dormitory that the police called the "innocent dormitory," was there any hope for someone like me—forgotten, neglected, not even knowing why he was here—to escape from this hell? Was the road to this jail just a one-way street? Was the expression that I heard repeated by the prisoners every day—"the one coming in is lost; the one going out is born again"—was it really true? I had never seen anyone who came into this prison leave it!

So when, when would be the hour of release? I didn't know. Meanwhile, either complete impotence and submission to fate, or suicide and release from the daily torture that appeared endless.

My soul was seething with anger.

■ ■ ■

Sandstorms, or *tawz,* as some people call them, occur in this desert two or three times every year, and in years of drought it might be two or three times more than that. The sandstorms blow up and fill the air with dust. This goes on for one, two or three days. Whether the wind itself continues to blow or whether it stops, the dust remains suspended in the air and we breathe it in. The nose, mouth, and eyes are all filled with dust. When we sleep, the dust still hangs over us, around us and inside us. We wake and find that all the orifices to be found in a man's head are full of soft, crushed earth. Our water is dust, our food is dust.

The wind had started to blow from the morning of the day before yesterday. It got stronger after noon, when the wind turned into a series of hurricanes. With the dust, these hurricanes hurled down slivers of plastic bags from the skylight in the roof, as well as a lot of straw, dry sticks, thorns, and all sorts of dry desert plants that weighed very little. Anyone who had an extra piece of clothing would try to wrap his head in it. Many people's faces were no longer visible except for their eyes.

Suddenly the wind blew a complete page of a newspaper onto the iron bars of the skylight, so that the page hung between the bars on the roof. The eyes of everyone in the dormitory were fixed on it. As the wind shook the paper, everyone could hear the sound of it rustling. I heard some people call out, praying to God to make the paper fall inside the dormitory and not let it fly away.

In normal circumstances, we would see the guard every few minutes, either leaning over to keep a watch from the skylight, or else passing beside it in such a way that we could see him or his shadow. Even when he was a long way from the skylight, we could hear his footsteps as he walked up and down over the dormitory roof. But now there was no sign of the guard. It seemed he must be sheltering from the wind and the dust in one of the corners of the roof.

Like everyone else, I too was wishing that the newspaper would fall inside the dormitory. Since arriving back in my home country, I had not seen a single printed letter. Everyone was like me, with a real yearning to see strings of letters, printed words! This newspaper contained news, and for more than two years, when the last resident in the dormitory had arrived, we had heard nothing of what was going on outside these four walls.

I heard Nasim say: "Come on, come down!" He was talking to the newspaper. I looked at him and his eyes were fixed on the newspaper high above him. Several people were standing up straight, and several had pushed back from their faces the pieces of cloth they used as veils. Those not standing sat up straight. Some of those standing headed spontaneously for the point below the skylight, heads held high and eyes fixed, as they followed the newspaper's dance between the bars. One of those standing under the skylight, one of the fedayeen, looked at everyone and in a voice that could be heard by everyone asked: "Come on, everyone! A pyramid?" As soon as he had asked the question, several more people jumped up, shouting: "Pyramid, pyramid, pyramid!"

The operation to build a human pyramid and retrieve the newspaper did not take longer than about ten seconds, but they were terrifying seconds, choking and almost taking away one's breath. It might have cost several people their lives, but it all passed off safely. And then we had a newspaper!

Abu Hussein immediately addressed the fedayeen who had retrieved the newspaper: "Quick, quick, to the lavatories, fold it up! Then someone read it and tell us what the news is!"

The fedayeen ran to the lavatory carrying the newspaper.

Everyone felt happy, really happy. Several people shook hands and embraced each other, congratulating each other. It was another victory! Nasim turned to me after embracing me and said: "You know that the first word of the Noble Qur'an to be revealed was the word 'Read!'"

"I know. And do you know that the gospel begins with 'In the beginning was the Word'?"

"I know. But what does this event tell you, mister film director?"

"Do you want me to talk big? Like films and novels? The event says: 'Man is ready to sacrifice his life for the sake of knowledge!'"

"That's right! Very clever!"

And we laughed as we hadn't done for months.

The contents of the newspaper were a bit disappointing. One side of the page was official advertisements and the other was a sports page, with news of the annual football cup. This page stirred a whirlwind of arguments that have not yet ended, for as the dormitory contained people from every province, it wasn't long before supporters' groups were formed for every club in light of the sports news to be found in the newspaper, and these groups then began to boast of the history and record of wins of the clubs they supported.

People even started to read the official advertisements with great care. Such an appetite for reading! Abu Hussein appointed someone to organize the reading of the newspaper by everyone in turn. The newspaper acquired an official, called by some the "Minister for Information" in jest, who organized the reading rota, passing the paper from one person to another and allocating the time for each person.

Today the wind had stopped completely, but the dust was still hanging in the air. Even inside the dormitory dust filled every empty space.

■ ■ ■

In the morning the police brought back to the dormitory someone who had been sent for punishment a month ago. They had caught him with his eyes open during the "break" in the yard. After they had flogged and tortured him in front of our eyes as we walked around the yard, the adjutant ordered him to be put in solitary confinement in Yard 5. When he had come in, and as soon as he was satisfied that the police had closed the door and left, he breathed a sigh of relief and started to laugh. He sat on the ground and told everyone of the month's journey that he had spent in Yard 5. "By God, my friends," he began, "I have missed you! When I came into the dormitory I thought that I was coming back home. My God! How sweet the dormitory is! Heaven, my friends, pure heaven! We are living here in heaven!"

Then he began to talk and give his account... and talk and talk!...

The toilet was inside the solitary cell, so to avoid the danger of rats he was forced to knead bread and make a stopper from it to block up the toilet hole. He swore that the rats in there were as large as a small sheep! Three times a day there was a torture party like the reception given to a new prisoner when he first arrived at the prison. Food was put on a dirty plate ten meters away from the cell door; then they opened the door, and the prisoner had to crawl out on all fours like a dog, barking all the time as he went and returned carrying the plate. All this time, the whips would have been tearing pieces of flesh from his back. And he slept on concrete, with no blankets, covers, or anything else!

He told us all about it with a laugh, his face lit up with laughter. *What was making him laugh?*

███

The dust was still hanging in the air.

People's eyelashes had become white. The policemen were tense but the supervision was slacker—slacker from above, from the skylight, and slacker from below, on the ground.

Two hours ago I heard a story which aroused my interest and which I still think about. We had four Bedouin with us in the dormitory. They were illiterate and did not know how to read and write. Their main employment was to herd sheep, goats, and camels. They had lived all their lives in this vast desert, moving all around it from place to place in their search for water and pasture. They were arrested, held, and brought to the Desert Prison on a charge of helping wanted men flee to a neighboring state. When they were interrogated here, they frowned a little, and their elder, called Shinyur, replied: "By God, my brother, a groundless charge, we are Bedouin, who wander God's earth. A group came to us, and we welcomed them as is the custom of the Arabs. We gave them hospitality, and afterward, my brother, they asked us for directions, so we showed them the way. Is there something wrong with that? Afterward, they told us, 'You're foreign agents, you're spies!' A strange thing, my brother, an extraordinary thing!"

Today, after Shinyur had told this story for the thousandth time, the conversation ranged more widely, though it was all focused on the Bedouin and their lives. Someone who lived in a city—one of those people who have known only three places in their lives: home, shop, and mosque— asked him if what was said about Bedouin hospitality and the reasons for it was true. He ended his question by asking in amazement: "How come, brother Shinyur, if a guest came to you and you had only one sheep, is it true that you would slaughter it and cook it to give it to the guest? Why would you do that? God willing, he would never eat, God willing, he would eat poison!"

"No, no, no! My brother, you should never talk like that," he replied in a broad dialect.

Shinyur then embarked on a long series of explanations, which I was forced to listen to as he was sitting by my bed, but he soon caught my attention with one particular idea: "Bedouin generosity has many reasons, many, many reasons, but the most important of them," so he said, "is that the Bedouin likes, even loves his guest. This is because the Bedouin spends days, weeks, and months living in this desert among sand dunes, dust, and mud in complete isolation. He doesn't consider his wife and children important enough to hold a conversation with them. For this reason, in many cases we find the Bedouin talking to his sheep and camels. When he is grazing his animals there is no one to listen to him, and because he loves his animals he holds conversations with them. It is fine for these conversations to be punctuated by oaths directed at the unruly animals. When the Bedouin reaches the stage of talking to his animals, this is a sign that his need for human contact, for meeting any human being, has reached its peak. At this point, if a guest arrives, he will surely find a person eager to shower him with an enormous number of signs of welcome and affection. The Bedouin gives the guest the best he has of everything, for he doesn't expect to be compensated for his coming, and he wants to tempt him to stay the longest time possible."

It seems that a solitary life teaches wisdom. This Bedouin was a wise philosopher! Thank you, Shinyur. You rid my soul of a vague anxiety that disturbed my sleep. My isolation in the dormitory was worse than the isolation of any Bedouin in the desert. But suddenly Nasim became my guest, and with Nasim came human contact and affection. So it was quite natural, according to Shinyur's account, for my feelings toward him to be impassioned.

I turned to Nasim with a loving, affectionate smile and he smiled back. Despite his continuing to take the medicine, his situation was becoming more normal. "I'm going to wash the dust off my face," I said to him, and he just nodded.

May 17

I don't know what time it was, I think it was after midnight, and Nasim was sleeping beside me. The medicine he was taking made him sleep very soundly. I myself hadn't gone to sleep yet.

I heard a movement in the yard and sat up. I wanted to look through the peephole to see what they were doing but before I could stretch my hand out to open the peephole I heard a policeman shouting at the top of his voice. I didn't understand what he was saying, but when he yelled it again, it was a man's name in three parts. I listened more carefully as he shouted: "Yard 6 dormitories, who's got this name?" And for the third time, he shouted the three parts of a name. It was my name! For a few fractions of a second, I had been wondering whose name it was. It sounded familiar to me, as if I'd heard it somewhere before. It was my name!

What was this, what was going on? Why were they calling my name? I felt almost numb as I looked around me in amazement. Abu Hussein had woken up and called out: "Have we got anyone with this name, my friends?"

I raised my finger like a young schoolboy, lifting it toward Abu Hussein's face without saying a word. The policeman shouted the name yet again. My numbness transferred itself to Abu Hussein.

He said nothing but his eyes widened in astonishment. "Is this your name?" I nodded. Abu Hussein quickly threw his heavy body against the door and immediately started knocking hard on it, shouting: "Here, sir, here, this name's in the new dormitory, number eight!"

Everything calmed down and suddenly no one was shouting any more. After a minute or a little longer the door opened, and the sergeant stood there with two policemen. He went over to Abu Hussein to ask: "Do you have this name, dormitory head?"

"Yes, sir, this is him!" he replied, pointing his finger toward me. The sergeant came up to me, looked me angrily in the eye and asked: "Is this your name?"

"Yes, sir!"

He raised his hand and brought his palm down on my right cheek as hard as he could. Then he turned his body ninety degrees, and with lightning speed followed it up with a blow to the left cheek that restored me to my natural position. Stars once again danced in front of my eyes.

"You ass, you son of a dog! We've spent two hours walking around shouting for you. Why couldn't you answer, you whore?"

I said nothing.

He stretched out his arm and dragged me hard by my chest to pull me out of the dormitory, then shut the door. The dormitory door slammed in my face for ever.

To the accompaniment of kicks and beatings, the sergeant and two policemen pushed me in front of them from Yard 6 to Yard Zero, and from there to the small iron gate. I was in front of the prison. I turned slightly and the stone inscription was still there: *In retaliation there is life for you, men possessed of minds!* I had read this inscription more than twelve years ago, when I was admitted, and now I was reading it as I left, but where was I headed? I didn't know.

Three men in civilian clothes came up to me. One of them was extremely tall, about half a meter taller than me. He came up to me, opened a piece of paper that was folded in his hand and asked: "Are you so-and-so?"

"Yes."

"Son of Y and Z?"

"Yes."

"Are you?…" "Yes." "Are you?…" "Yes."

He turned to the two men with him. "Give me the handcuffs!"

One of them handed him the handcuffs, Spanish handcuffs. I put my hands out in front of me and he put them on. There was a faint click and my hands were cuffed in front of me, then he signed some papers and dragged me fifty meters forward. There was a French Peugeot taxi, with a driver sitting behind the steering wheel. The tall man sat beside him, and I sat between the two others in the rear seat, as the car sped off into the darkness of the night, its headlights cutting through the darkness. They didn't say anything, didn't hit me or disturb me at all. They behaved as though I wasn't there with them. Soon after the car had sped off, the tall man asked the time and was told that it was around 2:30 in the morning. He said he would sleep for about an hour. After an hour they were all asleep, except for me and the driver, who looked at me in the mirror occasionally. I shut my eyes to make him think I was asleep and wondered where we might be going. I turned the question over from every angle, and concluded that wherever it was they were taking me, it would certainly be better than before. I relaxed a little and thought of Nasim. What would he say, what would he do when he woke in the morning and did not find me beside him? I missed him.

I relaxed a bit more and might have dozed off but suddenly the car swerved and the driver started to shout: "God almighty! God almighty!" Everyone woke up and shouted. The car's rear tire had burst. With great skill, the driver had managed to regain control of the car after it had left the road and ended up in the sand of the desert.

We reached the capital just before noon. Fixing the puncture had taken several hours, for we were in the desert and the nearest inhabited spot was several dozen kilometers away.

This was my city, but I knew nothing about the streets we drove through. My city, in which I had grown up, spent my adolescence, and thought myself an expert on, but I didn't know which street we were on or where we were heading. It had changed so much that it was difficult for anyone who had been away this long to recognize it, until we reached the city's main square. I was now returning to my city that I recognized. These fountains, they were as they were… when I was a child, I liked to stand under the spray, and feel invigorated. From this square I knew that the car was heading toward the security headquarters where I stopped on my return from abroad.

Do you suppose Abu Ramzat and Ayyoub could still be there? Ayyoub's cane, which now seemed to me like a child's toy compared to what I had seen and experienced there!

The car stopped at some traffic lights and I looked out at the people, looking hard into their faces. What was this indifference? How many of them, do you suppose, knew what went on, and was still going on, in the Desert Prison? How many of them cared, do you suppose? This was the people that the politicians kept talking about, singing their praises, and deifying them. But was it credible that this great people didn't know what was going on in their own country? If it didn't know, then that was a misfortune, and if it did know but did nothing to change it, that was a bigger misfortune. I concluded that this people must be either anesthetized or stupid.

A people of idiots. Did anyone in these crowds—this grocer, this happy, smiling girl walking arm-in-arm with her lover—did any of them know who Nasim was? Nasim, who was now crouching in the Desert Prison waiting for someone to give him his medicine; Nasim, who went mad because he couldn't make his peace with this reality.

I became conscious of myself. Why should I have such angry thoughts? Had I become a politician? I smiled despite myself. Was I expecting this people to go out on serious demonstrations demanding my release from prison? Who was I?

My God, how many people there were. I stared into their faces. Our house was near where the car was heading. Maybe I would be lucky enough to catch a glimpse of my mother or father or one of my brothers. No, any face I recognized would do.

The car turned off from the anticipated route leading to the grim building near our house and headed southwest, cutting through the city from north to south. We passed several landmarks I recognized and which I had missed. Here was the university, with students—boys and girls—going in and out. I could remember nothing of my life except that I had been a student, and now I was passing quickly through the fifth decade of my life.

The car pulled up in front of an enormous building with elaborate security. It was difficult and complicated to enter, even for security service vehicles. We waited for more than ten minutes; there were calls and queries, and then they allowed the car past the barrier and we went in and found ourselves in front of the building. They put us down in front of a wide glass door. The tiled floor shone, and everything suggested cleanliness and order. The tall man went off, carrying his papers with him, and went into the first room on the left. No one asked me to close my eyes or bow my head, though my head was half-bowed from habit. Then the tall man came back, handed the papers to the other two, and told them: "Take him down to the prison!"

Immediately in front of where we were standing, we went down some steps… more steps, then we turned, and there were more steps. A door made of steel bars, with an enormous lock. They knocked on the door, and a fat jailer came, carrying a bunch of keys in his hand. They gave him the papers, he opened the door and they pushed me inside, then the door was closed and the pair left. Then:

"Wait here, don't move!"

He went off carrying the papers to a room in the middle of a long veranda, then appeared at the door of the room he'd gone into and called me. I went to him and he let me into the room, where I saw a white-haired man looking at me from behind a table. He told me to take all my possessions out of my pockets.

"I haven't got anything."

"Nothing, nothing? Don't you have any money? Nothing at all?"

"I haven't got anything."

"All right, don't you have any ID? A passport?"

"No, no, I haven't got anything. They took my ID and my passport from me in the Desert Prison."

"Didn't they give them back to you?"

"No, they didn't give them back, sir."

"Alright. Is your body clean?"

"Clean, yes, sir, I had a shower this morning."

"I mean, you don't have lice?"

"Lice? I haven't got many lice, sir."

"And you say you're clean?"

He turned to the jailer and told him to take me to the bathroom, then after I'd finished in the shower, to put me in solitary number 17. Then he said to me: "The shower is hot. Go to the shower; wash all your clothes thoroughly the first time, then take a shower yourself after you've washed your clothes. Carry on showering and washing your clothes until you feel that you've no longer got a single louse. It's better not to fill the prison with lice."

"Yes, sir."

The jailer took me away and put me into the shower, which was filled with steam. "Do as the adjutant told you," he said before shutting the door on me. "Just knock on the door when you've finished. Understand?"

"Yes, sir."

The shower was enjoyable. I finished and knocked on the door, collecting together my clothes that I'd washed thoroughly. I couldn't wring them out properly because they were threadbare. Then the jailer knocked on the door and saw me trying to put on the clothes I'd washed. He told me to leave the shower before getting dressed. When I said that wasn't right, he shouted: "Get out! What's the matter, aren't you a man? What are you afraid of? Afraid for your arse, like a monkey's arse?"

I hid my private parts with my wet clothes in front of me and walked behind the jailer. We reached a room with number 17 on it, which he opened, then pushed me in and closed the door behind me.

Here I was, alone, in a cell painted bright green. There were blankets on the floor. It was a spacious cell, possibly more than three meters square. In the ceiling there were two openings, which I discovered were for ventilation—one for the extraction of stale air and the other to draw in air from outside. I spread my wet clothes on the floor and sat on the blankets, covering myself with one of them. The air here was warm. After a little I lay down and went to sleep.

I woke up to a terrifying sound, the sound of an iron key grating in the iron door, the sound of iron on iron. I sat down and wrapped the blanket firmly around my waist. Then the door opened and two men appeared, one middle-aged and the other younger, carrying a register. He asked me my name, age, and place of birth, and recorded all my relevant personal information. Then he shut the register and asked me why I slept naked. I replied that the only clothes I possessed had been washed and had not yet dried. He turned to the younger man and said: "Go to the dormitory and tell them that there's a prisoner without clothes."

"Yes, sir!"

The door closed and after a quarter of an hour the young man returned carrying a bundle of clothes, sports pajamas, a change of underwear, and briefs that reached the knee. They were all new, and I looked new as well.

May 20

In the three days since I'd left the Desert Prison and come here I hadn't seen anyone except for the jailers. Three times a day they opened the door to put food in. About an hour after putting the food in, they opened it again to take out the bowls, and for the prisoners to go to the lavatory and the wash-place. They called the lavatory here "the line," though I haven't been able to discover the reason why. The food here was better than there: each prisoner received a few pieces of meat, and the food was cleaner and more varied.

I waited with increasing anxiety whenever a day went by without my knowing the reason for my transfer. The treatment here was relatively good, however. With the exception of some blows to the face and neck while going out to the lavatory or returning from it, I had not been exposed to any direct physical mistreatment—but the sounds of torture that could be heard loud and clear in all the solitary cells became more alarming over time, and a cause of tension and fear. Every day from eight thirty in the morning the screams of pain and pleading began. They ended around two thirty, only for the music to start again from six in the evening till late at night.

I tried to ignore it, to forget it, or pretend not to notice. I did not succeed.

May 21

This evening they opened my cell door and a warden told me to come out. I went out and he took me by the arm and led me to the door to the steps with the metal bars. He opened the door and handed me over to another warden, who in turn led me upwards. We reached the shiny tiled floor and he led me along the right-hand corridor to the last room. He showed me in, then went out himself and shut the door without saying a word. There was nothing in the room except a table and a single chair.

A man in his forties came in with a bundle of white paper and a fountain pen in his hand. He asked me whether I was X, and I answered that yes, I was X. He put the papers and the pen on the table and ordered me to sit down. I sat down on the chair behind the table. This was the first time I'd sat on a chair for twelve years.

"You see this paper and pen," he said; "we want you to write your life history from birth till now, understand?"

"Yes, I understand."

He went out and I began writing. Recollecting, writing, and thinking: what exactly did they want? I didn't know, but I wrote. For one hour, two hours, during which the door opened twice, I wrote. When they saw that I was engrossed in writing they went out without saying anything. I was writing. Pen, paper, I had gone without them for many years; they were an ordinary, obvious thing, always to hand, but when you lose them, you think for a long time: how much time and effort did humanity spend to be able to invent and produce paper? How much time and effort was required to invent the pen that we write with so easily? How dear they were, how precious to my heart. Meanwhile, I wrote. I plunged into tiny details, I recalled the schools in whose classes I had studied, my family, my friends… the writing became a pleasure to me, and I didn't want to be parted from the pen and paper.

The man who had brought me came in, stared at me and said: "If you were writing the history of the world, you would have finished by now. For heaven's sake, why is it taking so long?"

"Give me a few minutes and I will finish."

After a few minutes I handed back the pen and paper. "Stay here," he said to me.

He went away. A little less than an hour later he came back with someone else, who looked as if he was important. The paper that I'd written on was in the hands of the important person. He stared at me for a moment, then said: "Everything you've written is like eating shit! Here's some new paper and here is a pen. Write us something useful and concise." Then they threw the pen and paper down on the table and went away.

I started to write again, but without the same pleasure. I simply wrote again what I'd written before. I had nothing new to say. I had been truthful in everything I'd written. They had asked for my life history and I had written it for them in a few pages. Everything that I had written was true. I had nothing to hide, nothing to be afraid of saying, but why did they want me to write again what I had already written? I didn't know. Once again they took what I had written, then after less than an hour the first man returned and said: "Come on, let's go!"

We went back by the same route and I returned to my cell.

May 22

That evening, my cell door opened and the warden told me to come out. I went out… corridors, staircases, iron doors, another corridor, the sparkling tiled floor on the right… the first room on the left.

A man wearing spectacles sat behind a black desk. In front of the desk was a plastic chair. He raised his head, took off his glasses, and gestured to me to sit down. I sat down on the chair. After a moment, he put on his glasses again, took the pen, and asked me some questions, recording my answers without looking at me: "Your name, father's name, mother's name, brothers, sisters, paternal uncles, maternal uncles, friends here, friends in France, everyone's full names, their party affiliations…" To this last question, I replied; "I don't know."

He didn't argue with me or accuse me of lying, he simply wrote "Not known" on the paper in front of him. He then asked me a lot more questions, all political—about the parties I'd belonged to. Finally, he asked me: "Have you anything else to say?"

"No."

"Stay here."

He collected his papers together and went out. After about an hour, a warden came and took me back to my cell, and I sat down. All the time, I could hear the screams of a woman being tortured.

May 23

At the end of the night, they took me back to my cell, shattered.

At the beginning of the night, they had opened the door of my cell and ordered me out. I went out as usual, but there were no stairs. They took me to the last room in the row of cells. The jailer put a blindfold over my eyes and shoved me into the room. "Has the honeymoon ended?" I asked myself.

The jailer's arms brought me to a halt, and I heard a voice in front of me say: "We've given you excellent treatment, because you're from a good family, but you seem to have no sense, all this drivel and empty talk. Look, either you tell me which organization you belong to, or else you'll see stars at noon. What do you say?"

"Sir, I've never belonged to any organization. I was taken to the Desert Prison on a charge of belonging to the Muslim Brotherhood."

"The Brotherhood? Shit! What's a Christian got to do with the Muslim Brotherhood? That was a mistake, and now we need to correct the mistake. What organization do you belong to?"

"I've never belonged to any organization."

"It looks like you are an ass! You don't understand! Anyone that talks the sort of rubbish you're talking must belong to an organization."

Then I heard him talking to the others in the room. "Take him to the flying carpet, and when he's decided to confess, bring him back here!"

They dragged me away by force. Despite everything, I'd relaxed a little, because I knew that my family were behind me. They threw me onto a wooden board, tied down every part of my body, raised the lower part of the wooden board up high then secured it. The beatings began, and with them the screams. I was in absolute agony but I wasn't afraid or agitated. By now I was an old hand. I had seen and heard a lot of such cases right before me, and I had learned and remembered from them. Just as the security men had their rules and lessons, so too the prisoners had their principles and pieces of advice. Here, the two most important of these were:

198

First: However much pain you are experiencing from the torture, do not confess to anything in order to escape the pain, because a confession, however small, will let them know that you have weakened. So, instead of ending, the torture will increase in quantity in order for them to extract more confessions.

Second: If they ask you to cooperate with them and become an informer in exchange for your release, on no account accept, because if you accept you will have put yourself in a compromising position that will continue for the rest of your life. And they always tell lies!

I was in agony, but I was not counting the blows. I thought of all sorts of things—of my family, of Nasim—all this while screaming at the top of my voice. After a little, I sensed that my feet were numb, and that my feeling of pain was much less acute. Things had become mechanical—they beat, I felt a little pain, I screamed out loud.

This rather childish game ended in my advantage. They had either become tired, or bored, or persuaded that I didn't belong to any organization. At all events, they gave up on me, on orders from the "Voice in the room." *Leave him, leave him. take him to the cell, his head's as thick as an ass's head!*

I walked with difficulty, shattered physically but in good spirits, as they took me back to my cell. It wasn't long before I fell asleep.

May 24

This morning they opened the door of my cell, took me out, and immediately blindfolded me. From the feel of the walk, I could tell that I was going upstairs. They led me on, in which direction I didn't know, and a warden knocked on one of the doors. "Come in!"

He went in, clicked his heels. "At your service, sir!"

"Take his blindfold off then go away!" said a thick, hoarse voice.

The warden removed the blindfold, and there were three middle-aged men. One of them sat behind a splendidly neat table, and the other two sat on either side of the table. They were all silent. Six eyes stared directly at me, scrutinizing me from head to toe. Six cruel, piercing eyes. I felt I was being stripped bare from the inside. Six eyes with a mixture of intelligence and cunning flowing from them. A mixture of cruelty and authority. A mixture of arrogance and pride. Eyes that had seen tens of thousands like me. Eyes sated with everything. Bored, sullen eyes.

I immediately calculated that that these three men were the most important officials or investigators I had met so far, and that my entire fate would be settled in this session. I decided to be bold, to defend myself forcefully, to take advantage of everything I had heard or seen. I would confront them. Before they could open their mouths, I summoned up all my courage and put a question to them: "Please could you let me ask a question. Why am I here? What crime have I committed that has kept me in prison for more than twelve years? What have I done? Could one of you answer this question?"

The man sitting behind the desk replied in the same hoarse tone: "First of all, shut up! Second, you are here to answer questions, not to put questions. Third, despite that, we will tell you why you are here and what your offense is, you criminal!" After a moment's pause, he added: "Draw up this chair and sit down!"

I drew up the chair and sat down.

"You're a film producer, right?"

"Yes, sir!"

"You say you've never belonged to any political organization opposed to the state. I believe you, but if anything becomes apparent to contradict this statement, I have the power to have you executed. Understood?"

"Yes, sir."

"Okay, I am going to read you a list of names. Any name that you recognize, tell me! Understood?"

"Yes, sir!"

He read out three names that I didn't recognize, then read a fourth name, the full name of my friend Antoine. I raised my hand immediately, as if to establish my trustworthiness.

"That's Antoine, sir, my friend in France!" I shouted.

"Okay, we've got something useful. You know that Antoine is a very dangerous person? He's a communist opposed to the regime—he's not like your uncle, I mean, despite the fact that your uncle is a communist. Your uncle is an extremely loyal and patriotic man, and we respect him greatly. Antoine, though… Antoine is an agent… Antoine is against the homeland! And it's well established that he incited you to speak against the homeland. Didn't he?"

"No, no, sir, Antoine didn't talk politics with me."

"Then where did you get this stuff that's written in the report?"

"What stuff? What report?"

"So as not to give you a headache, or you give us one, I'll read the report to you, and afterwards you can answer, agreed?"

"Very well!"

He opened a file in front of him, look carefully at a number of pages, pulled one of them out and studied it for a time, then began to read: "On such and such a date, I was invited to a party with my French girlfriend. The party was in the house of the said Antoine. X, Y and Z were present at the party, each of them with his girlfriend…"

He stopped reading for a moment to ask: "What do we want with this rubbish? Where's the relevant paragraph? Where is it? Yes, this paragraph…"

"*At the end of the discussion there was one person left there who hadn't taken part in the discussion and whose opinions I didn't know. He was someone called X, a student from the capital studying cinema production here in France. He had spent the entire duration of the discussion looking at us with a smile on his face, and occasionally talking to his girlfriend. I turned to him to ask his opinion on the discussion that had just taken place, and continued my attack on the political authorities in order to put him at his ease. He laughed and said something hurtful with regard to our comrade the Secretary General, the beloved President of the Republic. Under duress, I will now set down his words exactly as he said them, despite being greatly embarrassed and holding my pen in too high esteem to set down such expressions! You know that I am ready to cut out my tongue and not allow it to utter such slanderous expressions concerning a man whom we revere and respect, indeed, worship... the President, may God protect him and grant him victory, and may we sacrifice ourselves for him! The purpose of my recording these expressions, however, is so that that the security services who protect the security of the homeland should know everything, and be in the picture as regards the subject.*

"At all events, in response to my questioning, X replied as follows (verbatim): 'I really do not like or enjoy political discussions, and as a man who works in the field of cinematic art I am concerned with sound and visual effects. I am not interested in politics or political economy, and I cannot judge the regime or authorities by them, I judge through sound and image.

"'If a message can be known by its heading, the head of this regime is its President, so what does the voice say? The voice of this President is like the voice of a goat. And the goat, as you know, is one of the filthiest and most stubborn of animals. And I dislike filth and stubbornness.

"'As for the image, it says that his head is like that of a mule, and I hate mules a lot, for the simple reason that they are not authentic.

If they were asses, I would like them, because in that event they would belong to the genuine, authentic race of asses. For these two reasons, my brother, I don't like this President and I don't like this regime.'

"*Everyone sitting there laughed. That's the opinion of...*"

When he came to these words, the hoarse voice stopped reading, and he looked at me hard and angrily as he folded up the papers in front of him. Then, in a mocking tone, he said: "We have told you why you are here, and about your crime. Now you must tell us which organization you belong to. Are the words in the report yours or not? Tell us..."

While he was reading the report, my mind had been working at top speed. All my senses were heightened. I was listening with half my brain while the other half was thinking. I tried to recollect the evening but couldn't. I had picked up the date mentioned in the report, more than three years before I returned to my own country, to which was to be added the more than twelve years that I'd spent in prison! How could I possibly remember one of the hundreds of parties that we had held? Even among the people at the party, I could only recall my friend Antoine! And this was someone I was with more or less every day. I didn't remember, I didn't remember. As for my words in the report, they were a sort of joke, and there were thousands of jokes. A large proportion of them had something to do with politicians or the President in particular. As students, there wasn't a single party without scores of jokes, so why should this joke—even assuming that I said it—be so serious?

I replied to the question he had put to me: "This report that you read to me, which is more than fifteen years old... I don't remember saying those words, and even assuming that I did say them, it was a joke, nothing more or less. You know that there are hundreds of jokes of this sort."

"Even if it were a joke, this joke could be punished by one to three years!"

"But I've been in prison for twelve years!"

"Forget the twelve years, they are the result of an error for which we are not responsible. Your term starts from this moment. Now tell us about your organization. Which organization do you belong to?"

"I belong to the organization… of the Muslim Brotherhood!"

They burst into laughter, and the hoarse voice stretched out his hand to press the buzzer. A warden immediately appeared at the door. He spoke to him, the signs of laughter still apparent on his face. "Take him back to the cell, and tell the prison governor not to disturb him."

"Yes, sir!"

It seemed they had studied the case and taken a decision, and all the signs were that this decision was in my favor. But how did my uncle fit into all this? I didn't know.

June 10

More than half a month during which nothing had happened. The sounds of torture had weakened my nerves. To be tortured yourself is easier than to hear the sounds of people screaming night and day. I tried to divert myself by reading the names on the walls of the cell, all scratched out with a metal implement, possibly a nail, and daubed in bright green paint. There were several poems, the names of males and females, and some people had written the name of their city or political party. One person had drawn parallel lines beside his name. It looked as though every line represented a day. I counted them: thirty-three lines.

JUNE 21

The jailer let me out, telling me to carry all my things. We went upstairs with no blindfold or chains, and with the usual formula he let me into the room belonging to the "harsh voice," who immediately ordered me to sit down.

He spoke to me for more than ten minutes, in the course of which he gave me to understand that they had intended to release me; that they had great respect for my uncle, who had intervened on my behalf, because he was a good man; but that there were other security organizations who had objected to my release and demanded that I be handed over to them; and regrettably, they were obliged to do that.

For about a further ten minutes after that, he tried to make me understand something else, but by a roundabout route. It was clear to me that he did not want to address the issue openly and had therefore resorted to nods and winks. All I could gather was that, whatever methods they employed with me, I should not provide the other security authorities with more information than I had provided here, and that I should be grateful for the favor they had shown me here by not pressing me further in order to extract information (this was out of kindness to my uncle). This was because, if I supplied new information, the other security authority would appear as the more powerful and successful authority, and in that event I would be labeling the "hoarse voice" and his colleagues as failures. In particular, if I heeded these instructions, this would be in my favor, and would eventually work in favor of my release. He ended by saying: "I wish you all the best. If they release you, give my greetings to your uncle, and tell him that Brigadier-General "X" sends his greetings. Be a man, and do not be afraid. Goodbye!" Then he handed me over to the other security authority. Security men, a car, chains… we set off on the freeway toward the east.

June 24

At the other security authority.

Three days equaled three years in the Desert Prison.

The officer was waiting for me at the door of his room, seething with anger. He didn't turn around when the men saluted him, just asked me whether I was who I was, and I answered, yes. As I said the word "yes," he surprised me with a blow to my nose that threw me onto the chest of the man behind me. This man caught me and I stood up straight again. Then the officer took hold of my chest and pulled me into the room as he slapped me with the other hand. In the middle of the room he seized me by the neck, grabbed my Adam's apple and started to press it. I felt I was choking. "Kneel, dog, kneel down, you pimp!" he said, gritting his teeth.

As I knelt down, he let go of my neck and walked behind his desk. He grabbed a piece of paper, came closer to me, and began to read some paragraphs from it. With every paragraph he beat my face with the bottom of his shoe.

"Sound and image"—blow to the cheek—"you can tell a message by its heading"—blow just above the cheek—"voice of the goat"—blow to my side with the pointed tip of his shoes, throwing me to the ground, followed by more reading and more blows. He crushed my mouth with his shoe then put the shoe on my neck and pressed down, crushing me with his feet. I understood from him that what I said regarding "Mr. President" was in itself enough for me to be hung by the genitals!

He shouted instructions to one of his men, almost choking on his own voice. Three days I will never forget so long as I live. Floggings, beatings, in the tire, on the wind carpet, electric shock torture… He put the electrodes on the sensitive parts of my body and turned on the machine. My body started its electric dance. I felt that I would breathe my last, I was unable to breathe, my lungs almost exploded. With the blindfold over my eyes, I didn't know when he was using the machine or when he was stopping it; I was dancing, dancing with pain and convulsions.

On the third day the turn of the *shabah* arrived. When I heard the order for the shabah I didn't understand what it meant, but when they tied my hands up high with my whole body suspended more than half a meter above the ground, I recalled the crucifixion of the Messiah, and without realizing it shouted out "O Jesus, O Muhammad, O God!"

About half an hour later I felt that I had exhausted all my capacity to bear more; I felt an overwhelming weakness. I would confess to whatever they wanted me to confess to, and let the execution happen! Execution would be kinder! But how could I invent an opposition organization, apart from the Muslim Brotherhood... and how could I belong to it?

I recalled the dormitory, and the hundreds of stories of people who had weakened and confessed to things they hadn't committed. They confessed to crimes they had only heard about from the mouth of the investigator who accused them of committing these crimes. And what was the result of their confessions? Some had been executed, others rotted in prison, most had died or were well on the way to dying. I plucked up my courage. I was no longer the person I was twelve years ago. Experience had hardened me, and I began to persuade myself that I was a man, a brave man, a brave man who could endure it. And I endured it.

June 26

Were they satisfied with the three days of torture? Yesterday and today they didn't open my cell door except for food and the lavatory—food three times a day, and the lavatory three times a day immediately after the food.

I pulled myself together a little, cautiously and warily. Would they return to the attack? And when? I decided to relax and nurse my wounds. My hands were numb as a result of the shabah and I could use them only with difficulty. I tried some physical exercises on them, but found it difficult to clean myself after finishing in the lavatory.

I wanted my mother. O my mother!

August 22

A man of aristocratic appearance—which did not fit well with his heavy, uncouth mountain accent—spoke to me and gave me to understand that my days with them had come to an end, and that there was a third security agency that had asked for me to be handed over to them. I'd be able to avoid going to this third security authority and able to leave prison if I demonstrated some understanding and flexibility and was truly ready to serve my country. And now, he would send me to his adjutant, Ahmad, so that we could reach an understanding on the details.

The bell rang and the adjutant, Ahmad, appeared and led me into his room. He had a slippery look, a slippery smile, and his words were slippery too.

He put his hands on mine as he spoke. They were slippery, and dripping with sweat. He was such a slippery character he might have been a snake! He proposed to me—in such a repulsive and slippery way that it made one want to vomit—that they would release me and send me back to Paris. There, armed with my history (my long imprisonment), I would infiltrate the ranks of the opposition and serve my country through the reports that I would submit to the relevant security authorities, by revealing to them the country's enemies among its own citizens.

I refused, giving as my reasons... then maneuvering slyly,

I refused again. Then he tried… and I refused. He repeated his attempt, using enticements and threats, and I refused, recalling the lessons… He was trying to gain the favor of his superiors by succeeding in his job. He was trying to build some personal glory. He tried and tried.

His slipperiness, his smoothness, made one want to puke! But I continued to refuse. I drove him to such despair that he bared his teeth. The smoothness disappeared to be replaced by a petulant aggressiveness. I took no notice. Come what may, it could not be worse than it had already been.

He stood up angrily, hit me hard and in a tone that oozed failure and frustration said: "You're a stupid ass that doesn't recognize your own interest, you'll rot in jail, we'll turn you over to the mob and God willing they'll fuck your mother, you wretched dog!"

So they handed me over to the third security service. Security men, a car, handcuffs: the car sped off to the north, and we arrived at a street lit with reddish orange lights. A new cell, whose dimensions differed from the previous ones.

August 23

A meter wide, a meter long. This was the new cell. About a meter off the floor, there was a tile designed as a seat connecting the two walls. It was about a meter long and half a meter wide. The prisoner sat and slept on it. There was just one threadbare blanket in the cell. I was lucky, because it was summer. A lattice window with iron bars and grills took up half the outer wall and looked out over the security service office garden. I could breathe fresh air.

September 1

I'd been here for about ten days. For the first three days they didn't ask me anything. The food was just one meal, and was distributed at noon after the end of the investigation being conducted near my cell. After noon until nightfall was the only time I couldn't hear screams, crying, and swearing. Apart from that, the investigations went on throughout the twenty-four hours. This branch was well known among prisoners for its cruelty.

On the fourth day, the jailer opened the door of my cell in the morning, with another person standing beside him. He asked me my name and I replied. "Look," he said, "the boss, the *mu'allim*, has asked for you. You've certainly heard of the mu'allim. And I'm going to give you some advice, for God's sake. Whatever he asks you, answer frankly and truthfully. Don't be stubborn or try and make a hero of yourself. There are no heroes in this place. Everyone knows the mu'allim, and just so as you'll be in the picture, the mu'allim was once conducting an investigation with a dumb man and forced the dumb man to speak. And the dumb man spoke. So, brother, may God be pleased with you, in your own interest don't hide anything, tell everything, it's safer for you." Then they took me to the mu'allim.

They kept me standing in the luxuriously furnished waiting room in front of the mu'allim's room for more than a quarter of an hour. Their movements, their frantic racing up and down, and the hushed tones of their conversations—these were all things calculated to strike fear and terror into the heart of the person waiting. The mu'allim also kept me standing in front of his desk without paying me any attention for more than a quarter of an hour. He behaved as though he hadn't seen me, preoccupied as he was with reading papers and files, and with answering the telephones. But after that he devoted himself to me exclusively, for a period of four days!

From morning to afternoon I wrote the story of my life three times. Each time after I'd finished writing he took it from me and gave it to one of the junior officers, who returned after less than half an hour shaking his head and told me to write it again.

The office was a spacious and lavishly furnished hall. I had never seen such elegant or neat furniture. He sat me down at a conference table in a corner of the room with twenty-four chairs around it. While I was in his room writing my life story, he was conducting an investigation with three people, whom he tortured in front of me. I tried to concentrate on what I was writing amid the lashes of the whip and human screaming. Each time it ended in the prisoner confessing, at which point the mu'allim would order the torture to be stopped and tell one of his men to record his statements and confessions. Everything in the room was neat and orderly, except for me and the other prisoners in their creased and threadbare clothes, and the black tire and other torture instruments.

After noon there were no prisoners left in the room apart from myself. The mu'allim left his desk and sat down near me. He looked at me and said: "Look, two clean words are better than a filthy newspaper!" He started from where the others had left off and gave me a choice between two things: Either torture and a return to the Desert Prison, where I would meet my death, or… a confession and return to France to work as an informer in the ranks of the opposition. I did not make a choice, but denied any connection with any organization and refused to go back to France.

He tried all the means at his disposal. I had already become familiar with some of them elsewhere, but here they added to them by using the "German chair," which I thought had broken my back. They hung me up like a chicken, and contorted my body on the stairs… The last thing he threatened to use on me during the final day—in the final minute of the four days the torture had occupied, in fact—was to insert a soft-drink bottle into my anus. After they'd brought him the bottle, the telephone rang, and he spoke angrily on the phone then left the room—before he could carry out his threat—after ordering that I should be taken back to my cell and the torture stopped.

For four days I didn't eat or sleep for a single minute. They left me in the cell for three or four hours after noon with my hands cuffed and tied together with a metal chain, which was suspended from a ring in the ceiling. Then they pulled it so that I could hardly stand on tiptoe. I felt relieved when they released my hands and took me to the tire, the flying carpet, or the electric shock machine... Any means of torture was easier than being suspended like that.

I continued to resist, and this time I did not weaken completely. I kept saying to myself that these hours of torture were temporary, and would come to an end. I would console myself with other thoughts. I was probably helped by my concentration on daydreams in previous years, and the ease with which I could summon up any material to make a dream! I discovered myself, and I was happy with what I had discovered. I said to myself, with a ring that carried some pride: "This is a baptism to mark my coming of age as a man who respects himself."

Four days had now elapsed since the end of the torture, and I had had enough sleep, despite the fact that I had been sleeping in a sitting position. But one meal a day was not enough.

December 2

It was now one thirty in the morning, and for the first time since I returned to my country from France I was conscious of cleanliness all around me, surrounding me on every side. My bed was clean—a clean white sheet, clean blankets, clean pajamas, and new snow-white underpants—and around me were ten people who were clean in every way.

In the last few days of my spell in the one-square-meter cell, with just one threadbare blanket and a window opening onto the garden, I had suffered worst from cold at night. So I began to deliberately stay awake the whole night. Whenever I felt cold I would move around and do some physical exercises, insofar as the space available allowed. Then in the morning I would wrap myself in the blanket and sleep in a sitting position.

I was woken by the grating of the iron key in the iron door. It was the jailer I had come to know, and two other people with him. "Get up quickly!" he said. "Grab all your things!" I went out immediately. I didn't have anything with me except for some scraps of clothing. The procedures didn't take long, and very soon we were outside. A microbus with its engine running stood at the door of the station. They handcuffed me and told me to get in—there was a driver, four security men, and me.

"Trust in God, to the mountain prison!" said the man in charge.

The microbus headed off in a westerly or north-westerly direction, climbing up, and in less than an hour we had arrived. Set among the mountains, in a secluded place, was a large modern four-story building with hundreds of windows. It was the mountain prison. We got out, and after the usual handing-over and reception formalities they took us in to the prison governor, who asked me several questions. When he found out that I was a Christian he called a military police sergeant and told him to take me to the communists' wing.

While the policeman was occupied with opening the door to the wing, I looked in astonishment at the prisoners walking in the corridor. They were walking, chatting, and laughing in loud voices, eyes open, all with the policeman right beside them. Three or four prisoners stopped in front of the door to look at me. The policeman let me in and closed the door. "As-salamu 'alaykum" I said to them quietly.

"Wa-'alaykum as-salam! Greetings, comrade! Are you a comrade?"

"No, I am not a comrade!"

"Greetings, whatever you may be, come in, come in!"

They led me into the first dormitory and asked me whether I needed to go to the washroom before I sat down. I answered that I did so they took me to the washroom. Perfumed soap, new underwear, new pajamas. I went out, sat down, and told them my story. As I replied to their questions, a circle of people gathered around me to listen. One of them brought a large tray, with fried eggs, tomatoes, cheese, oil and thyme on it. Goodness, just like home! Was this prison? When I asked them this very question, they laughed and replied: "Yes, prison, but a five-star prison!"

One of them invited me to eat then finish my story. I was hungry as a wolf. I ate real food and drank real tea. Someone gave me a cigarette with the glass of tea and asked: "Do you smoke?"

"Yes, I used to smoke, But for twelve years, seven months, and twelve days I haven't smoked a cigarette."

"You seem to have forgotten to count the hours, minutes, and seconds."

The people around me split into two factions. One group told me to take the opportunity to quit smoking for good, while the other group said there was no harm in a few cigarettes after all this time. I took the cigarette and lit it, inhaled twice and felt my head spin! I coughed and carried on smoking. The session lasted from morning to last thing at night.

They asked questions, sought explanations, made laughing comments, and I told them everything. I was empty. I felt an overwhelming sense of peace, which I expressed by asking them: "Is this paradise?"

December 31

Today was New Year's Eve, and preparations were in full swing.

Everyone was busily preparing for the New Year's party, with colored streamers and balloons, pictures and colorings, meat and good food... as well as drink. They had wine and arak, all made locally.

I had been living among these people for almost a month. Most of them knew my friend Antoine when I mentioned him in passing in the course of conversation. Some of them said that Antoine was their friend, and they all knew my uncle. They all also had a negative opinion of him because he cooperated with the regime, but what surprised me was that my uncle had become a minister in the current government. "Is so-and-so your uncle?" shouted someone I was having a conversation with.

"Yes, my uncle."

"So why hasn't he tried to get you out of prison, now that he has become a minister?"

They said that he was an opportunist and that he had sold himself to the devil, himself and his whole party; and that because his party had shared power with the regime, it bore an equivalent share of responsibility for my imprisonment and that of the others, and for all the killing, destruction, and repression that was going on in the country.

My uncle a minister? A piece of news that stunned me!

JANUARY 6

Despite the absence of women, the New Year's party was enjoyable by any standard. They had a lot of wine and arak and some other unnamed alcoholic drinks, all manufactured here by themselves. They made these drinks from grapes, fruit, and jam. We drank, ate, sang, and danced until morning. Everyone was happy, and took part enthusiastically.

I was sitting in one of the corners of the dormitory sipping a drink and watching—watching their actions, their happiness, and their laughter—as I tried to guess their inner feelings. Could this happiness be genuine? I asked myself. Didn't each of them carry within his breast a woman—a wife, a fiancée, a lover? Didn't he wish this woman could be here with him at this moment to dance with and embrace? Didn't the painful absence of this woman cause bitterness and pain? So where did all the merriment come from that was spread throughout the party?

Everything gave the impression of simplicity and love, but I couldn't remain completely untroubled. Mountains of misery and dejection crouched on my breast. I tried to throw myself into it, but there was something inside me that refused to be happy—refused because it couldn't, couldn't jump over the high, solid wall of misery that had built up over all these years.

There, in the Desert Prison, during the sad, lonely nights—nights that seemed endless, when one became more and more certain that there was no way out; nights when life and death became equal, and for a few moments death became something to hope for—even my rosiest dreams at that time could not have aspired to the situation I was in now. I could never really have been persuaded—despite all my daydreams—that I might one day be in such an atmosphere of happiness as the New Year's party that I experienced here in this mountain prison! Yet despite that, I couldn't be happy, I couldn't give a single laugh from the heart. Had the joy died inside me in that crush of death? Would I remain like this? And why? Would I have to carry the threshing floors of death and torture on my chest for ever, to choke everything that was beautiful in life? I did not know.

March 2

Finally, the efforts of my uncle, so it seemed, had begun to bear fruit.

Among the first things I did on the first day I arrived at the mountain prison was to look at myself in the mirror. I felt afraid. The front of my head was bald. My hair, which had gotten a lot longer while I was at the local station, was turning white. My mustache was drooping and more than half of it had turned white; my eyes were sunken and surrounded by black rings. Pain, violence, fear, and humiliation had dug deep furrows on my brow and around my eyes. I quickly put the mirror away.

Today at ten in the morning a policeman came to the door of the wing carrying a piece of paper in his hand. He called my name and told Abu Wajih, the head of the wing: "Tell him he's got a visit!"

More than ten people busied themselves to get me ready and prepare me for the visit: shaving my chin, trimming my mustache; shirt and pants; shoes. They asked me what size shoes and brought me size 42, as I requested, but they were too small. My feet would fit into nothing less than a 44; they had grown two sizes! This was the first time I had worn shoes for about thirteen years; it was also the first time I had seen a mirror in the same length of time.

After they'd dressed me like a bridegroom, they sprayed me with perfume. I was tense, and my hands were shaking. I smoked a cigarette until the jailer came to take me away for my visit. I was confused and wary as I walked beside the jailer. Twice I almost fell after stumbling in the shoes I was wearing. *How difficult it is to walk in shoes…* We reached the room, whose door was open. A middle-aged man with white hair was sitting there, with a younger woman carrying a small child on her breast. The jailer put his hand gently on my back and said: "Go on in!"

I went in. It took several seconds of staring before I could recognize the features of my elder brother. He didn't recognize me at first either. Nineteen years had passed since I had last seen him. I shouted his name as I walked toward him. He embraced me and we burst into tears. We embraced each other, weeping, for more than a minute. My head was on my brother's shoulder, and I was crying from grief, longing, pain and happiness. I was also crying from relief, for here was the land of safety.

My brother moved away from me a little, wiped away his tears and handed me a paper handkerchief for me to do the same. I turned to where the young woman was sitting. She had put her child on one chair and sat down on another. She was sobbing and crying, with her hand over her face and her eyes; her tears were tears of pain. I looked at my brother curiously, and moved my head to ask who she was. Between his tearful eyes there appeared the suspicion of a faint smile. "You don't recognize her? Of course, you don't recognize her! This is my daughter, my brother! My daughter, Lena."

I turned to her. She had raised he head, and I saw tears tinged with red around her green pupils. "Lena, get up and say hello to your uncle!" he said. Lena threw herself into my arms. She squeezed me and I squeezed her back as we wrapped each other in our arms. I felt a powerful headache; I was suddenly weightless and floating in endless space. I could see nothing, and don't know how I managed to sit down on a chair. Lena sat on my lap as she used to when she was small, wiping away my tears, kissing and kissing me as she whispered: "Uncle, uncle. What are they doing to you? Uncle, oh uncle! By God, I have missed you so much! How have things come to this? How?"

Lena, the apple of my eye!

When Lena was born, it was I that chose her name for her, and she had never left me since she was two. *"Lena is her uncle's beloved,"* everyone used to say. She slept in bed with me. Even when I was late coming home, and she had gone to bed before me, I would wake in the morning to find her sleeping beside me. She would wake several times in the night, missing me, and when I came back, whether I was asleep or awake, she would slip in beside me.

When I went to France, she was just over five, and now here she was, a full-grown woman, and a mother as well.

My brother took hold of Lena's shoulder and shook her gently with a laugh: "Come on, get up off your uncle's lap. You're breaking his legs. Do you think you're still a little girl?"

As Lena sat beside me, she kept my hand between her own. She squeezed my hand and kissed me while my brother tried to comfort me. He said that my uncle was making huge efforts to get me out of prison; indeed, they were all behind me and had never abandoned me. He gave me to understand that my release from prison was dependent on the agreement of the President of the Republic: for more than ten years it had been the practice that any security service official could imprison whoever he liked, but the release of any prisoner could only be effected with the agreement of the Head of State, who retained personal files on every political prisoner.

I asked him about my mother and father's health, and he said that they were well.

The visit ended with Lena still clinging to my hand, squeezing it and kissing it. I returned to the wing, and to the dormitory, where I was welcomed with a smile by Abu Wajih. "Thank God you've returned safely, congratulations on the visit!" They chatted with me and I chatted back, still in a state of weightlessness, feeling light as a feather! They noticed this and one of them brought me a glass of arak, which I drank in one gulp. He laughed and brought me another glass. This time I drank it in several gulps, then asked Abu Wajih what I should do with the money my brother had given me.

"If you like, put it in the box," he replied. "Here no one keeps his own money; everything is shared." Their money was shared and put in a single box. Their food was shared, and their clothes were shared. I put ten thousand lira in the box. The person that took the money said I must be rich, because everyone here was poor and the most any prisoner received from his family was two thousand lira. I said that in the Desert Prison there were people whose families gave them half a million lira, and the man let out an incredulous whistle from between his teeth. I lay down on my bed, covered my head with the blankets, and fell asleep.

A summary of several long conversations over an extended period: I discovered from the younger prisoners—the *shabab*, as they liked to call themselves—that the main reason I was being investigated by multiple security agencies was the bitter rivalry between these agencies. Using a great many political expressions, the shabab explained to me the "essence of the political regime in the country," and the mechanics of the work of the security services, which the President of the Republic had made to compete in two basic areas: first, to establish their total loyalty to him; and second, to secure the greatest possible number of rewards and privileges.

As my uncle was a communist minister, and had intervened to secure my release, the position of the various security agencies—positive or negative—in relation to the communists was reflected on me. Some of the security agencies absolutely hated the communists and did not distinguish between those communists who were supportive of the regime and those who were opposed to it, while others hated them less comprehensively.

May 6

They took me back to the intelligence service station where I'd gone when I came out of the Desert Prison. My brother visited me three times in the mountain prison with his daughter Lena. On the final occasion, he told me they might be sending me back to the branch in preparation for my release; that I should be flexible and cooperative, and:

"Kiss the hand you can't bite, and pray that it breaks!"

The jailer came in the morning, called my name, and told me to get myself ready. My fellow-prisoners gave me five thousand lira, together with a lot of clothes, and some food, and Abu Wajih kissed me goodbye. "Be strong, don't ever be afraid of anything, we wish you good luck… and freedom!"

In the station, there was one staircase, then another, then the door with the iron bars, the grating of the circle of iron on iron, and another new cell, with new names carved on the bright green walls. Two days of solitary, with the sounds of torture, and screams of pain—the pain of men, women, and even children! I tried to ignore everything, and felt self-reproach because of it. Ignoring it was an invitation to simple-mindedness and dehumanization!

The jailer opened the door in the evening: "Get up! The branch head wants you!"

"Good evening," I said to the branch head, whom I had met some months ago.

"Hello, please come in!"

I sat down calmly.

He then embarked on a lecture about the progressive role played by the President of the Republic against reaction and imperialism, about his generosity toward people, and his wisdom, bravery, and skill. His account included a lot of things constantly being repeated on radio and TV. Finally, he concluded by saying: "We have decided to release you, because you are a patriot, and because your uncle has rendered great service to the homeland, and… We just want two routine things from you. We want you to sign an undertaking not to work in politics. And we also want you to write a telegram of thanks to the President, may God preserve him!"

"A telegram of thanks?"

"Yes, a telegram in which you thank the President!"

"A telegram of thanks? But what should I thank him for?"

He looked at me in amazement, and replied, "Thank him, because he has taken you under his wing and his mercy and has released you!" He was genuinely puzzled.

Once again, I was overtaken by the mulish obstinacy that had become my way of confronting them when they demanded something of me. As politely as possible, I said: "General, I am sorry, but I cannot sign either a political undertaking or a telegram of thanks." The general was stunned when he heard my words. He was silent for a moment, though he hid his amazement as an experienced man would.

"You know that we respect you out of respect for your uncle," he said. "So I hope that you will be a little more flexible. Being stubborn will do you no good. You must know that thousands of prisoners have written thank-you telegrams to the President in blood and not been released. Be sensible and sign, that will be the best thing for you."

I did indeed know that hundreds of prisoners had asked the prison authorities for syringes to draw blood from their veins to use as ink for writing telegrams of thanks or to beg mercy from the President of the Republic in the hope of being released from prison. When the prison authorities did not give them syringes, they scratched their fingers and wrote pleas or telegrams of thanks with the blood that flowed out. But I had already made up my mind. *No more humiliation. Let it be prison or death.*

The fact is that my long association with the prisoners in the Desert Prison and the mountain prison had taught me many things. The most important thing I had learned was the meaning and importance of generosity and manhood, two personal qualities that have no connection with organization or regime. Signing a thank-you telegram as a condition of release was these agencies' final test to confirm to them that the prisoner had drunk deep in humiliation, and had turned into a being who would never, ever stand in their way: indeed, since he was ready to thank their boss for everything he had suffered at his hands and the hands of his subordinates, he would presumably be ready to do anything they required of him.

I categorically refused to sign. "I will not thank those who imprisoned me all these long years. I will not thank those who stole my life and my youth. I will not thank those who made me lose the best years of my life!" I repeated these words and phrases to myself, to harden my resolve and firm up my will. I was afraid of myself, afraid of my weakness. I continued repeating these powerful words, to rid myself of weakness.

When the head of branch had finally despaired of me, he ordered me to be taken back to my cell. The way in which they took me back was conspicuously harsh. Half an hour after I had arrived back at my cell, the prison governor—an elderly man on the point of retirement—came in. He was an extremely good-hearted man, who secretly tried to help the prisoners to the extent that it was possible. In a fatherly tone, and with the best of intentions, he tried to persuade me to sign. He explained to me at considerable length the consequences of not signing, noting, among other things, that those who refused to sign were usually ringleaders, spokesmen, or people strongly opposed to the current authorities. Refusal to sign would therefore be interpreted as evidence that I fell into this category, and would reduce to nothing all my previous statements to the effect that I had not been active in politics. He carried on trying, and ended his speech with the expression that my brother had used: "Kiss the hand that you can't bite, and pray that it breaks!"

I continued to maintain my position. After the prison governor had left, I thought for a long time, and laughed. If I'd been in the Desert Prison they could have made me sign thousands of telegrams; in fact, they could have made me kiss the shoe of the humblest policeman!

The knowledge that my whole family—in particular, my uncle—were following me step by step had given me a sense that I was protected. This might be the real basis for the position I had taken in refusing to sign. But… wasn't there also something springing from the self?

JULY 3

At 9:37 in the morning, I found myself standing on the wet sidewalk in front of the station after they had closed the door behind me. At last! I was free!

Thirteen years, three months, and thirteen days had passed since the plane I was traveling on had touched down in Damascus airport. A headache, a ringing in the ears, a squint in the eyes. Dozens of yellow cars were speeding along in front of me in both directions. Hundreds of people were hurrying along in every direction. I heard someone call out behind me. I turned and saw the guard waving to me to leave the area in front of the station. "Is that the last of their instructions to me?" I wondered.

I walked on for something more than a hundred meters and stood on the sidewalk. A yellow taxi stopped in front of me and the driver asked me whether I wanted a ride. I got in, and the taxi sped off. The air hit my face. I shut my eyes and heard the voice of the driver asking where I wanted to go.

"Anywhere!"

The driver said nothing for a moment, then looked at me carefully in the mirror and repeated his question: "Where do you want to go, sir?"

I didn't want to talk to anyone. I wanted to shut him up, so I said: "I want you to take me on a tour, a tour of all the old quarters."

※ ※ ※

After I had left the head of branch and after the prison governor had tried to persuade me to sign, they'd ignored me completely for more than a month and a half. In the first few days of this period I was happy, proud, and completely at ease with myself, but as this treatment continued, a sense of annoyance and boredom began to overcome me. Every day I heard the sounds of torture and screaming, and one day I'd heard the sound of a young boy being tortured. I thought of banging on the door to demand a meeting with the branch head. Even the words I would need to say were already prepared. "Sir, I've thought long and hard and I'm ready to sign any paper you want!" I had walked two steps forward and two steps back with furrowed brow, then sat down with my head between my hands to think. I hit my head against the wall and cried and cried, then stretched out and went to sleep.

Around ten o'clock on the morning of June 23, the jailer opened the door and told me to prepare myself for a visit. It was my brother on his own, without Lena. He sat down beside the brigadier, who got up, saying that he would leave us alone so we could talk freely. He said it very politely. My brother started to speak. For about an hour or a little less, with many examples, he pressed me strongly to sign. As he went on talking, I had listened to him with bowed head, becoming more distant the more I listened. Was this my elder brother, who had once been an example for me to follow? Without lifting my head I told him that I would not sign anything, and that if I was a burden to him he should go away and not bother to visit me again. Then a lump of anger and annoyance welled up in my throat and I had shouted in his face that if he wanted to visit me again to make me hear this sort of thing—advice like this—then I very much hoped that he wouldn't visit me because I felt disgusted with him! His eyes widened in astonishment and his mouth remained closed, as he sat there silently with his head bowed.

The general had saved the situation by coming back in. He immediately grasped what had happened, turned to my brother, and said quietly: "Give my greetings to your uncle. Didn't I tell you he was stubborn?" My brother thanked the general and left.

Ten more days of being ignored, ten days of exhausting mental torture. Had I lost my brother? Was I just a small, empty, arrogant nobody? Did I want to clothe myself in the robe of a doughty fighter? Wouldn't such a robe be far too flowing for me? Wasn't the logic of my brother's words the prevailing one, if not the correct one? I was tossing on a bed of embers, and being burnt alive!

At eleven o'clock on the morning of July 1 they took me into the brigadier's room to find him standing respectfully, while my brother and another middle-aged man with white hair remained seated. I later learned that this middle-aged man was my uncle. The brigadier excused himself extremely politely and left the room after ordering three cups of coffee for us. After greetings and kisses, my uncle had embarked on a long lecture, which ended in reproaches and rebukes, then gave me a decisive instruction to me to sign the piece of paper that he held out to me. Completely calm, I refused.

For the first time, he had left his chair. How old he looked, I thought. He came up to me angrily then stopped and quickly turned to my brother, to ask him if he could sign the paper instead of me. My brother nodded his head in agreement then signed. My uncle bit his teeth, and said to me, "Too bad for you, if you say a word!"

The general came in, and my uncle had handed him the paper. The brigadier put it in his desk drawer and rang the bell. He told them to take me back to my cell. Two days later, at 9:37 in the morning, I was standing on the wet sidewalk in front of the local intelligence services building, a free man!

◼ ◼ ◼

The taxi took me around for almost an hour. I ignored the driver completely. I was in such a state that I could not think. Then I woke up and asked myself where I should go. Where, indeed? I felt an overwhelming desire to sleep. I wanted to sleep, I just wanted to sleep! I gave the driver the address of our house. I got out of the taxi after giving him half the money I had, and walked along the sidewalk. I looked at the sidewalk, fearing that at any moment it might split open and I would plunge into a bottomless pit.

I walked upstairs and rang the bell. Who would open the door? My mother, my father? No one opened it for me. Where was my father? Where was my mother? I sat on the stairs and stayed there for around three hours. Several of our female neighbors walked past me on their way up or down. They gave me strange, apprehensive looks but I didn't recognize any of them. A chic young man wearing glasses came up and gave me a curious glance then walked past me, opened the door to our apartment and went in.

I stood up and called him. Without turning around, he looked at me out of the corner of his eye.

"Yes, what do you want?"

"Who are you? Where are you going?"

We introduced ourselves. He was the husband of Lena, my niece. He welcomed me warmly and said that he would get the shower ready immediately, and that I must change my clothes. He asked me if I was hungry. I asked him for a cup of coffee with no sugar. One question was turning in my mind that I was extremely afraid to pose. I finished my coffee, sat up straight, and asked him: "Where are my father and mother?"

He was stunned. He looked at me with astonishment tinged with pity, and started to mumble: "I don't know. Lena and I, when I got to know Lena, they weren't around. May God have mercy on them. I never met either your father or your mother, and…"

What I had feared had happened. O my mother, my father! Did you, or either of you, say that you wanted to see me before you died? Did my absence and imprisonment hasten your deaths? I would have given half my life just to lay my head for five minutes on my mother's breast.

Anwar, Lena's husband, stood in front of me, looking at me in a confused way. I asked him whether he knew where they were buried and he nodded. He wrote something on a piece of paper, which he put on the table. We set off for the cemetery. When we arrived, my father's and mother's names were plain to see on the stone. Anwar made the sign of the cross on his chest.

I stood for a moment looking hard at the words without understanding anything. I clasped the cold stone and bowed my head over it. I shut my eyes, and felt a great comfort. I almost fell asleep but remembered Anwar and stood up again. Somewhere inside me, I felt I had a duty that I needed to perform in the face of death. I turned to face the *qibla*, the direction of Mecca. The grave was between me and Mecca. I opened the palms of my hands to the heavens and recited the fatiha, then mechanically said the prayer for the dead.

October 6

A week after I had left prison, my brother, Lena's father, invited me to supper at a restaurant outside the city. The restaurant was nice and quiet, with nothing but the sound of soft music to be heard, together with the ripple of the river coming down from the western hills. Over supper, he told me about my mother and father. He told me that, before he died, my father had provided for my financial situation by arranging that the family home that Lena was currently living in with her husband would become my property. He had also set up a trading partnership in my name with one of my relatives, the profits from which were being kept for me from that day hence. They amounted to a small fortune. "From that point of view, you will have no problems. Your material situation is sorted, thank God!"

He then asked me whether I wanted to live alone, and if Lena and her husband should leave the house. I refused point blank. I sensed that the decisive tone of my refusal made my brother feel reassured. When we had finished the second glass of arak, the atmosphere became more cordial and relaxed. We recalled some family memories. Then suddenly he sat up straight and embarked upon the very topic I had been afraid he would broach or at least hint at. "I'll be frank with you," he said, "about what you told me in the branch office during my visit. At first, I felt deeply wounded but after several hours I felt joy and pride because you are a man, a hero." I raised my hand to tell him to stop.

During these three months, the thing that annoyed me most was other people treating me like a hero!

The main thing in surplus in prison is time. This surplus allows the prisoner to immerse himself in two things: the past and the future. The reason for this may well be the prisoner's frantic attempts to escape from the present and forget it completely. Immersing himself in the past and the future may either make a man calm and wise, or else turn him into a withdrawn, narcissistic individual obsessed with himself, who only interacts with others at the lowest level—or else into a madman!

Since becoming conscious of this equation, I had tried hard to turn into that calm man, though I don't know how far I had succeeded. I therefore refused to trade on my imprisonment. I refused to be a hero when others wanted to regard me and treat me as a hero on my release from prison. I knew my potential well. Quite simply, I was a man, and a cowardly one at that. So cowardly, in fact, that I sometimes wet my pants from fear.

I was brave and strong and stubborn enough to resist the worst forms of torture. But in no way was I a hero, for my behaving in this way was not of my own free will, and a hero cannot be a hero if he behaves like that perforce.

I made a great effort with Lena and her husband, until I was able both to convince Lena that I was not a legend, and that she should therefore treat me extremely simply, and to persuade Anwar that there was no need for all this deference and respect in his dealings with me. There was no need to stand up out of respect when I entered or left the room. I was only about ten years older than Anwar.

※ ※ ※

Since 9:37 on July 3, I had noticed something that I'd never noticed in the city before. Dust. Dust covered everything in the city—lanes, streets, walls, everything was covered in a layer of fine yellow dust. The green tree leaves that I had known previously as a bright shiny green were now covered with this fine layer of dust. Even the faces of people walking along the streets, or loitering in the squares or on the sidewalks, were covered in this layer of yellow dust. They washed their faces, and dried them, but the dust did not go away. It seemed either to be clinging to their faces or to be part of them. The dust appeared most clearly when people smiled, for smiles—despite being so rare (almost nonexistent, in fact) that I suspected people in my city had forgotten how to smile—went well with this dust. If someone tried to smile, the smile seemed murky, and the person concerned seemed to have aged by several dozen years. The most important indication of the smile was the distinct appearance of the layer of dust clinging to the face. At this point the individual specks of dust could be clearly seen.

I was afraid to ask anyone about this dust.

■ ■ ■

Fifteen days after leaving prison, I thought of performing my first duty—to visit Nasim's family and try to reassure them about him. The fuss about my release from prison had subsided a little, and the number of visitors had decreased considerably. Visits were from family and relatives—uttering the usual expressions of congratulation, many expressions of respect, and more than anything else, advice.

"Praise God you are safe!"

"We're proud of you."

"Don't look back, the future is still in front of you!"

"May God preserve you! Do you have to work in politics? My brother, the eye cannot resist the awl!"

I listened to all this with a dumb smile on my face.

Two or three friends from the days of my childhood or youth sent me pieces of news in total secrecy: "We would like to visit you, but we are afraid what might result from this visit, so apologies!" I respected their cowardice enormously.

I told Lena and Anwar that I would travel to Nasim's city on the coast. Anwar made all the arrangements and accompanied me until the Pullman bus left, heading north. For the first time in several years, I felt as though I were a human being. The person sitting next to me and the bus conductor treated me as a human being, and when they spoke to me they called me ustaz! I leaned the seat back, closed my eyes, resisted all my neighbor's efforts to open a conversation with me, and tried to recollect Nasim. What was he doing now, I wondered?

In every part of this world, close relationships can be formed between two people, but when close relationships are formed between two people in prison, they will certainly have another meaning, another flavor, another aroma. We had spent many days, and many long nights, in conversation. I knew everything about Nasim's family, his father, mother, brothers and sisters, their habits, customs, and exact family details that could not be discussed except between two prisoners.

After this long period of conversations, each of the two parties to this prison relationship had two family lives: the life I had lived in my real family; and the life I had lived as a transmogrified dreamer in Nasim's family. I recollected the details afresh as the bus sped through the magical, lush-green scenery. During the final hundred kilometers I was so captivated by the beauty of the scenery that I could think of nothing else except for what I was seeing. To the left was the sparkling sea, with its various shades of blue, and to the right the towering green mountains. The road twisted around, drawing closer and closer to the sea until it was beside it. I watched the small waves breaking on the shore, and saw men and women swimming, embracing the sea and being embraced by it. Then the sea faded so far into the distance that it disappeared from our sight. To the right, I could see lemon, orange, and olive groves. All this verdant greenness.

The bus reached the city. It was a clean city. I got off and took a taxi. I gave the driver the address, which I knew as well as I knew the address of my own family. I arrived, got out, and without any difficulty stood in front of Nasim's family home. I pressed the bell. About three hours separated my ringing the bell from my departure from the house as a despised outcast.

The door opened and a small girl of about ten stood there. "Hi, is this the house of Dr. Nasim's family?" She didn't reply but ran inside.

"Mama, mama, there's someone asking for Dr. Nasim," I heard her say.

A few seconds later, Nasim's sister came out in her house clothes, having quickly put a covering over her head. Her eyes were heavy with a look that expressed both surprise and inquiry. I recognized her at once. I smiled and said: "Hello, are you Samira?"

For a moment, she froze in confusion where she stood, facing me. Her eyes were fixed on me. She took a deep breath and said: "Yes, my friend, yes, I'm Samira. But who are you? How do you know me?"

"I'm a friend of Nasim. I've come to pay his family a visit and reassure them about him."

"Welcome, welcome. Is it true? You mean, Nasim's alive? Nasim's alive?"

With the dozens of questions and greetings, not to speak of the copious tears, Samira began to go around in circles. She didn't know what to do. With her child at her side, she asked me a lot of questions without waiting for an answer, then followed them with "Welcome, welcome…" Several times she wiped her tears away with her headscarf. Finally she came to her senses, and said: "Sorry, sorry, come in, come in!" She led me in to the guest room, and I sat down. She went out for a bit then returned. "I've tried to contact my husband," she said. "My husband is in customs, but I couldn't track him down, so I left a message for him." She was silent for a moment then said emotionally: "For God's sake, my friend! Give me some good news about Nasim. Is it true that Nasim is alive? Where is he?"

I talked and talked, explained everything to her, told her lots of family gossip and stories—stories that only members of the family could know—and she believed me. I asked her about Nasim's mother and father, but this made her cry more, and her tears turned into wails. Through the tears and the wailing, I understood that they had died, died out of grief for their two sons. The first, who had enlisted in the ranks of the Islamist opposition, had been totally lost track of, and views differed on whether he had been killed in an operation, or imprisoned. As for Nasim, the family had waited on the day appointed for his return, having made preparations to celebrate despite the ordeal of the first son. But he did not return, and as the waiting continued, the father embarked on a marathon journey between the airport administration, the airline company, and the French embassy. After a month of waiting, the French consul confirmed that Nasim had left French territory to return home, but the national airline company and the airport administration gave only obscure replies that neither confirmed nor denied anything.

For six years, the father had continued his visits to the capital. Each time, he stayed for three or four days, during which he traveled between the French embassy, the national airline, and the international airport, but without success. The employees in the French consulate got to know him, and the reply was the same every time. The reply of the national airline was also the same every time: they absolutely refused to let him see the passenger list for the flight that Nasim was presumed to have been on. The security administration at the international airport gave him polite replies several times, then started to treat him more harshly. They eventually threatened him with arrest, and during his visit in August of the sixth year, a security man at the airport struck him twice on the face.

The father left, crying for the first time in his life. "Really, ustaz," said Samira, "we had never seen him crying. Even my mother—after they'd told her what had happened—said she'd never seen him cry or weaken, not one single time in their long life together."

The father suffered a stroke, which did not kill him but confined him to bed for four years, paralyzed and unable to move or speak. The mother forgot everything, even her children, and devoted herself to serving the man who had been her companion in this life. She never left his room except to relieve herself or for something that he needed. This state of affairs continued for four years, after which the father died, and the mother followed two months later. The girls married, and Samira and her husband, the customs officer, lived in the family home.

I gave her my telephone number and she gave me hers.

A silence followed, which lasted for more than a minute. I felt thirsty, so I asked the child to bring me a glass of water. I had decided to leave after drinking the water, but as I was drinking, the door of the house opened and I heard a man's footsteps. Samira leaped up and quickly went out. I heard whispering at first, then the sound of a heated argument, a man's voice that was getting constantly louder, while Samira desperately tried to keep her voice down and begged him to do the same. Despite that, I heard most of what was being said between them, in a harsh tone: "Hey, how could you let him into my house when I wasn't here? Do I need criminals and people just released from jail here?"

"God spare you and grant you a long life! This isn't a criminal, he's come from Nasim, he's Nasim's friend, and he's a good man... "

Samira's husband came in, in his customs uniform. He was tall, with light-colored hair, and he was scowling. "Hello," he said. His tone was cold and harsh. I stood up and returned his greeting. With a wave of his hand he invited to me to sit, while he himself remained standing. He immediately launched into his first question: "How can you allow yourself to enter a man's house in his absence?"

He didn't wait for an answer, but followed this question with a stream of questions to which he did not expect answers. Samira saved the situation by coming into the room. He turned toward her to tell her to leave. But she refused to go out, and held onto his hand imploringly. "For God's sake, I kiss your hand, I kiss your feet; this is Nasim's friend and his intentions are all honorable."

He pulled his hand away sharply and shouted: "Honorable? What do you mean, honorable? You know that if 'they' knew that people like this were visiting me, we'd be completely ruined, and I'd be in the same place as your doctor brother, or else this other criminal. Tell me, what would happen to you then? And to the children? Tell me that!" Then he turned to me and in a slightly calmer voice said: "Look, I shall have to tell security, but for the sake of Nasim, I will let you go! You didn't see me and I didn't see you! And you're in trouble if you come near our house again. Understand what I'm saying?"

I left without further ado, dripping with sweat, his words ringing in my ears. I threw myself into the first taxi I saw and told the driver to take me to the sea, but he stopped and said: "But this is the sea, in front of you, sir!"

"Then take me to some other part of the sea—outside the city, I mean."

I sat and ate in a seafront restaurant, about which I remember nothing. I don't know how or what I ate, and I don't know how long I stayed sitting. I woke up the next day when Lena came back in the afternoon, and she told me over coffee that a woman called Samira had telephoned her, asked after me, and apologized profusely for what had happened.

I recalled the events of the previous day in an attempt to absorb what had happened.

I tried to forget.

Leave me in peace, for I don't want anything from you.

I woke in the morning at no particular time. The house was empty, for Anwar and Lena were at work, and the little girl was at daycare. I stayed in bed for a little, then got up and dressed. Since leaving prison, I had slept naked. I went over to the locked door of the room, opened it, put a heavy coffee pot on the gas burner, and went to the bathroom. For an hour or two, sometimes longer, I sat on the sofa drinking coffee with no sugar and smoking. I went to the lavatory. I took great care to relieve myself while Lena was out of the house. I think the reasons for this were quite complex. For although I was annoyed that Lena should regard me as a legend, her attitude at the same time satisfied some inner worlds within me. And insofar as I was a hero and a great legend in her eyes— and despite my annoyance, I mean—I would try to confirm my status in more than one way, including not going to the lavatory in her presence. For the legend or hero that she had in her mind had to be preserved from everything that was hateful, being above such humble human needs. And for this reason, since I had been living with her in the same house, she had never seen me going to the lavatory.

I got dressed, went out, and wandered around aimlessly. No one knew me and I knew no one. I walked and walked, not thinking of anything in particular. I might buy a piece of good quality chocolate. I liked chocolate and I had plenty of money. I ate it, I smoked as I walked, and I often sat in a small garden near our house. I bought some things that I felt might save Lena and her husband some money, for my financial situation was a lot better than theirs. I was a millionaire by comparison.

■ ■ ■

Two things that terrified me.

Leave me in peace, for I don't want anything from you.

Some time ago, my uncle, the minister, came—he called on us regularly—and after a lot of the usual conversation, suddenly turned to me and asked: "Hasn't the time come to think about your future?"

I was stunned. The future? Did a man of my age and in my position have a future?

Like most of his colleagues, my uncle had firm, fixed views, which were not to be argued with. He always spoke in the tone of someone who knew everything, and assumed the air of someone—the only one—who was always right. For this reason, he asked his question in the tone of someone giving an order, as he embarked on the two subjects that terrified me: a job, and marriage. Everyone else who was there supported the idea. My uncle began to swagger about with a smile on his face, as he turned to some ladies of the family and said: "Leave the matter of a job to me. As for marriage, that's a job for these young ladies. Come on, show me how clever you are, and choose a bride who's pretty, and suitable for this millionaire groom!"

Shrieks and chirps could soon be heard from the women, as they immediately began to discuss among themselves the attributes of the looked-for bride. My uncle left, and everyone immersed themselves in the arrangements for the engagement and wedding. I said nothing. No one asked me for my opinion, and I remained silent. These two questions pursued me for a long time.

About two weeks later, a senior employee in the radio and TV department asked for me on the telephone. He introduced himself to me and asked me to come to his office to discuss the scenario for a TV series. "If you like the scenario, we can sign the contract for you to produce it immediately," he said. "Don't ask about the financial potential, which is huge, thank God!"

I needed considerable tact to excuse myself politely, but he continued: "Don't turn it down, my friend! Come to my office and I am sure you'll be convinced, I mean, no offense, you're a producer, sure, but you're an unknown name, and for reasons that I think you know I am offering you the chance of a lifetime on a plate of gold."

I refused.

The result of my refusal was a stern rebuke from my uncle that evening. He ordered me to accept the offer, but I refused. "You're an ass," he said angrily.

There remained the matter of marriage. Not a day went by without a female member of the family contacting me or coming to see me. Most of them would begin the conversation with the same phrase: "Well, I've found you a bride, a real catch, a real catch! And if all goes well, you'll have a house in heaven!" Then she would begin to expound the virtues of the bride, who might well be a relative or a neighbor of hers. One of them actually suggested to me her own sister. I needed the patience of Job, especially as the conversation was being conducted with a woman, for you can easily make any woman start talking but it's very difficult to make her shut up!

Leave me in peace, for I don't want anything from you.

Since coming out of prison, I had been conscious of an unbridgeable, unfillable gap between me and other people, even the people who were closest to me, my brothers or Lena. I carefully checked my emotions and did not feel anything toward them: neutral feelings, nothing attracted me, nothing aroused my interest.

Everyone has his own personal language of communication, which he uses to establish relationships with other people at a greater or lesser distance. This language—my own personal language for communicating with others—had been lost, it was dead. Worse than that, I had no desire whatever to invent a new language of communication, or to revive the old one. I always felt that they had their world and I had mine, or else that I had no world at all. Certainly, I did not belong to their world.

I was appalled by the idea of being forced to mix with people for the sake of a job or anything else. I wanted to keep as far away from them as possible… I craved total seclusion. I wanted to be forgotten and ignored by them.

Marriage? Oh my God!

For a female to come and share with me my bed, my food, my lavatory, my smells! Just to think about this subject made me tired and gave me a headache.

Leave me in peace, for I don't want anything from you.

In a moment of anger I told Lena to phone everyone, to tell them I didn't want anyone ever to speak to me on the subject of marriage after today. The result was that my uncle told me: "You're an ass!" As for the women who had been trying to marry me off, they regarded it as an insult to their honor, and their tongues set to tearing me to pieces.

"Don't bother to do good, or evil will come to you!"

"What does he take himself for? Does everyone who goes to prison for a couple of days behave as arrogantly as that?"

"People put up with trouble, but trouble doesn't do the same for us!"

"Just a worn-out old man, bald as a monkey, and because he's got two pennies, he doesn't like anyone any more… it's true, as the proverb says—someone takes a monkey for his money, the money goes and the monkey remains as he is."

All this and more. But many an injury has its uses. The relationships turned into something approaching a rupture. And finally, they left me in peace.

DECEMBER 25

Today was Christmas Day, and it was also the second birthday of Lena's daughter.

I really had lived a long time. Maybe longer than I should have done. I still remember the enormous enthusiasm with which we went to celebrate Lena's own birthdays—first, second, third, up to the fifth. And now I was looking (from a distance) at the enthusiastic preparations for the Christmas festivities and for celebrating Lena's daughter's birthday.

▧ ▧ ▧

During the last few months my life had been confined to a just a small group of actions. For the most part, one sort of action had provided the reason or justification for the second sort.

I would sleep, eat, and drink... and wake, shit, and pee.

I wandered aimlessly in the streets, lanes, and gardens, surrounded by many people, but without noticing their faces. I was aware of people as a glutinous or ethereal mass, a part of the atmosphere surrounding me. I noticed nothing, took no notice of faces. People do not usually see the air surrounding them.

I bought a new TV set and put it in my room. I only watched foreign films and serials. I didn't follow the news at all. I didn't miss a football match, whether local or foreign. Anwar, Lena's husband, worked as a computer programmer. He tried to persuade me to learn programming, and never stopped repeating the phrase: "In this day and age, anyone who doesn't understand computers is as good as illiterate." I learned it and bought a new, good quality machine, though I only used it to play games and especially the game called "The Spider."

I was completely isolated from everything going on in the world. Several times Lena tried to reconnect me with people and with my environment. I liked to walk with her sometimes and flatter her, but I steadfastly refused to change my lifestyle. I felt lonely and isolated in the company of other people. I felt that a heavy burden had been placed on my shoulders. This feeling only disappeared when I went back to my room. I would lie on my bed and stare at the ceiling. I would remain for hours, several hours, in this position, not thinking of anything.

Lena and Anwar were now moving very enthusiastically, decorating the Christmas tree, bringing the candles, arranging the table. There were several guests. I was thinking how to escape from this riotous party. There was a dark sadness inside me. I hadn't told anyone what had happened to Nasim.

▩ ▩ ▩

Ten days ago the telephone rang in the house. I didn't usually answer the telephone. No one contacted me. I stayed lying on my bed. "Uncle," called Lena, "it's the telephone for you!"

I started up immediately and went to the phone. Lena was holding the receiver. "Who is it?" I asked.

"Someone called Dr. Hisham."

I took hold of the receiver and spoke. He reminded me who he was, and I remembered him well. He was one of the doctors who'd been with me in the Desert Prison. He was also one of the first to have regarded me favorably, and he was a close friend of Nasim. I was taken by surprise. I asked him where he was speaking from, and he told me that he and Nasim had been released from prison, that Nasim had given him this telephone number and asked him to get in touch with me. "Nasim sends his greetings," he said. "He hopes you will come here." I replied that I would be with them the following day. He told me tactfully that I didn't need to go to Nasim's house: they'd arranged an appointment for the afternoon of the following day in a seaside café near Nasim's family home.

The café was almost empty. We chose a table at the side, with the small waves breaking below it, and sat there stealing glances at one another. Their hair was still short. More than half an hour had passed since we met and my eyes had still not met those of Nasim. Why didn't he look me straight in the eye? When we met, the three of us had embraced each other vigorously and started crying. We cried for more than five minutes. I don't know why we cried. Happiness at meeting? Or were we all crying for ourselves? Afterwards, the exchange of smiles began, but Nasim never smiled. He looked sideways, and did not speak.

Nasim and I drank beer and Hisham drank juice. It was Hisham who spoke, explaining to us his plans for the future. He had one simple goal: "Let me out of this country, and I'm ready to work as a garbage collector anywhere else in the world." Hisham was a cosmetic surgeon, and was regarded as an expert in his field.

Nasim said nothing, but sat staring at a point far away to sea.

I asked Hisham how they had been released from prison. One night—suddenly, and without any prior warning—the police opened the door and began to read out names. Everyone whose name had been called was released. When they compared notes with each other it became clear that they could be classified into three groups: the disabled, the chronically ill who were expected to die soon, and hostages… To these were later added a group of inmates from the "innocent dormitory," who were now young men in their twenties, having spent more than ten years in prison. They bused everyone to the capital, Damascus. The authorities had already released several news reports to the effect that the President intended to announce a general amnesty for prisoners. No one believed these rumors, either inside the prison or outside it, but they clung to the hope.

They spent a few days in the capital—in the capital's prisons, that is—where they tried to improve the prisoners' appearance somewhat. They bought them new clothes, and gave every prisoner the sum of two hundred lira as pocket money, plus the cost of a ticket to his town or city. On the day appointed for their release from jail, they put them onto buses, which took them to the biggest and most important square in the city, then handed the arrangements over to a senior officer in the security service. "Take them to the square, put the buses around the square, and set everyone down in the square. We need a demonstration in support of the President," were his instructions, and he interpreted them literally.

When it came to implementing the instructions, some people pointed out that there were dozens of disabled, and that they could not walk in a demonstration. But the officer insisted: his superiors had used the word "everyone." At the time specified for the start of the march in support of the President of the Republic, there were still about four hundred prisoners trying to unload nearly two hundred disabled. They got them off the buses and sat them in neat rows on the wide, circular area of asphalt. In front of them stood the chronically sick—men with cancer, heart or circulatory ailments, or tuberculosis—and the elderly. In front of everyone were the men from the "innocent dormitory," who were the youngest, together with some people from the hostage group. In front of them all was an enormous banner with bright, blood-red calligraphy, headed:

"A Pledge written in blood"

In this the demonstrators pledged their allegiance to the President of the Republic and swore that they were all his soldiers, who would give their blood and their souls for his sake!

The waves were still breaking directly beneath us. Some of the spray reached us from time to time. Nasim said nothing but smoked greedily, while Dr. Hisham steered the conversation, as he started to talk about his plans for the future. "The most important thing is to get away from this accursed country. Two or three days, and my affairs will be in order." He had a brother who worked as a sailor on a Swedish merchant vessel. By chance, this brother had been there when Hisham was released from prison. Hisham had told him of his burning desire to leave the country, so his brother arranged for him to work on the same ship that he worked on, as assistant chef. Dr. Hisham almost jumped for joy at the offer of this position, and the opportunity to flee.

Nasim was silent, and I was uneasy. Despite the fact that I had not felt the pleasure I expected to feel on seeing Nasim again, I was aware of him as an ordinary person—a sick person, indeed. He was constantly gazing at a particular point in the sea, and I took advantage of his preoccupation to ask Hisham by means of an inconspicuous gesture whether he was taking his medicine regularly. Hisham turned his lower lip over toward me without exhibiting any interest. He didn't know!

I felt that my coming here had been meaningless. What could I do here? I started to feel bored. I imagined myself stretched out on my bed at home, smoking. I felt relaxed just thinking about it. Generally speaking, I no longer liked to think. Merely exercising my thoughts or my mind with any matter, no matter how small, exhausted me. I felt that my head was swollen and my temples began to ache.

I decided to go back home, but how could I retreat? So far—and despite the fact that Nasim had cried like me when we embraced—he had not uttered a single meaningful sentence. "What do you think, Nasim?" I asked, with the idea of drawing him in to take part in the conversation. "Dr. Hisham here is planning to escape from this country. What are you planning for the future?"

He said nothing for a moment then turned to me, and our eyes met for the first time. His eyes were bloodshot. "I want to form a gang," he said, angrily: "a criminal gang." His voice was trembling.

Hisham laughed, and without thinking asked him as a joke: "Why a gang? Do you want to rob banks?"

"No, I don't want to steal, I'm not going to steal. Nasim isn't a thief, but there's a customs officer who stole my home and my sister from me. He violated my family home and every day he violates my sister, Samira. And now he wants to turn me out of the house. I'll kill this customs man, and every customs man in the land, I'll kill all these criminals, these dogs. I'll kill the people who are raping my mother and yours every day. My sister and your sister, my house and yours."

Hisham froze and said nothing. Nasim turned to the spot that he had been staring at far out to sea, and a deep silence settled over us as we sat there. I could see in Nasim's behavior the warning signs of an almighty storm, a violent storm that was threatening to explode. It seems that Hisham also sensed the danger. I exchanged looks with him without Nasim noticing; signs of unease and confusion were apparent in both of us.

I felt very tired. My head was throbbing and I had a headache. I made up my mind to leave and travel back, to go back home, with its peace and quiet and absence of thought.

The seaside café where we were sitting was near to Nasim's family home. While I was immersed in my thoughts, trying to take the first suitable opportunity to apologize and leave, Nasim stood up straight, turned to us and asked us to wait for him here.

He said he wouldn't be away for more than five minutes. I found this a suitable opportunity to say that we all had to go, and that I had to travel soon as I had some important commitments in the capital. I stood up, and Hisham did the same. Nasim said nothing for a moment, but gave me a searching look with his red eyes that I was unable to interpret. He then asked us to walk with him for a little toward the house because there was something he had to give me. I asked him for some more details and he said it was a gift from him to me.

In a minute or more we reached the front of the building, which was made up of six stories. A few months ago, I had left it a humiliated outcast. I stood on the sidewalk opposite the building with Hisham, awaiting Nasim's return. I told Hisham he should check Nasim's medical condition, because I believed he was on the point of a new attack; I thought he should speak to Nasim's sister and brother-in-law and put them in the picture regarding his health. Hisham waved his hand and said: "Nasim's brother-in-law is an ass. It's useless talking to him. And anyway, in a day or two I'll be saying bye-bye to this beloved country!"

Hisham hadn't finished what he was saying when we heard a shout from the roof of the building, and saw Nasim waving his hand and calling my name at the top of his voice. We understood from what he said that he would be giving me his death as a present. Then he jumped.

On the sidewalk in front of the entrance to the building, Nasim had turned into a mass of mangled flesh, smashed bones, and blood. In front of a large crowd of onlookers, and in front of our eyes, he had jumped from the roof of the sixth floor to the sidewalk in front of the building.

So Nasim died.

Hisham led me away by the hand. I thought of nothing as we

walked away. I wasn't sad, I had no feelings at all, either negative or positive.

Hisham put me in the first Pullman bus going to the capital. He advised me not to tell anyone that we were with Nasim just before his suicide, because this would expose us to an investigation and a question-and-answer session.

I reached home at one o'clock in the morning. I didn't take my clothes off as I usually did when I came in, but fetched a liter of arak from the kitchen and sat in my room, drinking and smoking. Lena woke up, and stood in front of me in her nightdress, staring into my face. "What's going on, uncle? Where have you been? And why are you drinking arak now?"

Lena had not completed her string of questions when Anwar, her husband, appeared, having also woken up. "Goodness me," he said. "Uncle's drinking arak as usual, but today it's later than normal. Give me a glass so that we can keep him company!"

He drank a glass of arak with me, and Lena drank a small glass, then Anwar excused himself and left to sleep. Lena was left sitting opposite me, looking at me with alarm. As I poured a third glass I noticed that Lena was about to speak. I raised my hand to stop her, and asked her to go back to bed, but she refused and told me that she wouldn't leave until she found out what I was about. Why was I burying myself alive like this? Why was I smoking so much and drinking this extraordinary amount of arak every day, as if I were trying to commit suicide? Why? Why? I drained the third glass in one gulp, and the arak began to go to my head. I looked at Lena and wondered: What does this pretty young girl, who calls me "Beloved uncle," want? I know that she respects me and loves me a lot. Despite this, I had no desire to talk. For a long time, I said nothing at all, while she waited for me to speak. I don't know how I started to speak, or what I said, but I talked a lot. "Listen, Lena, I wish my mother had been alive so that I could have relaxed in her arms, and put my head on her breast and cried, just cried. Crying for me is a need, a powerful need. Today, Lena, my friend and soulmate committed suicide. He committed suicide in front of me and presented his death to me as a gift. *Can death be a gift?* I didn't cry, I wasn't sad.

"Lena, I believe in the saying that a man doesn't die all at once. Every time a friend or relative, or one of his acquaintances, dies, the part that this friend or relative used to occupy dies in the soul of man. As the days go by, and the succession of deaths continues, the parts that die inside us become more numerous, and the area occupied by death grows larger. I hold a large graveyard inside me, Lena! These graves open their doors at night, and their occupants look at me, speak to me and chide me. I drink arak every day, Lena, to go to sleep!"

Lena took my hand and burst into tears. The last thing I heard her say was that she hoped she could take the place of my mother, so that I could lay my head on her breast and cry. I stood up and almost lost my balance. I took her hand and led her to her room. I pushed her inside and shut the door, then went back to my own room and locked the door. I don't remember when I went to sleep.

July 3

A full year had passed since my release from prison.

A man goes to sleep and is no longer conscious of what is going on around him; all his senses enter into a state of slumber. The man wakes up and his senses all wake with him, and he becomes conscious of what is around him. But between sleep and waking there is a moment, a second, more or less, that is neither sleep nor waking—the moment of transition between two states, or of moving from one state to another. This moment represents a state of semiconsciousness, of partial awareness, of partial comprehension.

In this moment, in the temporal space occupied by the moment, I still half saw myself—was half aware of myself—as being in the Desert Prison.

A full year had gone by and I still saw myself in the Desert Prison when I woke up. Could I really say that I had been released from prison in word and deed? I don't think so!

Every day, I undertook the same mechanical tasks, necessary for the continuation of life. I ate, drank, slept, and… Would I take my imprisonment with me to the grave?

In the Desert Prison, my double fear formed a shell, which I retreated into to avoid danger. Here—in what prisoners called the world of freedom—there was fear of another kind, as well as revulsion, anger, and loathing. Together they fashioned an extra shell, thicker, stronger, and darker. Because the hope for something better was only found in the first shell! In the second shell there was nothing, except… nothingness.

A man drinks wine, and the first glass may do nothing. He carries on drinking until he is intoxicated, which is the state in which a man's mind splits in two. The drunkard has two minds: a drunken mind—let us call it the "non-mind," though it is not a denial of the mind, not nonexistence, rather it is the opposite of the mind. The "non-mind" is something material that exists, like the mind itself.

The "non-mind" controls the actions and movement of the drunken man, and drives him to commit errors. The other mind of the drunken man is a wakeful, conscious mind that has no control over this person at this moment. It sees, watches, and records, without being able to intervene.

For a year, I have been living in a state like this. I know that my seclusion and withdrawal, my aversion to dealing with people, is an unhealthy state of affairs, but I have no desire or wish to change. On the contrary, I feel a backbreaking terror, when the idea flashes through my mind that I might go back to living as other people do. My God, how tiresome and stupid to live like them.

※ ※ ※

More than a month after Nasim's death, his brother-in-law, the customs officer, contacted me by telephone, and apologized. He told me about Nasim's suicide—they didn't know I had been there—and invited me to attend the forty-day commemoration. I didn't know the circumstances that led them to invite me, but I went on the appointed day; we all went to the graveyard, and I saw some faces that I recognized from prison. Afterwards, I went back to a hotel overlooking the sea, having decided to spend the night there. In the evening, I went to a restaurant, ate supper, and drank—so much that I could hardly manage to get back to my room by one o'clock in the morning. I lay down on the bed fully clothed, staring through the darkness at a point of light coming from outside, imprinted on the ceiling of the room, when Nasim appeared…

He stood in front of me at the end of the bed. He didn't speak and didn't move. He just gave me the same look that I'd seen deep in his eyes a few minutes before his suicide. Then I understood that the look was a look of mortal reproach: "Why have you abandoned me? Why have you abandoned me?"

It was like hearing Christ's cry at the moment of his death: a cry of reproach, protest, perplexity, and immense love: "*Eli, Eli, lama sabachthani?*"

Grief exploded inside me like a pent-up volcano. I sat up, and Nasim left, still giving me the same look.

I was seized by a single idea, almost an obsession, that I should take a bunch of roses and go to the cemetery, embrace the stones of Nasim's grave and cry, cry until I could cry no more. The roses for Nasim, and the crying for me. I went out into the street to look for a flower shop, but at two o'clock in the morning? There was no one in any of the streets where I wandered in my search for the roses.

A full year had gone by since my release from jail. The moment when I looked for the roses was the one outburst of emotion that made me feel I was like other people. But it subsided when I carried on looking until morning.

I thought that it would be selfish to go without flowers, just to cry. It would be selfish to satisfy my own need and not that of Nasim. Nasim wanted only me. And in front of me alone, he wanted to restore his self-respect. And I wanted to cry to empty some of the blackness which was filling my heart.

The blackness returned, effacing everything.

■ ■ ■

I spent thousands of nights inside my shell there in the Desert Prison, revisiting and drawing on hundreds of daydreams. I held out to myself the hope that if I was destined to escape from this hell, I would live my life to the fullest and would fulfill all the dreams that had come to me there.

And now... a full year has passed, and I have no wish to do anything at all.

I see that everything around me is just humiliation, misery, meanness. And my second shell, in which I am sitting now, is becoming thicker and blacker. I am not consumed by curiosity to spy on anything. I try to close the smallest peephole in my shell, not wanting to look out. I close the gaps in order to focus my gaze entirely toward the inside, toward me, toward myself!

And I peep...